I d  Mom had
moved I'd been
born in pened in
Nebrask already been
living somewhere in Iowa. Maybe it was Mom's family
who was from Nebraska. But where else in Iowa had
we lived? Des Moines, since that was the newspaper I'd
found?

Also, it occurred to me that it was weird we didn't
have much money. If all those people had died, surely
Mom inherited money or got insurance money. It made
no sense.

Googling everybody who had died brought up
records of long-dead people with similar names and
nothing more. What if it was all made up? What if those
weren't their names at all? What if I was adopted—or
worse, kidnapped? That would be crazy. But it also
would explain why Mom was so paranoid.

Could that really be it?

Praise for Kelly Vincent

Finding Frances

by

Kelly Vincent

Finding Frances

Cover Art by *Kim Mendoza*

The Wild Rose Press, Inc.
PO Box 708
Adams Basin, NY 14410-0708
Visit us at www.thewildrosepress.com

Publishing History
First Young Adult Rose Edition, 2020
Print ISBN 978-1-5092-2903-1
Digital ISBN 978-1-5092-2904-8

Published in the United States of America

Dedication

For every girl who doesn't know her own strength

Part One: Chapter One

Mom was holding my brand new white smartphone and acting strange again. "So, Retta, do I?" she asked, her expression still all intense.

I made the effort not to roll my eyes. "No, Mom, you don't need to put that number in. Yes, I still have it memorized."

All I wanted to do was to finish making this sandwich so I could get upstairs and start looking through my closet to pick out what I was going to wear to school tomorrow. And get my backpack ready, again. I spread the peanut butter across the slice of white bread, making sure to get the corners.

"Okay, I'm putting in my two work numbers in case you need them." Mom began typing on the phone's screen with her thumb, her hair falling forward to frame her tense face while the cigarette in her other hand became a stick of ash.

"Okay, sure," I said. That seemed unnecessary, as the numbers were already on the fridge.

"You know if anything ever happens to me, you call the other number and do whatever they say. I mean it—whatever they say."

"Are you some kind of secret agent?" I joked, not looking at her while I closed the top of the jar of peanut butter. "Is that why you don't have any pictures of you or my dad around here?"

"No, of course not," Mom said, not looking at me. "It's a backup number just in case, since I'm your only family. You remember what you're supposed to say?"

I sighed and opened the jar of grape jelly before saying in a monotone, "I need the three-by-four special."

"Right."

"Tell me again why I can't just go to the police?" I covered the other slice of bread with jelly. We'd gone over this point on more than one occasion, and she always said the same thing.

"You can't always trust the police. They don't always have all the information." The ash fell to the floor, leaving the cigarette tip glowing red.

"Whatever, Mom." My feelings at the moment were at odds with the note I'd written for Mom to go along with the sandwich. *Have the best day! Love, Retta.* Right now I didn't care what kind of day she had tomorrow. I put the jar back in the fridge and pulled out a mini-pack of baby carrots.

"Honey, you know I love you," Mom said.

"I know. I love you, too." I put the sandwich in a zip-close bag and pulled a brown lunch sack out of the pack on top of the fridge before Mom caught me in a hug.

"Thanks, honey," she said, nodding at the lunch bag and heading toward the den.

I opened the bag and put the sandwich and carrots in, then extracted the note from my pocket, laid it carefully on top of the carrots, and folded the top of the sack shut. I pulled a sharpie out of the drawer and wrote *Jenny* on the bag. This had been our little ritual for a long time. I made her lunches for her because it reminded her of me when she was at the school, surrounded by all those kids who weren't me. She worked in the local high school's cafeteria, which always seemed ironic since she was so adamant about homeschooling me.

Or not homeschooling me herself, since she had to work. I used to have babysitters who would help me work through all the material, but for the last three years, she'd left me alone during the day, and I'd stayed in and studied. It was more self-directed independent study than homeschooling.

She didn't realize how lucky she was with me. I could have been a much wilder kid, but instead I loved studying and had mostly always done what she said.

Once I'd put the lunch sack in the fridge, I went upstairs to figure out what to wear the next day. It was hugely important, since it would be the first day of school—my first day ever at a brick-and-mortar school. My first ever time interacting with other kids, except for the handful of other homeschooled kids I'd met when I was younger. None of those had become my friends because they were all super-Christian and we weren't.

On one of the occasions we got together with the area homeschooling set—the last occasion, as it happened—I managed to get myself ostracized by saying, "Oh, my God!" at a story one of the girls had told. The girls all told their moms, who then suggested to Mom that I not attend anymore.

I laughed out loud in my closet, remembering what had happened in the car on the way home. I thought Mom would be mortified since she was always so serious, but she actually giggled when we got in the car.

"Retta," she'd started in this super judgy voice, "how dare you take the Lord's name in vain?" Then she actually snorted and said, "Those self-righteous hypocrites." That was when I'd figured out we weren't religious.

I flipped through the Walmart clothes in my tiny closet. A blue and green striped T-shirt—a birthday gift from Mom—caught my eye. I decided on that and a pair of jeans. Would it be cool enough? I really had no idea. Fashion hadn't exactly been on the homeschooling curriculum, unfortunately.

Convincing her to let me attend the local high school in our little town of Buckley, Iowa hadn't been easy. I was fifteen years old and still wasn't allowed to go out. I don't mean I wasn't allowed to date. No, I mean I wasn't even really supposed to go outside. She was super worried I'd be kidnapped or something. So it had involved several fights, but I finally got her to agree when I pointed out that if I didn't learn how to talk to people my own age when I was still a kid, I'd never function as an adult. She was crazy nervous about the whole thing, even though she was trying to play it cool.

There were two real reasons I fought so hard to get her to let me go to school—and not because I wanted friends, though I obviously did. I wanted to join the cross country team. Mom didn't know that I had been going out every weekday. I had to run. She knew I ran, but thought I stayed in the neighborhood. That would be ridiculous because it was just one circular road, maybe half a mile around. I wasn't going to literally run in circles. No, I followed the country roads instead.

I needed to join a team because I had to see if I was

fast enough to get a scholarship somewhere. Which was the second reason. I had to go to college. I'd be the first in my family. But I didn't have much time, as I was already going to be a junior because of the extra classes I'd completed during my long days at home. I guessed that a couple years might be enough to impress some colleges.

But back to the immediate concern. Mom's grungy green Converse would be perfect for this outfit. Way better than my running shoes—the only shoes I owned. Mom never actually wore the Converse, but I remembered them from my dress-up days. Nope, Mom only ever wore her lunch lady shoes, which perfectly matched her life uniform, jeans and ratty T-shirts. She even saved her old pairs of shoes to wear for her afternoon shift at the animal sanctuary.

"Mom, can I borrow a pair of shoes for tomorrow?" I called from the stairs before I reached the living room.

Mom sat in the middle of the sunken couch with a navy blue throw wadded up behind her head. She paused the *Buffy the Vampire Slayer* DVD and looked up at me while taking a last drag off her cigarette and then snuffed it out in the giant ashtray on the coffee table. Her eyes narrowed as she frowned and said, "If you can find something not horribly out of style, knock yourself out." She lit another cigarette and focused back on the TV while starting Buffy back up.

Her apparent disinterest was very misleading. Normally she'd be all over every detail like some kind of stalker. Inside, she was freaking out since I'd be visible in the real world. But whatever—it was pretty much too late now for her to change her mind and pull me out. I flew back up the stairs to her closet and grabbed the Converse.

That's when I spotted the rounded blue toes of what turned out to be a surprising pair of lace-up boots rammed against the wall behind a shoebox, mostly covered by a folded blanket. The boots had chunky, plasticky soles that were a sort of see-through tan. There was something about the boots that made me like them. Something...bold, for the new Retta. The Retta who now had a chance at a normal life.

I sat on the bed to slide the boots on, pulling the laces taut. Nice—they fit like Christmas morning socks.

It was strange that I'd never noticed these boots before. I took them back to my room and sat on the twin bed to inspect them. Someone had obviously worn them—scuff marks lined both inside ankles, small rips made the leather jut out in a few places, and both laces had cracked end caps. But Mom? Not in my lifetime. And she never, ever talked about anything that had happened before I'd come along. I'd always assumed it was because of the whole rest-of-the-family-dying-tragically thing.

Maybe she'd even had them on in the car wreck. But why hold onto them if the memories were so unpleasant? She still refused to talk about it all. I knew very little about the wreck, except that my dad and all four of my grandparents died.

Mom didn't make a lot of sense. But I guess surviving that kind of wreck might make a person a little off.

I shook my head. I had the clothes sorted out, but now I had to figure out what to do with the rest of myself. Mom had blonde hair and an adorable snub nose. On the other hand, I must have gotten my deeply boring mousy brown hair and straight nose from my father. But the biggest problem was I didn't know how to "do" hair. Mom had never taught me because I'd never asked. But it was possible that she didn't know anything other than the braids she used to put me in, either, because she just blew hers dry and called it done.

I picked up a green and white hair tie in the bathroom and pulled my hair back into a ponytail. My hair was just past the shoulder so it wasn't a very long ponytail, but if I wore the little makeup Mom was going to allow—just lip-gloss and blush—maybe it would be okay. I also could wear it down since it had a little wave so it wasn't completely lifeless. Hopefully I'd be okay for the first few days and could look at what the other girls were doing to figure out what to do from there.

I went back to the closet and draped the shirt and jeans over the chair at my tiny black desk, also courtesy of Walmart. I'd put the thing together a couple years ago.

"Retta, are you—?" Mom called from the hall before appearing in my doorway and gasping like she'd just witnessed a murder. "What do you have those for?"

"What? You picked this shirt and—"

"Not the shirt, the boots!" She pointed at them with her cigarette. "Not those, you can't wear those."

"What? Why not?" I glanced at the boots, which looked like a simple pair of boots, not something to get all emotional over.

"You just can't," she said, free hand over her heart. She took a long drag.

I seethed. "Why not? Why don't you ever tell me

why you're so worried about stupid things?"

She squinted, obviously calculating, and I worried she might actually pull me out of school after all. But I was still mad, so I spat out, "And why do you have to smoke so much? It really stinks."

She looked off to the side. "Retta, you know I'm trying to quit."

Mom was always "trying to quit." It never took. There were ashtrays everywhere.

I sat down and took the boots off. I might have to compromise on this issue to make sure I'd still get to go, but I didn't have to be cooperative.

"Wear the Converse. You always liked those, anyway." She walked in and stuck the cigarette in her mouth so she could carry the boots out with that hand, still holding the other to her chest.

****

The ride into school the next morning was awkward. I was so excited I was practically bouncing around inside the car. And Mom's mouth was in a straight line that matched the lines of her tense shoulders and back.

"You be careful, Retta," she said as we pulled into the parking lot. "You don't have a lot of experience with other kids."

That was the understatement of the year.

"And you can't trust everyone," she continued. "Just remember that."

"Okay," I said, admirably not rolling my eyes. We'd been fighting enough lately that it was easiest to just agree. I still worried she'd change her mind and drive me home.

She didn't. We parked, and although I'd hoped I'd

have time to go by the office to ask about how to join the cross country team, I didn't think there was enough. I had my schedule printed off and made my way through the crazy busy hall—dodging kids left and right—to my first class, English. I was relieved to be out of the hall and in the classroom, which was blessedly quieter. My heart raced from all the people.

I looked around the room. At the front was a large tan desk with an older woman sitting behind it. She had reading glasses on a chain around her neck and stared out the window. There were several rows of matching tan chair desks, some of which were occupied. Some of the occupants looked at me standing in the doorway. There was a super-nerdy-looking chubby boy in a sloppy T-shirt. He eyed me, obviously bored. A girl in a long skirt sat in the front near the door. She could have easily belonged in the homeschooling set that had rejected me, so I took a seat across the room second from the front. I wanted to be close but didn't want to be like the teacher's pet.

Once I sat down, I could only see the girl and not any of the other kids, since I didn't want to be all obvious and turn around. She had long curly hair, and my intuition stated very clearly that it wasn't the popular style.

More kids came in and eventually a pretty girl with long, straight blonde hair sat in front of me. She talked to someone a couple rows over as she sat down and didn't even look at me. The bell rang right after that, and I was embarrassed I jumped a little. I hoped nobody noticed.

The class itself was fine—there was nothing surprising, though I was excited about the reading list.

Fahrenheit 451 and *The Scarlet Letter*. I'm a big reader and always enjoyed my English classes. That was how I'd managed to work a full year ahead.

When the bell rang to mark the end of class, I started again. I dug my schedule out of my pocket and went back into the throng of kids to navigate to my second class, Media Studies.

I was the first one to the room and sat in basically the same spot as I had in English.

As the kids started coming in, I glanced over as a boy sat next to me.

He smiled and said, "Hi. You're new, right?"

I nodded and couldn't help grinning even though he was dressed like a country boy, all the way from his ridiculous shirt with shiny snaps for buttons down to his cowboy boots. That was not going to be my scene. "I'm Retta."

"Nice to meet you, Retta. I'm Jack. And this is Gary." He motioned to the guy in jeans and a gray T-shirt sitting on his other side, who gave me a wave and a nod but didn't say anything. He at least wore normal shoes. Nikes.

Jack didn't look anything like the rest of the kids here, who were all as white as could be. Maybe Middle Eastern, with his shiny black hair and dark tan skin. He was tall and lean and—except for the cowboy look— kind of cute.

The class sounded interesting. We'd be doing a project where we had to create a blog and some other material. We'd be working in groups, but she'd assign them later.

When class was over, Jack arched his eyebrows at me and waved goodbye before disappearing into the crush of people.

My next class was French. I was pretty excited about this one. I'm a big language geek, and I'm pretty sure I'm going to end up being a translator. My best language is Spanish, but I also know a fair bit of French and German, both of which I'm taking at the junior level this year. I took my official lucky spot, since nothing had gone wrong yet.

The class was nice because we got to speak French. That was the problem I'd had studying languages on my own—no speaking practice. I'd found some free language sites online and could understand it okay, but I'd had few opportunities to speak it. But the teacher understood me, so I guess I did okay. By the end of the year, I would be totally up to speed.

My next class was also fine, and at lunchtime, I threw my books in my locker and followed the herd toward the cafeteria. I had to make sure I didn't interact with Mom. I'd already had a conversation with her about this, and she appeared to understand. Lunch ladies were not cool. I didn't know much about school, but I knew that.

I opened one of the weathered red double doors into the small cafeteria across from the main building. It was quite the spectacle. There were kids everywhere— in the line, filling the tables to bursting, and just milling around talking. My nerves started acting up, shooting daggers into my stomach, because I'd never been around so many people at once.

I'd never been around even a classroom's worth of people, since the only ones I'd ever known were my babysitters, both older ladies, and a few other homeschooled kids. The hall had been one thing, but the cafeteria was in another league.

I forced myself to find the end of the line, putting my green tray on the metal shelf in front of the glass sneeze guard. There was Mom, wearing a horrid hair net and some kind of stained white smock with snaps running down the front. When I got to her, she slopped a pile of chicken and rice casserole onto my tray and gave me a little smile, but I didn't think anyone noticed. I still glared. I poured a cup of water, paid, and then stood there, unsure where to go.

The room was so loud, which was both intimidating and exciting. My heart sped up. So many possibilities. If only I had some friends to sit with.

There, in the corner—a small and empty two-seater. I glanced around while making my way over to it. There were some people I recognized from my classes, but I wasn't gutsy enough to attempt to sit with them. I set the tray down on the tacky, fake-wood-grain table. The chair screeched as it scraped the floor when I dragged it out.

I observed the room while I ate. There seemed to be a lot more talking than actual eating. And kids were moving around all over the place, table to table, chatting with different people.

Then I watched the cowboy from Media Studies—Jack—walking purposefully toward me. Was he going to talk to me?

"Hi," he said when he stood before me.

"Hi."

"Why don't you come sit with us?"

My face warmed. Did he think I was pitiful for sitting all by myself? And did I want to sit with him and his friends? What if they were all country like him?

He laughed. "Don't worry, everybody's nice."

Now I was embarrassed by my overly long silence. "Okay, that sounds cool." Then I added, "Thanks."

"We're over in the east corner, by the fire exit."

I stood up—the chair screeched again—and picked up my tray. We snaked around tables to get to the corner table. He sat down, and the only open chair was next to him, so I set the tray down and squeezed in between him and a girl with long, blonde hair. A different one from the girl in English. There were lots of blonde girls here. I faked a brave face just as Jack said, "Hey, guys, this is Retta."

The brown-haired boy—Gary from Media Studies—nodded at me and the girls all said "Hi," in unison. Jack introduced everyone else around the table. Rachel was the girl sitting next to me, and then there was Lily and one other girl whose name I missed. She and Lily were both wearing cute tank tops that looked like they came from the same place.

Rachel turned to me while the three across from us started talking again. She said, "So Jack tells me you're in Media Studies. Do you like it?"

Jack had told them about me? My stomach fluttered. "Yeah, it's pretty good."

"I took it last year," Rachel said. "And if you're interested in that sort of thing, there's still time to join the yearbook committee for this year. We always need more people."

"Okay, I might do that," I said, feeling lighter. Maybe I was making friends, right now. Is this how it was supposed to go? Rachel seemed nice, and I decided I would stop being a snob about the country thing in order to ignore the fact that she wore a denim dress and cowboy boots with decorative stitching in pink and green.

Rachel went back to her lunch—just half a sandwich and a yogurt, from what it looked like—and I took a bite of my cooling casserole.

"I think I'm going to drop Media Studies and pick up Art," Gary announced.

"Who'll I do my project with, then?" Jack asked.

"You'll think of something, I'm sure."

Just beyond Jack, I saw Mom making her way toward our table. The bottom of my stomach caved in. Now she wore an awful grayish white apron with stains all over it, and of course her hair was still in the net. She looked positively humiliating.

And she kept getting closer and closer until she stopped at the end of the table and began wiping off the two now-empty spots next to Jack with a bleachy towel I could smell all the way from my seat. She looked at me several times while doing this and then looked at everyone else sitting there like she was trying to memorize their faces. I was frozen. Was she going to say something?

Then Mom gave the table one last swipe with the towel and walked away.

Lily said, "That was weird." Everyone watched Mom walking back toward the lunch line, and my face surged red hot, but I said nothing.

"It was almost like she was checking up on us," Lily continued. "What did she think we did?"

Jack glanced at me, and my heart twisted as I wondered if somehow he knew she was my mom. But instead he said, "So, Retta, what do you do for fun?"

Thank God. I tried to think of what to say while I

finished chewing. "Well, I read a lot. And I run."

"Oh, you're a runner?" Rachel asked, turning back toward me.

I nodded.

"I run cross country. You should join the team." Rachel waved her sandwich around as she talked with her hands.

"Oh!" I said. "I already planned to. How do I join?"

"Tryouts are next Monday. After school."

"That's awesome. Thanks." It *was* awesome. What were the chances I'd end up sitting with people who were into the same things I was?

When I turned back to my tray, I caught Jack watching me with a half-smile, like he was pleased with himself. I caught his eye for a second until he turned back toward his own tray. I wondered what that was about.

I didn't figure anything out by the end of lunch, but it didn't seem like anything to worry about.

I ate with them every day that week, and Mom didn't pull her stunt again. Neither of us said anything about it at home.

On Friday, I concluded that they definitely were my friends now. I'd talked to all of them some, and they seemed nice enough, but I spent most of the time talking to Rachel and Jack. Jack was in my last class of the day, too—Trig. Still, it was a surprise when Rachel said, "Who's coming over tomorrow?" while scanning the table. "You're welcome to come, too, Retta."

Whoa. I'd been invited to hang out with a group of kids *my own age*. It was a small miracle. "I'd love to," I managed. "I'll have to check with my mom."

Getting permission from her wouldn't be easy. She'd probably given the rope as much slack as she would.

Chapter Two

On Saturday morning, I listened for Mom's car to leave for her grocery run. As soon as it was gone, I went into her room to look for anything that might reveal the Big Secret. Because there had to be something to explain why she acted so strange and paranoid.

Friday night we'd sat down to dinner, and I'd asked to go over to Rachel's.

"No, I don't think it's a good idea, honey," Mom had said, dishing stir fry on top of the rice on my plate. The tangy scent of hoisin sauce wafted up my nose.

"Why not? Please, I really want to go." I had to focus to not sound like a whiny child.

"No." Mom served herself some of the stir fry and blew on a forkful of it, a green bean dangling.

"Mom, come on—what's the big deal?"

"No, Retta."

"But Mom, it's crazy! Nothing is going to happen to me in Buckley!" Why did Mom always act like everything was so risky? Like anything bad had ever happened to the two of us, anyway. Our life was boring, boring, boring.

"You don't know that." She paused, voice rising. "You don't know the world like I do."

"Well, why don't you tell me?"

"Retta, there are things you don't know." She'd

lowered her voice again and finally put the forkful in her mouth.

I was so pissed that I yelled, "Tell me, then!" My hands were on the edge of the table.

"No." Her firm voice made it clear she wasn't going to budge.

I'd pushed my chair back and spent the rest of the night in my room. Who needed dinner when it meant I had to spend it with Mom?

So now I sat down at the small desk in Mom's bedroom, careful of the medical thrillers precariously stacked on one corner. I pulled open drawers and scanned stacks of bills and other papers, trying to put things back where I'd found them.

Nothing jumped out, but not knowing exactly what I needed made it extra difficult. Everyone kept certain important papers around. Maybe birth certificates? They wouldn't tell me much, maybe, but it would be something. None of the things I found looked old—then again, it might not have to be something old. I didn't know.

Just bills, really. I'd hoped to find something related to my dead family. You'd think an entire family dying in one accident would make the news. My dad and both sets of grandparents, all at once. Mom had been in the van, too, but she was okay. I sat for a moment tapping on the desk before I remembered the shoebox I'd seen when I'd gotten the boots out.

When I opened it, the box had a bunch of baby pictures of me. I was sort of cute as a baby. My hair was a lot lighter back then. There were three CDs under the photos: *Pearl Jam Ten*, *Nirvana Nevermind*, and *Principal Pike*. I opened the jewel cases and noted that all the CDs looked like the real things, not burned copies. Weird—why in the world would Mom have these CDs hidden away instead of out on the shelf with all the others? I opened the cases and could see nothing unusual. Just the CD and the insert in each, which I unfolded to make sure there was nothing fishy.

There wasn't. I threw my hands up, sighed, put the box back in order and left it where I'd found it.

I was still sitting there when Mom called me from downstairs. I jumped up, panicked. How had I not heard the garage door? I ran out into the hall just before Mom turned from the top of the stairs.

"Hey, honey. Are you okay? You look pale."

"Oh, I'm fine." I willed the color back into my face.

"Guess what? I bought jelly donuts."

"Thanks." This must be a peace offering. We were both crazy about donuts, especially those stuffed with a gooey substance. Now I felt guilty about pawing through Mom's stuff.

I followed her downstairs, and she reached into a white paper bag to hand me a powdery donut with red jelly poking out the side.

"Thanks, Mom." I helped put the groceries away with one hand while stuffing my face with the donut in the other, powder sprinkling my shirt.

"Are you still mad about the party?" Mom asked, resting her hand on my shoulder. "You were pretty upset last night."

She could be so handsy. She'd been better lately, but still.

"Yeah, I still don't understand why you won't let me hang out with a few people." I swallowed a big bite of donut. "And it's not even a party. You don't want me to have any fun." I focused on the macaroni and cheese I was putting into the cabinet because I knew Mom well enough to know trying to convince her was pointless.

Mom loaded the freezer with bags of veggies. "Would you like me to make a grilled cheese sandwich? Some tomato soup?"

"No, I'm not hungry." Like comfort food would do anything. After everything had been put away, I went back to my room, shutting the door with a soft click. I spent the rest of the day alternating between reading for English and other homework. As I got ready for bed, I stuffed my favorite running shorts and T-shirt into my backpack for the tryout Monday.

****

Monday at lunch I talked to Rachel about qualifying for the cross country team at the tryouts, and she laughed. "You make the team just for showing up, basically," she said.

"Oh." I blushed.

"But it's the meets where it matters," Rachel said with raised eyebrows. "You know, if you're good you win, if not, you don't."

"So how come you didn't come to Rachel's on Saturday, Retta?" Gary asked out of the blue, glancing over at Jack as he said it.

My stupid face heated up again. "Oh...my mom wouldn't let me." I didn't know if I wanted them to know how paranoid Mom really was.

"That sucks," Jack said.

I nodded. It truly did.

Rachel said, "Maybe another time. We do something most weekends. I think we're all going to a movie this weekend, right?"

Lily nodded and Gary said, "*Final Destination*, the fiftieth incarnation."

I wasn't too keen on movies like that, but I'd still go if I could convince Mom. Which I probably couldn't. I stewed over that for the rest of lunch.

When I got back to my locker afterward, it was ajar and missing the lock. I must have not latched it properly. I swung the door open only to see no backpack. I spun around but the only things in the hall were other kids at their lockers and walking down the hall, nobody with an extra backpack that looked like mine.

"Are you okay?"

I turned around to see Lily behind me and realized my mouth was still hanging open. "Someone took my backpack from my locker!"

"Oh, no," Lily said, shaking her head. "Did you leave it unlocked?"

"I don't know," I said. "Maybe by accident?"

"Hold on a sec," Lily said as she leaned over a trash can a little way down the hall before coming back. "No luck. Sometimes they dump them in the trash."

"What do you mean?"

"There are some kids around here who think it's funny to raid unlocked lockers." She shook her head again. "You might check other trash cans around here, too. You should report it to the office, though they can't do much."

"Oh."

"Good luck." Lily shrugged but looked genuinely sorry.

I stood staring after her as she walked off to class,

still dumbstruck. Why would somebody take my bag? What were they going to do with it? But I went on to class. I'd already removed most of my books and notebooks that morning. In German I had to look over at my neighbor's book, but it was not a huge problem.

I checked all the trash cans I passed, plus my locker after each class, hoping to find the bag sitting in front of it, but no luck. By the time my last class rolled around, I was pretty stressed. Mom would be pissed if she had to buy a new backpack.

Jack came in right after me and sat down. "So Lily told me they took your backpack."

I nodded, my eyes wide at how I was being talked about among people who were now my friends. I knew it would happen, but it was still kind of surreal.

Jack said, "There are some guys who do this whenever they see an open locker."

"Lily said." I cocked my head. "Why?"

Jack shrugged, palms up. "Who knows, but I'll see what I can do to get it back. I know who usually does it."

"Oh, okay. Thanks." That was very cool of him.

His smile revealed some very nice, straight teeth I hadn't noticed before.

I managed to recover from blushing at how my heart had sped up ever-so-slightly, just in time for all the color to drain from my face. "My running clothes! They were in the bag!"

"Oh, man, and you have the tryout today."

I groaned and fell onto my arms crossed on the desk.

Chapter Three

After class, I raced into the office to see if my bag had been turned in, but it hadn't. I sighed as it hit me that I really wouldn't have my running clothes for the tryout.

I looked for Rachel, but she wasn't in the locker room or outside with the other kids. I plopped down on a bench in the locker room.

A couple of tanned girls glanced at me sitting there, but neither said anything before they left.

Rachel rushed in. "Oh, hi, Retta! What are you doing? Aren't you going to try out?" She dropped her bag on the bench and pulled out shorts and a T-shirt.

"Yeah, I want to. I hoped you had an extra pair of shorts I could borrow. Someone stole my backpack today."

Rachel slid her shorts on. "Oh, I heard about that. Your running clothes were in there? That's terrible. I don't! Maybe someone else does? Let's go ask." She threw her T-shirt on and tossed her bag into a locker, slamming it shut. "I'm running so late!"

We raced out to where all the other kids were standing, but a tall and slim bald man was already talking.

"—coming out for the tryouts."

Rachel looked at me with a shrug and a grimace. I was going to have to do it in jeans.

"As most of you know, I'm Coach Olson, and I coach cross country and track and field. I also teach English, but that's not important. The tryouts today are for cross country, but I always include some track and field work at the beginning so we don't have to do this in the spring. This isn't how most schools do it, but I do it this way since most of you end up doing both anyway."

His gaze fell on me and narrowed.

"You don't have any shorts?" he asked.

I shook my head slowly.

"You're new. Didn't know about the tryouts?"

"Um, yeah."

"Well, I suppose that will have to do." He cleared his throat and continued. "Everyone will do everything, but half of you will be working on sprints and hurdles while the other half tries out discus, shotput, and the long jump." He stopped and began counting us, finally saying, "Let's go to the track." He jogged off toward the back of the school, away from the football field, with everyone else following behind him.

It became clear that running in jeans was not ideal, but also that I could do it. At least I didn't have tight skinny jeans, although part of the problem was that the bottoms of my jeans kept scraping each other.

Once we reached the track, the coach sent kids off to the long jump, shotput, and discus, telling the last two groups, "Just pick them up and feel them in your hands. Do not throw *anything*. Until I get there." Then he motioned for everyone else to follow and jogged toward some set-up hurdles.

I was curious about hurdles but even more about sprinting. I'd only ever done distance running.

Coach Olson said, "We're going to try out the 100-meter and 200-meter sprints, and after that you can try jumping hurdles if you want." He showed us how to measure the distances on the track and then told us to run on our own—first slow, then faster each time—without worrying about timing. "I'll be watching you as you practice but don't worry about it. Don't try the hurdles yet. We'll do those together as one group. Go ahead and get started."

I followed some of the other kids trying out the 100-meter sprint. I found it super strange—it was over so fast, even at my probably slow speed. Nothing like running for an hour and the sense of true freedom it brought. It felt more like running from something. I tried it again a few times, and then worked on the 200-meter sprint.

I cycled through the discus, shotput, and long-jump stations. I kind of liked the long jump, probably because of the running part, but didn't care for the shot put or the discus. I practiced my sprints a bit more until the coach said it was time for the hurdles. He rounded everyone up and demonstrated the technique, telling us to practice by running and jumping next to a hurdle a few times.

After several trial runs past the hurdle, I decided to try to actually jump one. I started running, and as I closed in on the hurdle, I pumped my right knee up and lifted my foot, pushed off the ground harder than normal, saw my front leg clear the hurdle, then felt my back leg tap it and drag it down. Hitting the hurdle threw me off a little but I managed to keep going and slow down without tripping. I flushed with the effort and embarrassment at knocking it down.

When I turned around and walked toward where the coach stood, he was watching me—and he wasn't the only one. I looked down at the track before leaning over to set the hurdle upright again.

Coach Olson yelled for everyone to come in. "Now we're going to do the longer run. Everyone back to the football field." We took off.

As soon as everyone arrived, he said, "You'll all run around the field nine times, which is about two and a half kilometers, or just over a mile and a half. You need to keep track of your own laps. There are too many of you for me to do it. Just raise your arms on your last lap so I'll know you're done." He paused with a stopwatch in hand. "Everybody get in place."

Most of the kids clambered for front spots, but I hung back. I retied my shoes nice and tight. The coach started a countdown, then said, "Go!" and everyone was off.

I started pretty steady. One lap in, many of the kids had shot way ahead. Maybe I wasn't fast, despite what I'd thought. But there were several kids—girls, mostly—around me. Maybe they were all just running smart. Rachel fell back to run with me, though she didn't say anything.

As the laps passed, I concluded that running in a big circle was pretty boring. I used to do it in my neighborhood, but at least houses broke up the scenery. Running on grass was another matter—pretty cool. I'd never done that before.

I entered the seventh lap and still felt really good. Rachel touched my arm and said through heavy breaths, "I'm going to have to slow down."

I nodded and picked up the pace some and soon

finished that lap. Then I started running even faster, leaving just enough energy for later. Halfway through the last lap, I kicked it up to my max, and ran past the coach—the finish line—arms up and feeling powerful and completely in control. He shouted "ten thirty-two!" as I passed.

There was only one other kid who had finished—a slim brunette girl, one of the ones who'd stayed back with me in the early part of the run.

She came over to me, still breathing hard. "Nice run you just did. In jeans, no less."

My face was already red from running, so the blush wouldn't show. "Thanks. I didn't know if it was a good time or not. The, uh, jeans are because someone stole my backpack today, and it had my running clothes."

"Oh, wow. That's rough." She grimaced. "I gotta go, but nice meeting you. See you next time." She trotted over to talk to the coach and then back to the gym.

After she'd left, I asked Coach Olson, "What do I need to do now?"

"That was a great run. You would have had a good shot at finishing first if not for the jeans. And that hurdle!" He shook his head, eyes wide.

"Well, you're free now. We run together four days a week after school, Monday through Thursday. Be here tomorrow. The first meet is in two weeks."

"Oh." I still didn't know if Mom would let me do this. And of course I hadn't asked yet. "Um, Coach Olson?"

"Yes?"

"If I can't participate in the meets, can I still train with you?"

His eyes narrowed, and he frowned. "Why wouldn't you be able to?"

"My mom. She's very...overprotective."

"Please see if you can think of a way to convince her to let you compete. It would be really good for you. But yes, you can still train with us regardless."

I smiled. "Okay, I will. Thanks." He seemed to mean it.

I tightened my shoelaces again and started on the three-mile trek home after saying bye to Rachel. Soon I was running, feeling like life was on track.

****

By the time I neared my neighborhood, I was covered in sweat. My cotton shirt stuck to me, which was pretty uncomfortable, and the jeans were so damp they seemed gummy. Yet I felt fantastic.

I was about a quarter mile from my street when I passed a green mailbox with *Singh* written on it in neat white block letters. I'd passed it hundreds of times out on my regular afternoon runs and hadn't paid attention. This must be Jack's house. Indian, not Middle Eastern. Still interesting. I wondered how his family ended up out here in the boonies.

I intended to take a slow loop around my neighborhood to cool down. But when I got closer to my house, I could see Mom standing inside, in front of the living room window.

I stopped. I was dead!

Why was she home early? She should still be at the animal sanctuary.

I tried to think of a story, something about how I missed the bus, and it took two hours for me to run home...even Mom, who knew nothing of running times, wouldn't buy that.

So I'd just tell the truth. Whatever I said, I'd be in huge trouble. This way at least I wouldn't have to worry about keeping a story straight.

I inched toward the house, more nervous with each step. I walked up the porch steps and opened the front door.

"Oh, thank God! Where have you been?" Mom shouted, cigarette in hand. "I've been going out of my mind! I was about to call the police! And why didn't you answer your phone?"

"I—I missed the bus and took a wrong turn coming home." So much for telling the truth. "And you were going to call the cops?"

I pulled my phone out of my pocket and realized I'd left it off after the tryout. I wasn't used to people trying to get in touch with me.

Mom glared at me but stepped aside so I could squeeze past her. "Why are you all sweaty?"

"I ran." The lack of music was eerie.

Mom grabbed me by the arm. "What were you doing running all the way from school?"

"I told you—trying to get home."

"Why didn't you call me? I could have come by to give you a ride home—you know you're not supposed to be out like that!"

"Can I please sit down? I'm tired." I shook my arm free and fell into the couch, arms crossed. I deflated. "Why are you home now, anyway?"

"They're training a new cleaner today, so my shift is covered. Where's your bag?" Mom asked.

"I don't know. Some kids took it today."

"What? What do you mean, 'took it'?" She ran her

free hand through her hair.

"I mean, someone took it out of my locker," I said, shrugging and not looking at her. I put my feet on the coffee table and untied my shoelaces.

"Did it have anything valuable?"

"My German book, some homework, then just some notebooks and pens and pencils." And my favorite running shorts and shirt. "So, no, not really."

"You know you're not supposed to be out alone wandering around. Why did you miss the bus?"

"Because I was looking for my backpack." I surprised myself.

"Ah." She nodded but didn't look much calmer. "But, Retta, I'm so mad at you right now that you need to go to your room. I'm going to make dinner, and then we're going to talk."

I lay on my bed. Now Mom would never let me do cross country. She might even quit the sanctuary so she'd be here when I got home from school every day. I wouldn't be able to run at all anymore. My stomach was a mess from this realization.

After I spent an hour and a half with the unread book open on my chest, fretting, Mom called me back downstairs. The plaintive sounds of Snow Patrol were coming from Mom's Pandora station playing on her laptop.

"Let's eat," Mom said, motioning to the table.

I sat down, waiting for it to start, but Mom just dished up a ham casserole and glanced at me. Neither of us said anything while we started eating.

I stared at my plate, full of dread, but Mom still didn't say anything. We finished, and I stood to take my plate to the sink. "You done?" I asked. I usually did the dishes since she cooked.

"Yes," Mom said, handing her plate over.

I rinsed the plates off and scrubbed them clean with lots of soap. I rinsed them again and put them in the drying rack. Mom was still sitting at the table with her back toward the kitchen. I stood at the sink, not wanting to go back in there.

"Retta, I'm really angry at you. Why don't you care about your own safety?" Mom's shaky voice made her ooze tension. She lit a cigarette.

This was beyond stupid. "I do care about my safety, and I made it home fine!"

"You have no idea what's out there!" Mom yelled. "The fact that you made it home just means you—"

The doorbell ringing interrupted her.

Mom stood and walked toward the door but turned back to finish, pointing her finger at me. "It just means you got lucky this time." She opened the door.

I could hear a voice ask, "Hi, is this where Retta lives?"

Was that Jack? That made no sense. What would he be doing here? How did he even know where I lived? I rushed over to the door as Mom glared at me.

It was Jack, cowboy boots and all, and he held my backpack in his left hand. I stared at him and the bag he held.

"That's my daughter's backpack!" Mom said.

"Yes, ma'am," he said.

"And how did you come to have her backpack, exactly?" she asked, not in a very friendly tone.

"I heard the kids talking about it at McDonald's. They said they'd dumped it outside the school, so I looked for it. I thought you might want it back tonight.

So here it is," he said, holding it out to me with more confidence. "I know it looks kinda rough."

I stepped forward to take it. He'd meant it when he said he'd try to find it for me.

His eyes widened like he'd had an idea, and he said, "I didn't open it, but you might be careful. They might have put something in there before they dumped it."

"Oh. Well, thank you very much for bringing it."

"By the way," he said, grinning, "have you seen your video? It's wild!"

Chapter Four

I gaped at Jack. "What are you talking about? What video?"

"From the tryout. It's on YouTube. Just search for 'hurdles jeans,' and you'll find it."

"I'm on YouTube?" The backpack was ten times heavier.

He nodded. "Yeah, running and jumping hurdles."

My face flushed, and my eyes widened. "What—how—but I only jumped one hurdle! And I didn't even make it."

His eyes scrunched and glimmered like he'd burst out laughing, but he glanced over my shoulder at Mom and said, "Okay, I'd better go. See you tomorrow." He raised his hand in an awkward wave as he backed off the porch.

The wheels rolled as the truck drove off. Any second now, the argument would pick right back up but even worse. I was tired of all the fighting. A year ago we'd gotten along fine, before I'd asked for a few simple freedoms. What was wrong with wanting to be allowed out of the house now and then? Or being able to have friends?

"What is he talking about, Retta?" Mom asked, alarm in her voice.

"I don't exactly know. I didn't know anyone took video of me." I put my finger to my lip. "I guess that's why those kids had their phones out."

"But what is he talking about? What hurdles?" Mom strode into the dining room, where her laptop lay open on the table, and typed in the search terms in YouTube. I stood hunched behind her, hands in my pockets to keep them still.

Our newest cross country team member: Jeans! screamed the headline for the top hit. The thumbnail clearly showed me running. My stomach fluttered at the thought of all the kids who might see it. God, Mom was going to freak out. I needed to watch it to see how bad it would be.

Mom clicked play, and we watched two different videos packaged into one. In the first, I stumbled over the hurdle. But the second showed me running around the field. The camera was shaking like the videographer was also running, but despite that I looked like I was going fast—like a real runner.

"What is this?" Mom demanded.

"Well…" The video had 1114 views. That was way more than there were kids in the high school.

"This is on the internet!" Mom said, her voice shrill. "Everyone can see it!"

The panic in Mom's voice made me say, "Yes, that's YouTube."

But Mom didn't quite blow up like I expected. Instead, she said, "Oh, my God. Oh, my God." She looked off into the distance. "It was all for—" Tears fell from her eyes, and she whispered, "He'll find us."

"Who will find us, Mom?"

Then she smashed her cigarette out even though she'd just started it. When she saw what she'd done, she quietly said, "Dammit," and lit another.

I stared at her, unsure what to think and even less sure what to do. What was happening? What was she going on about? I knew how to handle yelling and knew with yelling things would eventually be resolved. But this felt different.

I put my hand on Mom's shoulder and said, "Mom, I didn't exactly tell you the truth about why I was late today. It was because I tried out to join the cross country team. That took an hour, then I ran home after. I thought I would have time to change before you got home."

"Hold on, Retta," she said, putting her hand over mine. She muttered, "Let me think. I have to get this video taken down."

I let go and fell onto the couch.

Mom Googled a few things and filled out a form before turning around and asking, "So is this something you do often?"

I stared at my feet. "Try out, no. But I do run for about an hour every day before you get home from work. I don't stay in the neighborhood, either, because it's boring."

"Retta!"

"I'm sorry." I focused on keeping my voice level. "But it's like I need to run. I'm good, you know. That's why they were recording me. Nobody could believe how good I was, even in jeans. The coach thinks so, too."

Mom's cheeks glistened with tears. "Really?" she said, her voice cracking.

"Yes." I nodded.

Mom cleared her throat. "Well, that is beside the point. You disobeyed me, knowing how I felt!"

"What else am I supposed to do? Parents are supposed to let their kids grow up."

Her face softened a little. "I know it seems harsh. But I have my reasons. I've seen things. There are things you don't know."

"Of course there are things I don't know! You won't tell me! Or let me learn them on my own like a normal person!" I was going to explode.

"Retta—"

"What are you hiding from me, Mom? I know there must be something! The way you're acting—it's just not normal. Who's going to find us?"

"Retta." Mom took a long drag on her cigarette. "I'm not hiding anything from you." Her free hand was clenched into a tight fist.

I didn't say anything because that was a lie. What else had she been lying about? Was anything true?

"So what does being on the team entail?" Mom ran her hand through her hair.

"They have practice Monday through Thursday after school. Everyone runs together." I knew Mom would say no, and I chewed on my lip.

"Is that it?" she asked, gaze boring into me.

"No, there are races against other schools, too. I told the coach I didn't know if I could do them or not."

"What did he say?"

"He said okay, but he thinks I should because I am fast. I know I could get a college scholarship."

Mom looked into her coffee cup. "Retta, no. Not if it gets your name out there."

"Why not?" I snapped. "Who doesn't want their daughter to get paid to go to college? What is wrong with you?"

"Honey, I..." Mom's voice trailed off.

"Of course. You can't even answer."

****

I sat down next to my backpack and leaned against the bed. The green bag looked quite beat up, like it had lost a duel with a monster truck. Dark, oily marks streaked across it, and a small tear flapped open near the top. I unzipped it and extracted the German book, notebooks, and my clothes; they seemed okay. But in the front pocket all of my pens and pencils were broken. Somebody had probably thrown the bag out of a moving car. Maybe even run over it.

I found some very surprising pornographic cartoon drawings in my extra notebook. My face felt hot, even though no one was around to see. The pictures were actually sort of well done but pretty offensive. I tore the pages out and buried them in the trash.

I picked up the clothes and tossed them onto the bed, which revealed a patch of bright red on my shorts. Somebody had taken red lipstick and dragged it along the crotch of the light yellow shorts, from front to back. That made me flush again.

I jumped up and ran to the bathroom to wash the shorts out with Woolite. Of course, the lipstick had stained them—my best running shorts.

I tiptoed to Mom's room and picked through the few sticks of lipstick, not that she ever wore it, looking for the right red. I found one that would do. I added streaks all over the shorts to match the original mark. After I'd added enough to make the design look intentional, I left the shorts to steep in the color for a while.

Afterward, I tried to do homework, but it was

hopeless—I couldn't even focus on French or German.

I opened up YouTube on my computer and checked the number of views—1423. My stomach went all twisty. All those people watching me. Who were they?

****

The next day, I convinced Mom to let me stay home with a fake queasy stomach.

After Mom left for work—ham sandwich, celery, and note in tow—I went to the garage and took photos of the stacks of boxes so I could put them back in the right configuration.

I had never looked in the handful of boxes out here but figured I could pick through them enough to rule them out as sources of information. But really, why didn't I know what they held, anyway? It now seemed weird that I never used to be suspicious or very curious. But now that I'd started questioning, there was no stopping it.

I stuffed my phone in my pocket and lifted a large box off the stack of three in the front corner. It weighed virtually nothing and contained only wadded-up packing paper. No secret stash of passports or mysterious plastic-wrapped white blocks.

I found the same thing with the next two I opened.

Another stack of smaller boxes, the tops closed with interlocking flaps, contained books, which didn't surprise me. I pulled enough out to make sure it was books all the way down. That took care of four more but yielded nothing.

The last two boxes in the back corner looked promising but were filled to bursting with crumpled old newspapers. They were all from the Des Moines

Register, from April and May of 2002, which was a little strange—it was after we lived here. Maybe Mom subscribed for a while? There was nothing else in them.

I put everything back and checked how it looked against the photos I'd taken, which I then deleted. Maybe paranoia ran in the family. I'd found a clue— Des Moines—but made no actual progress.

There had to be something, somewhere. Didn't there? Was Mom really a spy, maybe? It seemed crazy, but what rational mom gave weird instructions to follow in case something happened to her? Well, probably not a spy since she was worried someone might find us. Maybe a former spy? Either way, there must be some reason she hated the police so much.

I went inside to the little area we called the Reading Room, just a wide hallway running between the living room and the kitchen. A comfy recliner nestled up against a tall bookshelf overflowing with paperbacks, and a lamp stood guard next to the chair. When I was little, I'd had my own small chair, and the two of us would sit there and read together. I remembered how proud I'd been when we'd thrown it out because I'd gotten too big for it, but then I'd missed sitting in there with Mom.

That was a different time.

We did still exchange books quite a bit, however. I didn't go in for Mom's sci-fi or medical thrillers, but she'd turned me onto Barbara Kingsolver and Pat Conroy.

Even though it probably was overkill, I took pictures of the bookshelf, then pulled all the books off the top shelf and set them next to the recliner before falling into it.

I picked each book up and flipped through it, looking for any hidden documents.

Going through each shelf took almost two hours. And I'd found nothing except a few old receipts serving as bookmarks. Albertsons. Walmart. Greg's Used Books & More. As I put the last set back, I saw that I'd disturbed the dust on each shelf. Now I'd have to dust the whole shelf and act like I felt better and got bored if Mom noticed.

After that task, I sat back down in the chair and leaned it back, pondering. That's when it occurred to me that I hadn't searched all the books in the garage, which was more likely to be where stuff might be hidden. Crap. But I was sick of digging through stuff at the moment.

Anyway, maybe the key to the puzzle was not in Mom's possessions but instead in the story of the past. I remembered nothing before this house and hadn't even been there at the crash. I'd always believed the whole family except Mom had been killed in the van wreck, but one thing that had bothered me on occasion was why I hadn't been with them. Where would my parents and both my parents' parents be going without me? Maybe I really had been there, too? Plus, it now seemed weird that Mom didn't have some kind of permanent injury or scars from such a terrible accident.

I Googled everything I knew about the crash. I had the rough date, so I searched for news records of wrecks then. But there were tons, and the old newspaper records required payment. I found a few sites that would let me search accident reports by state, which made me realize I didn't even know for certain where the crash had happened.

I did know that right after it happened, Mom had moved us to Buckley and rented this house. I'd been born in Lincoln, Nebraska, so maybe it had happened in Nebraska. Yet I'd always assumed we had already been living somewhere in Iowa. Maybe it was Mom's family who was from Nebraska. But where else in Iowa had we lived? Des Moines, since that was the newspaper I'd found?

Also, it occurred to me that it was weird we didn't have much money. If all those people had died, surely Mom inherited money or got insurance money. It made no sense.

Googling everybody who had died brought up records of long-dead people with similar names and nothing more. What if it was all made up? What if those weren't their names at all? What if I was adopted—or worse, kidnapped? That would be crazy. But it also would explain why Mom was so paranoid.

Could that really be it?

Chapter Five

The next day, Jack arrived in Media Studies after me and nodded at me as he took his seat.

Jack turned and whispered, "So was everything in your backpack?"

"Yeah. They did some decoration, but it was all there."

"Certain drawings?" he said, nodding.

"Yeah." I was not interested in telling him about the decoration on my shorts.

"Alex does them." From his bag, he extracted a beat-up notebook with a pen crammed into the spiral.

"I don't know him."

"She"—he emphasized the pronoun—"is friends with Quentin Bird and that crew."

My mouth fell open. "A girl did those?"

"I know, right?"

"Also, Quentin Bird as in Bird Diner?"

"Yeah, that's the one."

"His dad is our landlord." I shook my head. That was just rich.

The corners of his mouth quirked up. "Ah. In Buckley, it's more like three degrees of separation, not six."

I laughed. I turned back toward the front but stole another glance at him.

A few minutes later, and we'd been assigned to the

same group for the project—just the two of us, Jack and me.

He asked, "So you want me to do all the blog entries?"

"No, no—we have to split the writing work according to the instructions, right?"

He glanced at his paper and nodded as Mrs. McIntosh walked by, so I continued, "But you could do the blog layout design and plan other stuff like which posts we will include, and I'll do the same for the print part."

"Ah, I see."

"We don't have to do it that way—I'm just suggesting it."

"It sounds good to me."

"Okay, but now we need to pick an actual topic."

"I have an idea for that," he said, before I had even brought my list out. "Unconventional exercising."

"Um, what do you mean?"

"We can use a still in the print section or an edited video of you running the hurdles. It's so funny." He grinned. "But in a cool way, I mean."

I had to put my hands on my cheeks to cool off. "My mom was so freaked out by the video. She made YouTube take it down."

His grin went away. "Really? Why?"

"I don't know," I said. "She's just like that."

"Well, if we could find it, we could use it."

"Sure," I said. "But what else could we write about?"

"We have to do two print articles and two blog posts, right?"

"Right."

"One of the print articles could be an overview of everything. The two blog posts could each cover some specific exercise or sport that's unconventional. Or a family of related activities. 'Unconventional' doesn't have to mean 'weird;' it could just be an activity not many people do."

"That sounds kind of cool. The second print article could be an interview if we could find somebody appropriate for it."

"Yeah, that would be awesome."

"Ooh, I know one!" I exclaimed. "I saw it on TV—what's it called—Parkour! You know, running across an urban landscape or whatever."

"Oh, perfect." His eyes gleamed. "See, this will work."

"I also swear I saw something on TV once about Extreme Ironing, which they claimed was a sport because you'd take an ironing board up mountains and stuff. It was crazy."

"What? That is crazy. Oh, another one—planking."

I looked at him blankly.

"You know, when people lie face down in weird places with their arms glued to their sides, like planks."

"Oh," I said. "I didn't know about that one. But there's always Quidditch for Harry Potter fans."

"Also, the one where you use GPS devices to find stuff…"

"Geocaching?"

"Yeah, that's it." Jack grinned, obviously proud of himself.

"Okay everyone, start wrapping up," the teacher said. "You have two more days to do your planning, and then we're going back to lectures, and you should do your work on your own."

I said, "This project could actually be sort of fun."

"I know. We should get together to plan it out more."

My stomach fluttered. "Oh, maybe." That would never fly with Mom.

"What about after your practice today?" Jack asked. "You know, I can give you a ride home after your practice. I usually wait around for Rachel. We both live out near Reginald Heights."

That was my neighborhood. Would Mom be more pissed if I took a ride from a boy I hardly knew or ran all the way home alone? Hard to say. "I'm not sure. My mom…"

"Okay, well if you want to, let Rachel know at practice. Unless you think you're too good to ride in my grungy truck." He grinned at me.

"My mom just doesn't like me doing stuff with people."

"Ah. Well, she doesn't have to know. I won't tell her."

I grimaced and didn't answer.

Jack said, "Okay, so anyway, this blog post. Did you think of anyone we could interview?"

We talked until class ended and continued that conversation at lunch.

After my practice that afternoon, he was standing there talking to Rachel. He seemed to be everywhere.

He spotted me looking and waved at me, his gaze traveling down toward my legs. I had on my decorated yellow shorts, which had ended up looking kind of cool.

Then he called my name. "A ride home? I'm taking

Rachel."

"Oh, uh…I'd better not. But thanks."

"Okay," he said, but I thought he frowned.

Rachel gave me a friendly wave, too, and she and Jack headed toward the parking lot. They seemed close. He even waited for her after school. Were they an item? I found I really wanted to know this.

But I had another task to distract me. I walked to the bank in town, which I'd found on Google maps. The day before, I'd printed an application for a copy of my birth certificate from the Nebraska Department of Health and Human Services website. It would have both my parents' names so I'd know something after I got it. I used some of the little cash I had to buy a money order and felt a rush of excitement as I dropped it in the mail slot. They said seven to ten days for processing.

My heart grew lighter with every step on the walk back home until my thoughts meandered back to Jack.

Maybe I should have accepted his offer.

****

Just before Media Studies ended Monday, Jack talked me into accepting a ride home. I guessed I'd get in trouble, but I decided to see what would happen if I forced the issue with Mom. Maybe ultimately she'd see he was a decent guy.

After the run, Rachel said, "I'm going over to meet Jack."

"Cool."

As we walked to the locker room, Rachel said, "I'm glad you're on the team—you should be able to help us in relays. You are so fast."

"Oh, I'm not sure if my mom is going to let me

compete. Actually, she said no, but I'm going to try and talk her into it." I had no idea how.

"That sucks. Why won't she let you?"

"I don't know; she's just a control freak."

When we got to the library, Jack started packing his bag up. Something about the way the sun beamed in through the windows and lit his hair made me really look at him. Although his black hair was cut in a generic guy's short style, the natural sheen it had gave him a glamorous look. Yet he dressed a hundred percent country boy, in everyday cowboy clothes— Western jeans, long-sleeve button-up shirt. Everything but the cowboy hat. My face warmed.

We got to his gray pickup. This was a real farm truck—mud-streaked, faded paint, a scratched-up bed. You had to respect that more than the glossy, perpetually-waxed ones the rich town kids drove.

As soon as we got going, Rachel switched on the radio, and the twang hit me like a too-hot summer wind.

"Uh," I said. "Can we change it?"

"You don't like Jason Aldean?"

"Who? No, this isn't my thing at all."

"What, country?" Rachel asked.

"Yeah."

Jack and Rachel both laughed. "You'll have to suffer then if you ever hang out with us," Rachel said.

Rachel and Jack chatted a bit about what sounded like a recent party, while I tried to imagine hanging out with them. I had to convince Mom.

Rachel said, "Retta, you really should come over sometime. You're not afraid to do something crazy now and again." She laughed, and I smiled.

"Wait," I said at the next song, "did he just ask if

47

she thought his tractor was sexy?"

Jack and Rachel cracked up.

"You're not kidding," Rachel said, still laughing.

"Sorry. My mom taught me to hate country music before she taught me to tie my shoes." I gave a clipped laugh. "Sounds like I might have to unlearn that."

We all laughed. Soon after, Jack dropped Rachel off and drove on to my house. It was a quarter to six, so we had about a half hour before Mom would get home. We got set up at the dining room table to work on the project.

Jack said, "I worked on this last night instead of math, so I've got a good list already. And I thought of another angle to cover: normal activities done in unusual ways. There is this group of skydivers who like to jump naked, which makes for some pretty uncomfortable viewing." He stretched out the "pretty" and "uncomfortable" when he said it.

I felt my face turn red yet again, but I laughed. "I don't need to see that," I said, going over and sitting down at the table across from Jack.

"No, you don't. A little imagination goes a long way."

He showed me the list he'd made, and I added a few I'd thought of. The list was impressive—thirty-one weird sports or physical activities.

"So who is going to do the overview article?" I asked. "Do you want to, since it was your idea, and you made the big list? And do you have any ideas for the second article? I've got nothing."

"Maybe we could pick a few of the activities to focus on that have a lot of high-school-age kids who participate. Or more rural ones. Or ones that are more about real exercise. Or maybe ones that are team sports. Or more…coed ones." He stopped.

I laughed. "Are you done?"

"I think so," he said, also laughing, blushing. "I sometimes get carried away."

The side door in the kitchen that led to the garage opened, and Mom came into view. She looked over and spotted Jack sitting there with me. Her expression darkened, but she recovered and said, "Hi, I see you have a friend over." Looking at Jack, she asked, "What was your name again?"

"I'm Jack. Pleased to meet you, ma'am. Sorry for delivering and dashing the other night."

"Nice to meet you, too." She looked at the table, with the backpacks and all the papers spread out, and asked, "What are you two working on?"

I said, "It's a group project for our Media Studies class. We have to create a magazine with a blog."

"Ah. What is it going to be about?"

"Jack had the idea of extreme or weird sports."

Mom gave a tight laugh. "That sounds like fun. Okay, I'll leave you to it while I make dinner."

I said, "Okay, thanks, Mom." Was this a good sign, or was she just waiting to freak out?

"So," Jack said, "we can start with Wikipedia for info on these and narrow down the list to the ones we're most interested in and see if there's a theme."

We talked more about the topics on the list, but I was distracted by Mom being right there. Probably because she kept glancing over at us.

Finally, Jack seemed to catch on to my discomfort and said, "I should get going. But why don't we each pick five we like the most tonight and decide tomorrow if there's a theme?"

"Yeah, that sounds good. And tomorrow we can also decide who's doing what."

"That's what I was thinking. Cool. So I'll see you then." Jack stood up and packed his backpack.

"Okay, thanks for coming over." I walked him to the door. At the door he turned around and looked into the kitchen before smiling at me.

Once he had driven off, Mom said in a tight, angry voice, "How could you just invite someone over without asking me first? What were you thinking?"

"It was spur-of-the-moment! It's not a big deal. He's in my last class, and that's when he suggested it. He's friends with Rachel and gives her a ride home after cross country, so he offered to bring me, too, and stop in." It all sounded very logical and reasonable to me.

"Why didn't you call me?"

I said nothing. Because she would have said no.

Mom shook her head. "Retta, I don't know what has gotten into you. Do not bring people—any people—here without my permission. You could have at least called me on your way here or when you got here. The fact that you didn't call tells me something: I can't trust you. At least not right now."

"You can't trust me?" I yelled. "You're the one who's lying to me about something huge!" It seemed so obvious now with the weird stories, all the paranoia.

"What are you talking about? I don't lie to you!" Mom shouted back.

"Yes, you do! I know it!" I'd been so naive to take so long to see it. "Why don't you tell me more about the van accident? Why won't you tell me about my dad or my grandparents? Why are you so against the police?"

"Retta, you need to calm down." Her voice was still raised, but she ran her hand through her hair, and I could tell she was trying to regain her composure.

But it wasn't enough. I yelled, "You can't just force me to relax! You're the one who's wrong here!"

Mom looked at me, her face like steel, and said, "And how do you know this boy Jack isn't horrible?"

"What are you talking about? He's obviously not."

Mom sighed and softly said, "I know he's different and kind of cute, but you don't know anything about him."

That hit a little close to home, and I blushed. I managed to say, "I know he got my backpack back when he didn't have to. I know him better than you do. And anyway, we were only working on a school project!"

"Still, you don't know him."

That got me going again, my head pounding. "How am I supposed to get to know anybody if you won't let me?"

"Retta, just don't spend time with people you don't know, for one. Just don't."

I narrowed my eyes and said, "Why are you like this? What happened to you? Why can't I have a remotely normal life?" I cradled my forehead in my palms, elbows on the table.

"I've told you before, there are things you don't know—"

I looked up and shouted, "What does that even mean? I've asked you over and over to tell me!"

Mom blinked once. Twice. "Okay, Retta. Once I

was in a relationship with a man who hit me. He seemed very nice at first. I'm not going to say anything else about it. You just need to be careful, for your own good. I'm not trying to ruin your life."

I already felt dizzy from being so mad, and the revelation that there truly was something Mom was hiding made it worse. Was the man my dad? Was Mom glad when he died? When I turned to go upstairs, I looked at Mom and could see she was crying. For some reason, it made me angrier. I was the one who was suffering, not Mom, and it was Mom's fault. Her choice.

I stomped up the stairs and slammed my door hard, embarrassed even as I did it. Then I lay down and cried, unable to think of anything else to do. After a while, I heard Mom at my door. "I'm leaving your backpack with all your stuff outside your door. Just say something to let me know you're there, and I'll leave."

I took a breath. "Okay."

"Okay. Good night, honey. I love you."

This made me want to scream again. The tears started with a vengeance, but then I remembered the way Mom had sometimes held onto me when I was little like she thought the wind was trying to carry me away. Mom had cried when she'd done this, and it always scared me.

I was on to something. Mom had admitted that there was something to tell, but that she just wouldn't.

****

Before French the next day, Jack said, "If you want to come over to work on the project, my mom will be there in case that matters."

"Sounds good." I paused, tensing inside. "But I'll

have to check."

When I called Mom, she naturally said no.

"Please, Mom, it's to work on our project."

She was quiet. Then she said, "You said his mom will be there?"

"Yeah."

"Give me her phone number, and I'll call her."

"Okay, but I'll have to get it."

I called Mom back with the number after school and had a message from her after practice, saying it was okay, amazingly.

Rachel and I headed to the library to find Jack.

"She said it's cool," I told Jack, "but I have to call her for a ride home."

"Great. Let's go."

When we pulled up to his house, I could tell it was pretty close to my house if I cut through the field. The route would be a bit circuitous sticking to roads.

I must have looked nervous, because Jack said, "Don't worry—my mom's nice."

I smiled and said, "Cool." This was the first time I'd ever been to a friend's house, unless a couple of the homeschooling kids' houses counted.

A tall blonde woman emerged from the back of the house after we walked in. "Ah, you brought your friend."

"Mom, Retta; Retta, this is my mom, Janie."

"Retta. That's an unusual name." Her eyes glowed as she looked at me and then at Jack.

I nodded. "Yeah, it's short for 'Loretta.' "

"It's nice."

I followed Jack into the dining room, where we got everything out to work. We hashed out the plan in about half an hour. Then we were quiet, just sitting there until Jack said, "So did you convince your mom to let you compete yet?"

"How'd you know about that?"

"Oh, Rachel mentioned it." His face looked red.

I experienced a little thrill at the thought that they'd been talking about me, but then I wondered why. "No, I don't know how I'm going to. She's impossible."

"That sucks."

"Yeah. I really want to race."

He nodded, twirling a pen. "So it's kinda weird that your mom hates country so much, but she named you 'Loretta.' It seems like a pretty country name to me, especially when paired with the last name Brooks."

I squinted at him.

"You know, Garth Brooks—famous country star of the nineties?"

"Oh, right. Yeah, it is weird. I have no idea." I shrugged. "So is 'Jack' short for something?"

He laughed. "Sort of. When I was a kid, I tried so hard to be all American, and I hated my name. It's Joginder. Plus, nobody could say it, even though it's not hard." He shrugged. "I guess that's rural Iowa for you. Anyway, I saw that movie Jack with Robin Williams and thought it was the funniest thing ever, so I made everyone start calling me that. My dad still won't do it, though."

"That's pretty funny. How old were you?"

"Four or five."

"So where is your dad from?"

"India."

I laughed. "I guessed that. I mean what part."

"Oh. I'm not used to people knowing there are

different parts of India. The northwest. The Punjab. He grew up in a small town about thirty miles from Pakistan."

"I can't imagine you at five years old."

"That's funny," he said, looking at her. "Because I wasn't much older than that when I saw you for the first time."

Huh? "What do you mean?" I asked.

"A while after you moved in. I was over at Gary's when you and your mom were outside trying to catch butterflies or something, and we watched you while we rode our bikes around. Gary had told me a girl had moved in, and we were disgusted." He laughed. "But then we noticed you were wearing these camo pants, and decided you might be okay, for a girl."

"What are you talking about? We've always lived here. Well, since I was a baby."

"No, I remember the people who lived in your house before you. It was these grumpy old people who would get mad at us for using their driveway curb as a ramp."

I stared at him. "I remember going through a camo phase, but we've always lived here."

"Well…"

"My mom! She couldn't tell me the truth to save her life!"

"Okay, sorry," Jack said with both palms up. "I didn't mean to bring it up."

I was mad but not at him, so I bit my lip and took a deep breath. "Sorry. My mom is keeping something from me, and I don't know what it is."

"That really sucks." He shifted in his chair. "Do you have any idea?"

"No, I've been looking, but I can't find anything. And you're sure I was just moving in then? I couldn't have already been there for a while?"

"Well, I am sure there were these old people there. Gary and I were in kindergarten then."

We were quiet again. I tried to remember moving into the house but couldn't. But now that I thought about it, I had some early memories that never seemed to fit in the current house. They must have been from the last place we lived. Why didn't I remember? It was too strange.

I remembered the newspapers I'd found. They must have been from the real move. But that still didn't tell me anything. How could I not remember?

Mom picked me up, and on the short ride home, I asked, "Mom, when did we move here?"

"What do you mean? You know we've lived here since you were small. After the accident."

"How small?"

"You were two."

I focused on not getting mad, but my heart raced. "Jack remembers me moving in when I was older than that."

Mom looked at me with a bit of a deer-in-the-headlights look. "Okay. You were older. Almost four."

My heart jumped. Was I finally going to find out the truth? "Why did you always tell me I was younger? And why don't I remember moving in?"

"Look, things were a bit rough after the accident. We moved around a lot. I didn't want you to remember those days, so I told you we'd been here longer. You probably just forgot because you heard that until you believed it."

I was stunned and had nothing to say. Was this it? The newspapers were dated before we moved here, after all.

"I'm sorry," Mom continued. "I thought it was best." She squeezed my arm. I didn't react.

"So where did we move from?" I managed.

"Nebraska."

But that didn't fit. The newspapers were from Des Moines. Mom was still lying, and I couldn't call her on it without playing all my cards.

Chapter Six

"Hey, Jeans! Wait up," Rachel called, catching up with me in the hall. "I'm having a few friends over Saturday afternoon and evening, if you want to try to convince your mom. We're going riding."

"Oh," I said. "I've never been riding before. I've never even been within ten feet of a horse."

"Really? I have one horse that's super easy to ride. Jack or I should be able to show you how, and you can always chicken out." She smiled. "It's cool. You could hang out with my sister. You can tell your mom that my parents will be home the whole time. Did I mention Jack will be there?" She arched an eyebrow ever so slightly.

What was that about? "That sounds pretty cool. I'll have to ask. I know what she'll say, though."

"What is it with her?"

"I have no idea." I frowned. "Wait, do you know my mom?"

Rachel nodded. "Yeah, everyone knows who she is, from the cafeteria. She's kind of famous."

My heart nearly stopped, and I had to make myself ask, "Why?"

"I don't know; it's just one of those things. I didn't know she was your mom until a couple days ago. I guess that's why she came over to the table that day, huh?"

"Yeah, checking up on me," I said. "So, I mean, do people think she's weird?"

Rachel shrugged and looked away. "I guess. But it doesn't matter. Don't worry about it. It's not like we can change our parents."

That was generous of her.

I'd been to Jack's house a couple more times to work on our project, but I hadn't hung out with anyone else yet. Mom did seem more comfortable with me going to Jack's, but she was still uptight about it.

After Mom got home from work the next day, she started a tuna casserole while I worked on homework at the dining room table.

I set my pen down and started to ask but chickened out. I knew what Mom was going to say and dreaded it. Until I asked, it was still a possibility. I moved my pen so it lined up with the edge of the placemat and took a deep breath. "Mom, Rachel invited me to go horseback riding Saturday. Can I go?"

"Who is Rachel?" Mom asked as she chopped the celery for the casserole.

"Come on, I've told you about her. She's on the cross country team, and she's the one that lives nearby."

"Is Jack going to be there?" Mom added the celery to a large bowl.

"Yeah," I said, my cheeks warming.

"No, I don't think so. I was hoping we could go shopping Saturday." She dropped some broccoli into the bowl. "Besides, I know you want to have time to study."

I ignored the study comment. She was just trying to distract me—she knew I could manage things fine.

"Why couldn't we just go on Sunday? I really want to go with them."

"No." She added a can of soup and started mixing.

"Why not?"

"You know, Retta, you think these people are nice, but you know nothing about them."

"That's crazy! I'm trying to get to know them. This is what people do with people they don't know." I slammed my math book shut. "I eat lunch with them every day!"

"Retta, I wish you wouldn't get so mad. I'm just trying to keep you safe." She poured the mixture into a casserole dish and topped it with breadcrumbs.

"You're trying to turn me into the Unabomber." I looked back at my homework but couldn't concentrate. Did Mom want me to have no friends at all, or was she that scared of...whatever she was scared of?

****

As soon as I sat down for lunch Friday, Rachel asked, "Is your mom going to let you out on day-release tomorrow?"

I started to say no but instead said, "Yeah, I think so. She said it was okay as long as I did some cleaning around the house," surprising myself. I was sick of everyone knowing how incredibly predictable Mom was, even if it was true. Plus, it was embarrassing.

"Great!" Rachel said. "Jack, she's never ridden before, so you get to teach her."

Jack grinned at me but said nothing. I smiled back.

Later, Jack drove me over to his house to work on the project. As soon as we walked in, Jack's mom yelled from the kitchen, "Hi, sweetie!"

Jack said, "Hi, Mom. Retta's with me." We headed

toward the kitchen.

"Hi, honey. I baked cookies for my meeting if you two want to steal a couple."

Jack said, "You baked? That's different."

"I know, I know. Come on, take a cookie. They're chocolate chip." She held up a plate, and we each took one.

"Thanks, Mom." He took a bite.

I said, "Thank you." His mom looked like the classic 1950s homemaker, standing there with a plate of cookies and her blonde hair and perfect fine-boned face.

"Sure. Now go study." She set the plate down and shooed us with both hands.

As we were walking off, she said, "Jack, your dad will be home at five."

"Okay." He checked his watch.

I'd learned it was easiest to be gone by the time Jack's dad got home. I'd only caught a glimpse of him once as he'd come in the front door. His complexion was darker than Jack's, and he'd worn a blue turban crowning a face that was probably handsome for an old guy. Even though he'd smiled at me as he passed us, I had the feeling he didn't like me being there, though I couldn't pinpoint why. Maybe he was like Mom—anti-relationship.

Jack sat on the living room floor and opened his laptop. "So what's your idea?"

"Oh, it's not that big a deal. Just, have you heard of Bobbi Gibb?"

"No."

"She was the first woman to run the entire Boston Marathon, before they allowed women to compete. She snuck in, in 1966."

"They didn't let women in?"

"No, they said women couldn't handle it physically. All that stupid crap."

"Huh. That's just weird. Glad it was a long time ago."

"Anyway, I've always sort of admired women like her because I'm also not supposed to run—for different reasons, but whatever—though I do anyway. Women have been excluded from sports for a long time, and I thought that might be a nice point to make for the historical perspective."

He nodded. "I like it. So I also had an idea," Jack said, glancing off to the side.

"Yeah?"

"So you know how we're going to do the video montage of different unconventional exercising?"

"Yeah. Oh, you know my mom got that video of me taken off YouTube, right?"

"Yeah, you mentioned that. Well, I can get it from…whoever made it. We won't upload it anywhere for the assignment—we can store it locally. Anyway, my idea has to do with audio. We haven't talked about that. Have you heard of Bhangra?"

"No…wait, isn't that some kind of dance or something?"

He laughed. "You know the most random crap! Yeah, but I'm talking about the music, not the dance."

"Okay, no."

" 'Kay, hold on." He started fiddling with his laptop. "So I'm going to play this for you." His cheeks reddened slightly. "Don't judge me."

I'd had no idea what to expect, but definitely not

this. The music was jangly. Some high-pitched string instrument played fast, accompanied by alternating male and female vocals in a foreign language I didn't recognize. The woman sang in a very high-pitched voice. Drum beats pounded the whole time, and I could pick out the occasional English word. It sounded very strange, very foreign.

Jack stopped the track.

"It's definitely different from anything I've heard before," I said.

He gave a clipped laugh. "That's diplomatic. So how does it rate next to country?"

"Oh, miles above." I laughed. "But where did you find it?"

"Well, it's kind of a long story, but let me play you a couple other tracks I think we could use for the video." He played two instrumentals, both pretty fast and with the same string instrument and bass beat. They still sounded peculiar, but the regular beat was catchy somehow.

"These would go well with anything we call 'unconventional,' " I said. "They'll seem that way to people around here."

Jack nodded.

"So where'd you get it?"

He twirled a pen. "My dad has never forgiven me for naming myself 'Jack.' He thinks I'm too American, that I don't know anything about Punjabi culture. We used to argue about what my real culture was."

I nodded.

"So a couple summers ago, my dad made me spend the whole summer in England with my cousins. Most Indian extended families are really big and have relatives all over the UK and the US, but my dad's family is pretty small, and nobody's here except him. He has a younger brother back in India, but he doesn't talk to any of his family there. There was some kind of falling out, and England was his only option. So off I went."

"Wow. Weren't you at least a little excited?" I would have been. I leaned forward.

"Yeah, but I had no idea what to expect. I knew my Punjabi was pretty weak. I didn't know how much I would need. Plus I was afraid all the aunts and uncles would be like my dad. You know, all conservative. And they sort of were, but the cousins were cool."

He looked at me and stopped talking. We locked eyes for what seemed like a long time to me, and my heart sped up.

He broke the look. "Anyway, it changed the way I saw things. It actually sort of had the effect my dad wanted." He laughed. "Though not exactly like he expected. I think he was thinking more Ravi Shankar than Bhangra. I think he hoped I'd stop cutting my hair and start wearing a kara."

I stared at him blankly.

"Oh, sorry. Those are things Sikhs do. A kara is a simple metal bracelet we wear on our right wrist. He wants me to be a good little Sikh, but I'm agnostic."

"Yeah, same here, I guess." After a moment I grinned and said, "So you got more in touch with your Indian half, then?"

"Yeah." He laughed. "But I didn't tell people here about that summer."

Even Rachel? I wondered, feeling my face—and heart—warm from knowing he'd chosen to tell me.

"So what did your mom think about you going?"

"Actually," he said with arched eyebrows, "I think she thought it was good for me. She always wanted me to know my Indian heritage better. She's sort of big on diversity."

"What does your mom do?"

"She teaches kindergarten. They have some meeting at the school tonight. Thus the cookies."

"Well, I'm glad I got one. My mom makes cookies about never."

Jack smiled at me, which was distracting, but I was curious about something.

"How come your dad is so traditional? He married your mom. That doesn't seem very traditional."

He cocked his head to the side and arched his eyebrows. "Yeah, it's not. He used to be really relaxed and happy. Everything changed about five years ago, when my grandpa died. My grandparents sort of disowned my dad when he married my mom. I know he always wanted to fix it. He thought about taking me over there to try to patch things up."

"You never met them?"

"No, and then when my grandpa died, that was it. My grandma died right after. My mom says he can't forgive himself for letting them die angry at him." He shrugged.

That sounded sucky. "So now he takes it out on you?"

He looked at me again. "No, it's not like that. He's not bad."

I nodded because I knew what it was like to have a parent you loved but who also drove you crazy.

****

I was walking across the field back from Jack's. He'd only invited me over there to work on our project, but we didn't need to spend this much time on it—it would be the best one in the history of Buckley High School at this rate.

No, it seemed like he might like me. I believed that to be true. There was that look we'd shared. At the realization I felt light and weirdly warm everywhere, like I could melt into the field. And I had a big, stupid grin splashed across my face, which I'd need to get rid of before I saw Mom.

I picked up the mail at the box at the end of the driveway on my way in, like normal. As I flipped through the envelopes, I found the one I'd been waiting for, from Nebraska—my birth certificate. I stuck the letter in my back pocket and put the rest on the counter, then raced upstairs to open it in my bedroom.

I sat on the edge of my bed and slipped my finger under the flap and dragged it across to tear it open, giving myself a paper cut in the process. I stuck my finger in my mouth and pulled out the letter.

This was not what I expected. At all. My finger fell out of my mouth and landed in my lap.

The letter said there was no such birth on record in the vicinity of the date I had given.

What? How could that be?

The letter fell to the floor.

I'd never been born? Certainly not where Mom claimed I'd been born.

My mind was an Arctic wasteland.

When it started to thaw, I knew this just proved with absolute certainty that Mom was a liar. What could it mean, exactly? I was so angry that my hands shook as

I stared at the letter on the floor.

I watched a bead of blood form over the paper cut. I wouldn't say anything about it yet. I had to think.

Chapter Seven

Friday afternoon, I put my "muddy" shoes just outside the back door as step one of my escape plan. I mean, they weren't actually muddy, but that's what I was going to say if Mom wondered. Later that night, I picked a fight with her. Step two. It started off about the get-together—I tried one more time to convince her to let me go, even though it was pointless.

"No, Retta, I already said no." She shook her head while standing in the doorway to the kitchen.

"Fine. I am not going shopping with you. I am going to spend the weekend studying." I sat at the dining room table staring at my history book lying open.

Mom sighed; hand on the fridge door. "Retta, you know I'm not comfortable with you being out with so many people I don't know. Please don't get so angry with me."

"I'm not angry," I lied. I stopped, and everything boiled up. The birth certificate. Mom's admission that there was something she wasn't telling me and her lie about when we'd moved here. "I just want to know what you're keeping from me and why!"

I looked her in the eye as her expression shifted. It was both hard and soft at the same time.

Finally, Mom said, "Okay."

We said nothing. What did she mean? I thought my

heart had stopped beating. "Okay, what?"

"Okay," Mom said. "I will tell you what you want to know." She was still holding onto the fridge, white-knuckled.

I was stunned. "You…will?"

"Yes," she said, glancing away and running her free hand through her hair. "But not now. You have to give me some time."

"When?" My heart had started back up, twice as fast as normal.

"Soon." Mom let go of the fridge and pulled a cigarette out of a pack on the counter. Her hands were shaking when she held the lighter up to light it. "I need some time."

"Okay, thanks." This could be another lie. "I'm still not going shopping."

Mom's face was in a light grimace, but she nodded. "We'll wait until next weekend."

****

On Saturday, I spent the whole morning hiding in my room. Mom left me alone.

In the afternoon, I listened until Mom went into the bathroom. My heart started thudding over what I was about to do.

I slipped out of my room, turning the doorknob when I shut it so it wouldn't click, and crept down the stairs. I shook all over but made it out the back door where I stuffed my feet into my shoes and crouched down to tie the laces, blood rushing to my head.

I speed-walked away from the house and looped around the neighborhood in order to stay out of sight. I listened for Mom's yell, but it didn't come.

The farther I got from the house, the twistier my

stomach got. How could I possibly get away with this? But really, the plan was only to get away with it long enough to have a little fun. I'd deal with the consequences later. Which would probably be not being allowed to do anything.

I tried to think of other things. When would Mom tell me what she was going to tell? And what was it? The thought that I might be kidnapped rolled through my head. If that were the case, my other family was probably desperate to find me. They might also be the type who would let me hang out with friends every once in a while.

But no, that couldn't be it, since Mom wouldn't be willing to tell me. Would Mom give me the truth? Would I even know?

It took me about twenty minutes to get to the mailbox marking the entrance to Rachel's. When I made it all the way to the barn, four people stood outside it, including Rachel and Lily. I knew the others but not as well.

"Hi!" Rachel said. "I wasn't sure if you'd make it, with your mom and all."

"Yeah, actually, she doesn't know. I sort of snuck out."

"Seriously? In the middle of the day?"

"Yeah. She thinks I'm hiding in my room being mad at her. But instead I'm out here being mad at her." I forced a laugh. The others laughed, too.

Rachel turned to the others and said, "I already brought in a horse for everybody, so go ahead and pick the one you want. But leave Matilda for Retta. It's her first time riding."

One of the girls said, "Oh, fun! Matilda's a great

horse for noobs. Unless she's in one of her moods."

Everyone laughed, including me, maybe too quickly. I was getting nervous.

We all turned to go into the barn when Lily asked, "Who else is coming?"

"Just Jack," Rachel said.

My heart sped up a bit.

"Cool." Lily nodded and followed the rest of them into the barn.

"So what is it with Matilda's moods?" I asked Rachel, trying not to let my nervousness show.

"Oh, nothing bad. She's super calm, and sometimes she gets so calm she doesn't want to move at all, so she doesn't. I have to take her out and ride her hard to remind her who's boss."

"Oh," I said, following her in. A pungent smell so strong it was almost visible invaded my nose. This must be what horse things smelled like.

"I don't know where Jack is…he's probably trying to make himself look perfect or something. He likes you."

I stopped in surprise and had to run a few steps to catch up. I was glad Rachel walked ahead of me. Did she mean like like, or just like?

"So let's go on in, and I'll at least let you meet her."

We walked through the barn to a pen where a couple of horses meandered while the other girls were saddling theirs.

"See that chestnut mare off to the side? That's Matilda." She grabbed a couple carrots from a bag nearby, and Matilda ambled over like she knew they were for her.

I gazed up at a giant horse inches from my face. The horse lifted her lips so her closed teeth shone, which scared the crap out of me for a second. I took a step back.

Rachel laughed, "Don't worry. She's just being friendly. Here, give her one of these." She handed me a carrot. "Hold it at the end—be careful of her teeth. Hold your hand open, palm up."

I took the carrot and stepped forward to gingerly hold it to Matilda's mouth. The horse took it with a slightly manic look in her eyes and crunched away until it was gone. I calmed down and stepped back to study the rest of the horse.

Rachel said, "She's big, but she's tame, like I said."

I nodded, still looking. I stared at Matilda's legs and feet. They seemed so small compared to the rest of her body.

"Hey, Jack!" Rachel said.

I looked up. Jack wore a cowboy hat today. He did make a striking image, if only because he just looked so thoroughly country, like he'd just posed for an album cover and then actually gone out and wrangled a calf. Mom was right—he was cute. And I was glad to be on the receiving end of his smile and wave.

He stopped in front of Matilda and stroked her head. "Hey, girl. How's my little lady?"

Okay, I definitely, definitely liked him. That was too sweet. Even if he did sound like an old man just then. I felt warm and wobbly.

"Okay, guys," Rachel said, "I'm going to leave you to it. Jack, you get Phoenix."

"Okay."

"We'll probably leave soon, but you can catch up, or just go off on an easier ride. Up to you." She walked over to where the others were saddling their horses.

"So," Jack said. "You've met Matilda. She's a good horse. I like her." He stroked her head again. "They like this, you know."

I forced myself to run my hand above Matilda's nose. The horse did seem happy if her calmer eyes were any indication.

"So since you've never ridden, I'm going to handle the saddle and all that for you, but I'll tell you what I'm doing so you'll know, for future reference. Then I'll help you get on a few times so you can get the hang of it. We can ride around the pen a bit before heading off. Matilda used to be a lesson horse they used for people nervous about riding, so she's easy."

"That's good. I am slightly nervous," I admitted.

"It's okay. We'll be gentle," he said, smiling.

Jack disappeared and came back with the saddle, which he draped over the fence. I was hit with the pungent, earthy aroma of the leather. Jack went into the pen, saddled Matilda, and put the bridle on, explaining things as he did them. Seeing Matilda calmly accept all this relaxed me.

"Is it okay if I come in now?" I asked, the fear finally lessening a bit.

"Sure," he said. His hand still rested on Matilda's neck.

I latched the gate behind me and stood against the fence.

"So the saddle is how you stay on, obviously, but it also helps you stay in control. It can slip around a bit, so it's important to get the cinch right. Let me show you how to tighten it—it's not really a knot, because we want it to be easy to release. Here, come a bit closer so you can see."

He showed me how he fastened it and shook the saddle to show how stable it was.

Jack worked on saddling a spotted gray horse across the pen for himself. Watching him was so nice— he totally knew what he was doing, and seeing him moving around so purposefully made my heart go faster than it needed to.

Jack had his horse ready and tied him to the fence near me. "This is Phoenix," he said. "He's a bit more of a handful, though he's being good for now."

Jack demonstrated how to get on the horse a few times and then had me try. I stuck my left foot in the stirrup, grabbed onto the horn, and pulled up, swinging my right leg over and landing perfectly in the saddle, almost like I knew what I was doing.

"Awesome!" Jack said with a grin.

My heart skipped, and I looked down to avoid his eyes, but he'd already turned to get onto Phoenix. Once on, he showed me how to kick to get the horse moving and how to use the reins to direct her. We spent some time moving around the pen until I felt like I had some sense of control.

We were soon following a narrow trail that ran between a farm and the edge of the woods. I wished I knew more about trees because there were several different kinds of them, and from this height everything seemed majestic. I felt large and powerful, like anything was possible.

I also admired the other view. Jack turned around occasionally, but mostly he looked ahead, and I noticed his shirt was tight across his back muscles. My gaze strayed farther down. Most impressive was that he knew horses well, and I filed this observation away for further thought. Seeing him so confident and good at something sent my mind in a direction I wasn't used to. What would it be like if he really did like me back?

I tried to distract myself by paying more attention to Matilda. Soon I was thinking about going faster. I kept having the urge to kick Matilda's sides harder just to see what would happen.

Jack turned around and asked, "So what do you think?"

"Yeah, this is really cool. I feel…empowered, I guess. Definitely different."

The trail widened, and he slowed down so he was riding beside me. "There's nothing like riding a horse. It's like riding off into another world where things are only good."

I looked ahead again to watch where Matilda was taking me. "So what do you do, with riding? I mean, do you do shows and that sort of stuff?"

"No way." He snorted. "I just ride for fun. My mom got me started when I was young. We used to have horses."

"Ah."

"I shouldn't mock it. Lily does show jumping and dressage. But Rachel and I have just been riding around our farms since we were little kids."

Rachel again. I didn't like it. "So…you and Rachel have been friends for a long time, then?"

"Our moms are best friends, so yeah."

He was quiet for a moment, like he was trying to think of something to say. Was he as nervous as I suddenly was? He finally said, "So, yeah, we called ourselves best friends for a long time until it got kinda weird. We're not a thing or anything."

I blushed again, but my heart felt like it floated on air. He must have said that on purpose. I realized I needed to say something. "That's cool."

Jack continued, "She has a boyfriend in Cedar Rapids. A guy she met at camp. They visit each other on the weekends sometimes." He laughed but was looking straight ahead. "He doesn't like me at all. I think he might be coming tonight."

I was glad but still felt too awkward to turn toward him. I concentrated on the swaying of the saddle and the thick, tough reins in my hands.

"So anyway," Jack said, "you like riding so far. It's even better when you learn to go fast and really push the horse. You feel like you own the world."

"I bet." I glanced quickly at him and flashed him a quick smile. I got panicky when I tried to think of something else to say and couldn't.

So we were quiet for a bit. Had we run out of things to talk about, or was it just that we were both still nervous?

I looked toward him and said, "So you're a senior, right?"

"Yeah. And you're a junior?"

"Yep. Are you going to college?"

His eyes crinkled. "I'm going to apply to Iowa State."

Our gazes were still locked. "Is that in...uh...Ames?"

"Yeah."

"What's that, like two hours from here?" His gaze

made me dizzy, like I might fall off the horse. I looked ahead only to see we were as stable as ever.

"I think it's closer to three," he said.

I was very aware of the motion of riding again. Back and forth like a sideways rocking chair. "Your parents ought to be happy you're staying close. I am hoping to get a scholarship for running. I should be able to get an academic one, too, though." Oh, why did I say that? It would sound like I was bragging.

He glanced over at me. "Iowa State has a cross country program."

I laughed. "Did you check?"

"Heh. I've heard you are pretty good, from what Rachel says. Plus I saw the video."

"Oh, I don't know how good I am. Really, I'd love to be good enough to join the team in college, even though my mom might try to keep me from going."

"Same here. I mean, I'm applying for scholarships, too. My dad said he would only pay for half of my expenses and I have to cover the rest, either with scholarships or work. And he doesn't want me to take out a loan."

"Wow." *Poor guy*, I thought at first, but then I realized I'd have to pay for all of it myself. Mom couldn't really help even if she were willing.

"So why doesn't your mom want you to go?"

"You know how she is. You and the rest of the town, apparently."

He chuckled.

"She probably thinks if she isn't there, some man will break into my room and stab me to death," I said.

We both laughed.

"It's idiotic," I said, more forcefully than I'd

intended.

We were quiet for a moment, until Jack said, "So I was curious. You take German, too, don't you?"

"Yeah," I said, wondering why he was asking that.

"How'd you manage to take two language classes at once? I mean, why did they let you?"

"Oh, it's because of the homeschooling. I finished more than the normal sophomore curriculum. I already took American History, so I had some extra free periods."

"Ah. I was just wondering. So you really like languages, then?"

"Yeah. I read Harry Potter in Spanish last year. I was pretty impressed with myself."

Jack laughed. "Nice. But seriously, Spanish, too?"

I blushed. "It's my best language. I have a bit of a knack for them. But I've been studying it the longest."

"That's cool."

We continued on along the woods, and I noticed the leaves were starting to change. Yellows and oranges mixed with the greens. I was so pleased with the way things were going with Jack that I had to concentrate in order not to be constantly wearing a silly smile.

We rode along in comfortable silence for a while. I felt the sway of the horse, smelled the crisp fall air. It was nice to have a friend.

"Hey, let's start heading back," Jack said. He turned us away from the woods and back toward Rachel's farm. I could see the barn in the distance. I wished the day wasn't almost over.

When we got to the barn, the others had finished unsaddling their horses and were releasing them back into the field.

Jack dismounted. "Careful getting down," he said. "It's not that hard but—"

I threw my leg over and slid off, but my foot twisted and caught in the stirrup just long enough for me to lose my balance and hit the dirt.

"—it isn't hard to mess it up, either," he finished. He offered me his hand. "Are you okay? You didn't hurt yourself?"

When I took it and he lifted me up, the heat of his hand coursed through me, warming my whole body. I stumbled and struggled to say, "No, I'm fine."

Jack looked away quickly, but not before I saw the color in his own cheeks. He let go of my hand.

Jack tied Matilda to the fence and showed me how to take the saddle off and brush Matilda's coat. He left me with the brush while he carried the saddle back. "Just leave her there when you're done," he said.

I began brushing Matilda, noticing her damp coat and the earthy scent of sweat. I was having trouble standing still because my legs were so wobbly from exercise they weren't used to. My inner thighs felt like they were made of jelly, and my butt was one big bruise.

After I finished, I noticed a fire burning out beyond the entrance to the barn. I checked my phone to see if Mom had called, but she hadn't. Lucky. I walked closer and saw it was a small bonfire in an area cleared of grass. The others were gathered around it.

"Oh, hey, Jeans," Rachel said. "Come sit." She patted the ground.

I sat on the ground next to Rachel. I didn't know where Jack was, but there was room for him next to me if he wanted to sit there—and I really hoped he did.

Lily asked, "So how was the ride? You guys never caught up with us."

"No, it took a while to get going. I guess I'm not a natural. But it was a lot of fun."

Jack appeared and sat next to me. "Actually, she wasn't half bad once we were out." He turned to look at me. "I think you were just scared of Matilda until you were in the saddle, when you couldn't tell how big she was anymore."

I laughed. "Yeah, I hadn't realized how huge horses are before today. It seems obvious, but I just have never been around them."

"We all remember how big they seemed when we first learned. But that was when we were young enough to be fearless," Rachel said.

"Or crazy," Jack said.

A couple of girls I didn't know arrived and sat down, and Rachel introduced us. More people started arriving, and someone backed a truck up toward the fire, the local country station blaring. Rachel and Jack looked at each other, and then at me, and we all laughed.

Not long afterward, another car pulled up. The door clicked shut, and a guy called, "Rach!"

Rachel said, "Ooh, Daniel," and jumped up to meet him. As he came into view, I could see he was tall and blond and slightly chubby, but he wore it well. Rachel had to get on her tiptoes to kiss him. She took his hand, and they started toward the fire.

Daniel's gaze fell on Jack, who stared at the fire and not at them. A dark look passed over Daniel's face, and he abruptly stopped, yanking Rachel's hand to pull her back a few steps.

I turned away, but I could still hear everything even though they were talking low.

"Why is he here?" Daniel hissed.

"Babe, I've told you. He's just a part of my group of friends. I can't not invite him. I love *you*." Her voice shook.

"No. Just no. I've told you."

"Daniel, come back!"

But his car starting and roughly backing up showed he wasn't.

I glanced up, but nobody else looked at Rachel as she sat back down, rubbing her wrist like it was sore. Lily gave her a hug and said, "He'll calm down." Then it was quiet until Gary showed up a moment later.

"What?" he said, glancing around.

Jack said, "It's nothing, man."

Gary shrugged and sat down. The conversation got started again.

After a while, there were about ten kids sitting around the fire talking and listening to the radio. I wasn't sure what I had expected. Some of the girls were dancing to the radio, and I saw a couple disappear into the dark. Still, it wasn't a wild party, for sure. Not that I'd seen one to know.

I just took in the whole scene, enjoying sitting next to Jack.

At one point, his hand brushed against mine, and I almost moved mine away, but the side of me that had recently emerged dared me to leave it. After a moment, he wrapped his hand around mine and held it, where anybody glancing in our direction would be able to see. I felt like I would disintegrate, and I couldn't say or do anything for a while. Jack seemed similarly afflicted, so we simply sat there, watching the others.

A small pipe and a lighter got passed around. I tried not to look too surprised. But no way was I doing that. When Rachel handed it to Jack, he held it out to me, but I shook my head, and he passed it to the guy next to her.

Gary said, "Really, Jack?"

"Don't feel like it tonight," he muttered, squeezing my hand.

Maybe he didn't want to let go of my hand—it took both hands to smoke the pipe. This sent a thrill down my back.

We sat a while longer, when I remembered Mom. "What time is it?" I asked.

He checked his phone. "Almost ten."

I wanted to check mine for messages I might have missed, but it was in the wrong pocket, and I'd have to let go of Jack's hand to get it.

Finally, curiosity took over, and I let go of his hand, which made him glance over. I was focused on the phone. No messages. "Oh, wow. I can't believe I'm getting away with being gone this long. I don't know how my mom hasn't figured out I'm not there. It wouldn't be that hard for her to figure out where I was."

"That does seem strange, considering. Maybe it's just karma paying you back." He grinned at me.

"Yeah, I don't know what's going on. She's been so weird lately." I was still staring at the screen and thought about mentioning the birth certificate but decided it might weird him out. It still freaked me out. "I wonder if I should go." I put the phone back in my jeans.

"You could go now if you want." He paused,

taking my hand again. "But you should stay longer. If she hasn't noticed, why leave now?"

I considered this. "Yeah. Plus, if I go in now, she will probably still be awake. She usually goes to bed around eleven. If she really thinks I'm still in my bedroom, maybe I'll get away with it."

"There you go."

We sat together a bit longer, talking about nothing. "It's pitch black tonight," Jack said.

"Yeah, I can't even see the moon."

He nodded, but neither of us said anything. I checked my phone again. It was eleven thirty. "I should probably go." I hadn't even thought about getting home. I hadn't realized I'd be out past dark. "Can you give me a ride home?"

He laughed. "Sure." He let go of my hand, and we both got up. Jack said to those closest, "I'm going to take Retta home. See you guys later."

Rachel and Lily both waved at us as we left. Gary nodded at Jack.

We walked toward the truck, and Jack took my hand again. The whole way home, I wondered if he would kiss me. I thought I wanted him to—no, I definitely wanted him to—but my insides jiggled like gelatin.

"You want a Coke?" Jack asked as we approached the gas station on the corner of my neighborhood. "I suddenly want one."

I shook my head. "I'd better just get home."

He stopped the car in front of my house. We were both quiet for a moment, until Jack said, "Huh, it looks like you have an out-of-towner in the neighborhood."

An old gray Cutlass with South Dakota plates was

parked across the street from my house. "That's new," I said, still wondering how I could turn this conversation into a good-night kiss.

But he wasn't facing me and had both his hands on the wheel. I must have messed it up somehow. I got out, both disappointed and a tiny bit relieved, and he looked at me and the side of his mouth quirked up. "See you Monday."

I looked over at the house again. The lights were still on. Mom must be up waiting—she would kill me.

The whole way to the house, I remembered how happy Jack looked when he said he'd see me. Maybe he was just scared, too? He was still parked when I reached the front door, but the truck left as I unlocked it as quietly as possible.

Chapter Eight

I pushed the front door open gently and stepped in, surprised Mom wasn't already yelling.

Instead it was dead quiet.

I tiptoed through the downstairs, past the living room, before peeking into the Reading Room. No Mom. My stomach was heavy. I backtracked past the stairs and toward the kitchen. One of the dining room chairs was on its side and several papers were strewn across the floor near it.

A sharp metallic smell invaded my nose just before I rounded the corner to the kitchen.

My gaze followed dark streaks on the floor toward the back door. Mom lay on her stomach, her arm reaching out to barely touch the bottom of the door.

A large pool of blood surrounded her. I gasped and lurched forward. I knelt and grasped Mom's shoulder and shook her. There was no response. That's when I saw her face—several cuts covered it, and her eyes and mouth were wide open. I shook her again. But she was in a sea of red. Mom didn't move.

I moaned while rocking and staring at her glassy, unblinking eyes. I couldn't stop making the noise. A shuffling sound came from upstairs.

I jerked upright and grabbed the door handle. Just as I threw it open, it sounded like someone brushed against the wall next to the stairs, and then a deep, loud voice yelled, "Princess!"

I looked at Mom once more, and then I was running, running, running out the back door and around the house.

I headed out of the neighborhood toward the highway. Toward Jack.

The front door slammed open, and now the man was running after me, shouting words I couldn't make out, except for "princess" again.

My heart was exploding. The night's darkness enveloped me, but I knew where I was going, yet each step jarred every bone from my toes up to the back of my head, so much that I felt like disintegrating chalk.

I'd gained some distance from the yelling, but it was still way too close.

I could see the light from the convenience store now—just a little farther and around a corner.

The man was still shouting. I ran faster than I ever had in my life, and then slowed down so I could turn the corner into the parking lot.

Everything came into view—two gas pumps, the dirty orange walls of the store itself with windows covered in cigarette ads. And a gray truck backing out of a spot.

Jack!

I raced over toward the truck, but he'd already started pulling forward. I ran toward the passenger side as he stopped to turn onto the highway. I slammed both palms onto the door. He jerked, and the cup he'd been holding bounced off the seat onto the floor.

There was another shout way too close.

I yanked open the door and climbed into the cab.

Jack leaned over to pick up the spilled cup. "Retta!

Are you okay? What are you doing here?"

I slammed the door shut and shouted, "Just drive! Away from here!"

"What?"

"Drive!" I screamed.

The cup fell as he grabbed the wheel, and the tires screeched. "Okay, okay! What is going on?" Panic laced his voice now.

I looked out the window as we drove past a man at the end of the road shaking his fist in the air. He turned around and ran back into the neighborhood as the truck passed some trees, and I couldn't see him anymore. My heart was still sprinting faster than it ever had, and I had to fight the urge to throw up. I put my hands on the dash.

"Retta, what is happening?"

The world stopped spinning, and clear-headedness descended on me. "Okay, look," I said loud and fast, "I just found my mom—stabbed—dead—"

"Oh, my God, Retta! Are you okay? Oh, my God!"

"I know!" Tears burst free, but a part of me must have been listening all those times Mom had pounded the emergency plan into my head. "The man was right behind me! He chased me all the way to the store!" I sobbed, feeling sick again.

Jack started slowing down and said, "I need to turn around so we can go to the police station!"

"No, no, no! I can't go there!"

"What? Why not?" He stopped the truck.

"Look, I can't totally explain it, but this is what my mom made me promise. Not to go to the police if anything terrible ever happened to her!" I looked at Jack, whose eyes were full of terror.

"But that doesn't make any sense!" He shook his head.

"Please, keep driving!"

"Okay," he said, pulling back onto the road. "But you still need to convince me."

"Look, I don't think it was random. My mom has always been so paranoid about something, and I never knew what. But now it's finally happened!" My voice had risen again. "I promised her. And now she's dead! I have to keep my promise!"

Headlights appeared behind us.

Jack's hands gripped the wheel tightly. "Retta, I don't think—"

"There's a number I'm supposed to call." I grabbed my phone and started to dial the number.

"But Retta—"

A sudden, scraping sound filled the cab as the truck lurched forward. The phone flew out of my hand.

"Shit!" Jack said, holding the wheel tighter and punching the gas.

"Did he just hit us?" I asked, turning around. I couldn't see anything behind us except the vague shape of a car with a silhouetted driver—it was so close the headlights weren't visible.

"Yes!"

We were speeding up, already going way too fast for this road, but the car was still right on the truck's bumper.

I clutched the dashboard as Jack tried zig-zagging a bit to shake the guy, but it didn't work. Then the truck accelerated, and finally the guy fell back. Jack hit the brakes pretty hard, and I hit the door and was jerked to the floor as we took a corner sharply.

"Retta!" Jack yelled. "Are you okay?" He leaned over and gripped my arm, helping me back into the seat before speeding back up.

I put the seatbelt on before stealing a glance behind us. "I don't see him."

"No, I think he might not have made that corner. It's what I was trying to do, but I never would have if I'd realized you didn't have a seatbelt on!"

"I'm okay, it's fine." I shook my head, having to extricate myself from the top half of the seatbelt to pick up the phone off the floor.

Jack slowed down to a more normal speed and turned to me. He looked freaked out. "I can't believe I nearly killed you."

I dialed again and only glanced at him. He turned back toward the road.

"Tito's Pizza," the woman's voice in the phone answered.

"Hello, hi, I need the...uh, three-by-four special," I said.

"What?" the woman asked.

My stomach dropped. "The three-by-four special?"

"Oh. Oh! Hold on a second." After a click, another voice came on the phone, this one sleepy. "Hello?"

"I need the three-by-four special?"

"Oh, okay." A rustling sound and a pause. The new woman said, "You have reached a safe number. How can I help you?"

Now I wasn't quite sure what to say. I hesitated before deciding to go with the blunt truth. "My mom always told me to call this number if anything happened to her, and I just found her murdered."

"Oh, no! I'm so sorry." Her voice cracked on the

sorry even though she still sounded groggy. When I didn't say anything else, she continued, "I'm very glad you called us—you did the right thing. Are you safe right now?"

"Yes, I'm in a friend's truck."

"Do you trust this friend?" The woman sounded almost business-like, as if this were a normal conversation.

"Yeah," I said in a clipped voice.

"Are you on your own, except for your friend? And you're under eighteen?" I could hear shuffling paper.

"Yes. I'm fifteen." I sniffed.

"Did you call the police?"

"No."

"That's good," the woman said, exhaling. "What's your name, honey?"

"Retta Brooks."

"And where are you right now?"

"We're near Buckley." Tears dripped off my cheeks.

"What state?" There was some typing in the background.

"Oh, we're in eastern Iowa."

"Okay, give me a minute. Don't hang up, okay?" I heard more typing and a shuffling sound before the phone went mute.

I waited, my stomach turning in on itself. It was pitch black outside with no streetlights. I took the opportunity to turn around—no one was behind us. I glanced over and saw Jack's face was a strange orange from the lights on the dash. I caught his worried gaze.

"What's going on?" he asked.

"I'm waiting to hear back. I guess just keep

driving." We were heading north.

There were several moments of tense silence, the drone of tires on the road the only sound.

"Okay," the woman's voice said. "We can help you. You are in a friend's car, right—not your family's?"

"Yeah."

"Good. Drive to 1511 Del Mar Avenue in Ripton. How far away are you?"

"Jack, give me your phone," I said. After he handed it over I punched the address into the map app.

"It's about an hour to get there," I told the woman.

"Okay, someone will be waiting for you. It's a library—you'll be looking for someone waiting for you in the parking lot. Please take the battery out of your phone as soon as we hang up. The police may track you if they figure out you're missing."

I hung up and took the battery out and put it and my phone in my pocket.

"Where do I go?" Jack asked.

"Stay on Highway 136, then turn onto 52 in a bit."

"Okay. Now tell me what really happened!" Jack said.

I groaned. "Oh, God. When I went in after you dropped me off, I found my mom in the kitchen. Then a man yelled and chased me."

"Oh, my God! I can't believe—" He stopped. "I can't believe you were that close to him! Thank God you run fast."

I stared out the window at the rushing black trees. "I know." My heart was still racing, and I couldn't stop the tears.

"I can't believe your mom. God, your mom. Your

poor mom."

I couldn't talk. When I did look at Jack, he seemed shaken up, but he was focused on driving. I felt unusually safe, right at this moment, in this small space, with him.

As we got closer, I helped Jack navigate to the address—a small brick library. He turned into the lot that held two other cars. He switched the lights off after we pulled into a spot two down from an older dark Toyota with someone inside.

"What time is it?" Jack asked.

I checked his phone. "Just before one. I can't believe everything that's happened. It doesn't feel at all real." My voice was flat.

"I know. Just a couple hours ago, we were sitting in front of a fire with a bunch of other kids, listening to music."

We sat there not talking. Jack stared straight ahead, hands still on the wheel.

Whoever "he" was, he'd found us. But who was he? I couldn't think of a single possibility.

After a moment, I said, "Okay, I guess I should go talk to them. Whoever they are."

I reached for the door handle but then found I couldn't get myself to pull it. I closed my eyes and remembered my promise to Mom. The least I could do was honor that now. I got out of the car and looked at the person in the Toyota.

Jack followed me out and said, "Wait. I'll come, too." He walked over to me and gripped my hand firmly. I held on just as tightly as we neared the back of the truck.

A lumpy middle-aged woman wearing jeans and a

gray hoodie stepped out of the Toyota. "Can I help you with something?"

"Hi, someone just directed me here. On the phone."

The woman said, "Yes. Okay. What's your name?"

"Retta." It came out in monotone.

"You took your phone battery out earlier, right?"

I nodded, still squeezing Jack's hand.

"You can call me Irene." She glanced at the two of us and then looked at me and said, "Please say goodbye to your friend. You might never see each other again." She walked back toward the car.

"Oh," Jack said, not looking at me. Then he turned to me and said, "Are you sure you want to do this? You don't want to go back and talk to the cops?"

"No." I was numb. "I promised my mom." This time I wouldn't break my promise.

"Okay." He frowned, which made me feel weird. A little better, a little worse. Then I felt sick about feeling any bit better under these circumstances.

We stood in front of the truck in silence. Jack took my hand and said, "Did you know I've liked you since that first time I saw you? When you'd just moved in?"

I blushed, and my heart pinched.

"I used to watch you when you would go running after school. You look incredible when you run. Like a gazelle or something."

I still didn't know what to say and started crying again. Maybe I should stay. Surely they'd catch the guy.

But no. I couldn't. Even with all the fighting Mom and I had been doing, she hadn't always been so horrible. And she'd been about to tell me what she'd been hiding.

The woman came back over, her long gray hair falling forward. "Okay, time to go." She looked at Jack and said, "Son, it's very important that you never mention this to anyone. Not just for me, but also for the women and children who need our help."

"So first tell me what's going to happen," Jack said, squeezing my hand tighter.

"Son, I can't tell you the details. But I'm part of a network of people who help women and their families get out of dangerous situations. I'm assuming we helped Retta's mother at some point, which must be how she knew to get in touch with us. We don't just give the number out to anyone."

"But why can't we just go to the police?" Jack asked, holding my hand so tightly it hurt.

The woman sighed. "Sometimes people need to go into deeper hiding. Even though things are better now and the police take domestic violence more seriously, there's no way to control true stalkers."

"Okay. I won't say anything." He relaxed his grip, glancing at me.

I stood there for a moment longer, just feeling the warmth of Jack's hand. I was so queasy from everything going on that I was afraid I'd throw up, so I concentrated on his hand. His strong grip.

"Come on," the woman said.

I had promised Mom.

"Well," I said, "it was nice meeting you, Jack Singh." I was crying again.

"You, too, Retta Brooks." He sounded choked up and still hadn't let go of my hand. "Would you...let me know you're okay, somehow? Any way you can think of."

The woman touched my shoulder. "Come on, we have to go."

I nodded and started to extract my hand, but Jack pulled me back.

"Wait," he said. Then he reached up with his free hand and touched the back of his long fingers gently to my cheek.

I'd never felt anything like it.

Eyes on mine, he said. "I'm really going to miss you."

I let go of his hand and hugged him, tears dripping off my cheeks.

Finally, I broke away from the hug and started backing up toward the car, watching Jack the whole time. His face was dark and sad.

The woman waved Jack off, and he backed up and turned out of the parking lot.

Chapter Nine

"We need to get you moving," the woman said. Before I could get in the car, she continued, "I need you to lie down in the back with a blanket, like you're sleeping even if you can't."

I arranged myself with the blankets as the woman backed up. I got situated, and the car backed onto the street and headed in the opposite direction from where Jack and I had come.

The woman continued, "Make sure to keep your legs and arms down and out of sight. If we do get stopped, don't hide, but act sleepy, like it's totally normal for you to be asleep in the back of your Aunt Irene's car at two in the morning. Don't say anything unless you have to. To the police, I mean."

I was wide awake, so I didn't even try to sleep. I couldn't get the last image of Mom out of my head. I cried and cried but managed to stay quiet, just sniffling.

Irene was talking. "—to know what's happening. We're heading into Wisconsin. I only know about this part of the journey, but you will be heading north."

I thought I should say something. "So did your group help my mom? Before?"

"Maybe." She paused. "Why don't you tell me what happened tonight? If you want to."

I closed my eyes. "I snuck out this afternoon and stayed out late. When I got home, I found my mom in the kitchen. Dead." My voice thickened. "Then a man yelled from inside the house, and he chased me, but I got away."

"Could he have followed you here?" Irene asked.

"I don't think so," I said. "He did chase us in his car, but we shook him. There were no headlights behind us all the way here."

"Is there any way she could still be alive?"

"No. There was so much blood!" I sobbed, her glassy eyes in my mind.

"Oh, I'm very sorry, dear. But it's good you didn't call the police. You might be in more danger if you go to them. Maybe not, but we just don't know at this stage. You never saw the man?"

"No."

"Do you have any idea who he was? Could it have been your father?"

I hadn't thought of that. "I don't know. I always believed my whole family was dead. My mom always told me that, although I just found out I wasn't born where she said."

"It sounds like you might have gotten new identities. Your mom probably couldn't have done it without help, so she likely utilized our network. That must be how you knew to call us. Did you have the number memorized?"

"Yeah, since I was ten. How does your group help people?"

"We help women in dangerous situations. We don't always help lone kids, but the woman who took your call felt you were in enough danger that it was worth the risk, and I agreed. The fact that you hadn't called the police helped. With anyone underage, we always run the risk of being accused of kidnapping, even if you willingly come with us. Even if it doesn't come to that, the network risks being exposed."

I was too stunned to say anything else. I closed my mouth, which had been hanging open from listening to what Irene had said, and then closed my eyes. Tears formed in the corners as I thought about how Mom had been right, so right, all along. The tears crept down my cheeks.

****

I woke up cold and uncomfortable. One of the blankets had fallen on the floor. I could see the woman driving, and it was still dark out. Where was Jack now? Was he home yet?

"Where are we?" I asked.

"Southern Wisconsin. We made it over the border okay. We're about half an hour away from the changeover."

We drove on. Just as morning light was starting to snake over the horizon, we pulled into a farm house drive. The car continued past the house and stopped next to a three-walled carport painted red and white like a barn. I could see an RV and an older silver or white extended-cab Ford inside.

"Stay in the car," the woman said as she got out and went into the RV. I could see light shining in the windows from a flashlight.

After Irene came back out, she said, "Okay, it's not much, but I have these for you." She handed me a bag containing a four-pack of dinner rolls, a jar of peanut butter, and a plastic knife. "It's all I had. A woman will come for you at about eight thirty."

"What time is it now?" I asked.

"A little after six. So you should sleep. You should be safe here. Come lock the door after me. It will be dark—there's no light in there."

After I was inside the RV and Irene had shut the door, I locked it and felt my way back to the bed I'd seen. I was exhausted. But I couldn't see anything, and it didn't take long for me to imagine all sorts of terrible things in the RV with me. What if he had followed us?

I lay there, trembling and listening to my racing heart, too terrified to move or even to breathe, until the RV got brighter and brighter with the rising sun. My heart pounded like I'd been sprinting for hours.

Still, I was so exhausted that I passed out.

Something woke me, a sound like someone walking on gravel. Mom...oh, God. I put my hand over my mouth, willing the fresh nausea to go away.

A light tap sounded on the door, and a voice called, "Hello? Are you in there? My name is Becca. I'm your next ride."

I froze. My heart was racing again, and my stomach wavered.

"I'm going to come in, okay?"

"Okay." It came out like a squeak. I cleared my throat. "Yes. Okay."

A woman unlocked the door and stepped in. She was younger than the last woman had been, and looked like a perfectly normal soccer mom—blonde and slim.

"Hi," the woman said. "Are you about ready to go? What is your name?"

"I'm Retta. I'm ready to go now."

Becca held up an empty blue plastic bag and a large trash bag I hadn't noticed until just then. "Find a couple things in here to change into, and do you normally wear your hair down?"

"Yeah."

"Can you pull it back in a ponytail? Or do a quick braid? There are rubber bands in the bag."

I took the bag and started rifling through it. "I can do a ponytail," I said, pulling out a pair of cargo pants and a monster truck T-shirt that looked like they'd fit.

"Good. When you're ready, come on out, and we'll go. You can keep your clothes but just stick them in the plastic bag." She left the RV.

I changed quickly, noticing dried blood on my shoes and hands for the first time. I scraped at my hands until it flaked off. I pulled my hair back, grabbed the rolls, and opened the door.

Becca said, "Okay, into the truck. Let's go."

We got in, and Becca pulled onto the driveway. After we were on the highway, she glanced over at me and said, "How are you feeling?"

"Pretty crappy."

"I'm sorry. How did you end up here?"

"My mom was killed—stabbed," I said, my voice cracking, "last night."

"Oh, honey, I'm so sorry to hear that." She squeezed my arm. "How are you doing right now?"

"I don't know. It's only been a few hours since I found her. I think I still don't believe it." I heard my own voice as a strange monotone.

"You found her?"

"Yeah. I only got away because I caught my friend before he left."

"That's awful. I'm so sorry you had to go through that." She patted my shoulder. "You seem very composed for having just gone through something so awful."

I just stared out the window. "I can't get the image out of my head," I said, sobbing again.

"I'm so sorry, honey."

I missed Mom and felt so guilty about how pissed I had been at her. She hadn't been wrong after all. I'd had no right to be so angry. *Oh, Mom, I'm so sorry.*

I leaned my head against the window and cried as quietly as I could until I noticed how hungry I was. I pulled out one of the dinner rolls. They weren't very good, but it was better with the peanut butter.

Becca seemed to understand I needed to be left alone, which was nice. She said, "We will stop for lunch in about two hours. There's bottled water behind your seat if you want any."

"Okay," I said.

We were quiet for the next hour until Becca said, "So do you have any family you know of?"

"No, I don't think so. I don't know. My mom always said they had all been killed in a car wreck when I was a baby."

"Even your grandparents?" Becca asked, sounding surprised.

"Yeah. They were supposedly all in a van together that crashed."

"Wow, hopefully that's not true."

"Oh." I didn't know what else to say. I hadn't actually considered the idea of a whole family.

Becca said, "You will be staying with someone at the end of the journey, and she will be able to help you figure out what to do."

"Okay." I had no idea how to feel about that. "What…what are you all doing with me?"

"You mean the drive?"

"Yeah."

"We are just trying to get you away from a situation that was too dangerous and risky for you. I don't have the details, but from what you've told me, it sounds like there's a chance your father might have murdered your mother. If that's the case, and he were to get away with it, he could get custody of you since you're under eighteen. We are giving you options. The last person you stay with will help you figure out what the safest options are."

"Oh." Everything was so overwhelming. We were quiet for a few minutes until I asked, "Do you mind if I sleep for a bit now?"

"No, of course not. There's a blanket in the back if you want it."

"Thanks." I turned back to grab the blanket and glanced out the back window. "There's a cop car behind us!"

"I see it," Becca said tensely. "Okay, go ahead and get settled. If they pull us over, just act calm and uninterested. But don't go out of your way to avoid eye contact—that would seem suspicious."

I nodded and focused on being calm and acting normal.

When I leaned forward, I could see the car in the side mirror. It was definitely gaining on us. And then it got worse.

"The lights—"

"I see them," Becca said in a strained voice. "Just lean back and act like you're trying to sleep. You're my niece, Jenny Stanford. Like the college."

I couldn't see the car from this position, so I kept

glancing at Becca and her white knuckles gripping the wheel. Becca sighed a couple times and whispered something to herself.

Becca slowed down, signaled and started pulling over to the shoulder.

The police car blew past us, lights still going.

"Oh!" Becca said. "Thank goodness! I thought we were in real trouble. I wondered why he never turned the siren on."

I also was relieved, but now the idea of a family was back in my head. Why hadn't Mom been honest with me? And, God, she'd been just about to tell me everything.

****

I woke as we were pulling into a gas station with a Subway restaurant sign.

"Hey, you're awake," Becca said.

I nodded.

"I'm going to go in and get us some food. What would you like?"

"Oh, um…a turkey sub with no onions will be fine. Mustard. Thank you."

Becca started to get out and said, "Don't look around much." She pulled a book off the back seat. "Just act like you're reading, in case somebody sees you and might recognize you. I don't know if it's hit the news yet."

I nodded, and Becca got out to go inside.

I pretended to read, but I was thinking about Jack. Did he make it back okay?

Over my book, I saw a grungy and freckled older man looking through the windshield at me. Actually, he was leering at me. I held the book higher, but he didn't leave.

Mom was probably still lying alone in the kitchen, which made my stomach ache, and I teared up again.

Becca returned with two sandwich bags and leaned into the car to hand them to me. After she got in and shut the door, she asked, "Has that man been staring at you?"

"Yes," I said, sniffing. "He is creepy."

"Yes, he is. Hopefully he's just a dirty old man and doesn't know who you are." Her voice was shaky.

I unwrapped Becca's sub and handed it to her.

Becca said, "Oh, thank you, honey."

"How much longer before we meet the next person?"

"About two hours."

****

I'd fallen asleep again and woke as Becca parked the truck beside a small gas station.

Becca disappeared inside and returned with a Snickers bar and two Diet Cokes and handed one of the drinks to me. "Sorry, I forgot to ask you what you wanted. But I figured, what teen girl doesn't like a Diet Coke every now and then?"

"I usually drink Coke Zero."

"Oh, I'm sorry I got you the wrong drink."

"No, that's not what I meant. I like Diet Coke fine." I started crying and said, "I'm sorry. I didn't mean to be ungrateful. It just got me thinking about my mom."

"I get it, honey," Becca said, patting me on the shoulder.

"She once told me about how they replaced real Coke with New Coke when she was young and how it was so bad, but then they came back out with regular Coke with a new name."

Becca said, "Yeah, I remember hearing about that."

"But she told me Diet Coke started tasting like New Coke to her as soon as she first tasted Coke Zero. So that's all we had around." I exhaled in a short laugh before feeling terrible again. But I'd managed to stop crying.

A dark Volvo crept in and parked in the space next to Becca.

The driver, a black woman with hair clipped so short she was nearly bald, got out of the car and headed inside. She came back out with a bottle of Diet Coke and a Snickers. Becca took a bite of her own Snickers and then took a sip of the Coke.

The other woman watched this and approached Becca's window. Becca rolled it down. "Marilyn?"

The new woman nodded. "Yes. Are you Becca?"

Becca said, "Yes." She turned to me and said, "Ready?"

We got out and Becca gave me a hug. "Good luck, honey," she said.

Marilyn picked up an atlas and handed it to me as I got in. We pulled onto the road.

Chapter Ten

Despite Marilyn's silvery gray hair, she didn't look old. She wore a flowing, orange, wrap-like shirt and a bright, striped scarf.

Marilyn glanced over at me. "How are you doing? I understand you've been through quite an ordeal."

I nodded and glanced at the atlas, which showed eastern Wisconsin.

"Do you want to talk about it?"

"I don't know. I guess not really."

"That's fine. You can sleep or keep quiet, whatever you like. Feel free to ask me any questions, if you have them."

I tried and failed to get comfortable enough to sleep. I wasn't tired anymore.

Talking about something else might keep my mind from going back to the image of Mom. "Actually, I guess I'm curious how everyone got involved with this group."

"You mean those of us driving you?"

"Yeah."

"Well, a variety of reasons. I am a college professor and have always had an activist streak, so when I was asked by someone I knew professionally if I would be willing and able, I of course agreed. With other people, they—or someone they love—sometimes have experienced some type of domestic violence themselves. Some of them even went through the network and are living with new identities, still willing to help."

"Wow. I guess my mom used it a while ago. I had no idea until last night, really. Is it normal that moms don't tell their kids?"

"Well, it's not uncommon when the kids are too young to remember. Young kids can accidentally give information away or sometimes do it on purpose, not realizing the severity of the consequences. And teenagers...they're unpredictable. I think most women tell their kids when they're older. Adults. If they ever tell."

"That makes sense, I guess. It still feels like she lied to me." Saying it aloud made me feel so bad I started crying again.

"Well, she did. But sometimes it's the best way."

I sniffled. "Sorry."

"Don't worry about it, honey. Cry all you want."

"Thanks." I paused. "So, um, what do you teach?"

"Sociology and Women's Studies."

"Cool." I was quiet. The crying had passed for the moment. "What is Women's Studies, exactly?"

"If only we really knew." Marilyn laughed lightly. "But seriously, it's an umbrella term referring to study in several fields like history and literature from a more women-specific perspective. The idea is that in these fields women have been invisible, or only relevant in relation to the men around them, and so on. Women's Studies tries to provide some balance."

"Ah, okay." This was a good distraction. "Balance is good."

"Personally, I think a lot of the time it misses the

point by overemphasizing the so-called feminine perspective and romanticizing it." She gave a laugh that sounded self-conscious and added, "I only teach the classes because I have to. We offer a minor."

"I think I know what you mean. Two wrongs don't make a right and all that."

"Exactly."

We were quiet until Marilyn broke the silence. "So are you planning to go to college?" Her clipped laugh filled the car. "Sorry, this is my area of expertise. Feel free to tell me to be quiet if you don't want to talk."

"Well, until yesterday I was set on it. It's been all I've wanted forever." I remembered talking to Jack about our plans, which seemed so innocent and oblivious now. Naive again. "Now I'd give it all up to have my mom back."

"Honey, I know. It must be so hard."

"Oh, my God!" I exclaimed. "I actually made a joke yesterday about getting stabbed, and how paranoid my mom was, all probably while it was happening to her!" Dizziness rushed through me.

"Honey, you couldn't have known what was happening. Your mom was trying to protect you from the truth, and it sounds like she did a thorough job of that."

My stomach lurched, and I held onto the seat and door to steady myself as I stared at me knees.

"None of this is your fault," Marilyn said, like she'd read my mind.

"Do you know why my mom always told me not to go to the police?"

"At all?"

"She always said not to if anything ever happened

to her."

"Ah. I don't know, but sometimes the family circumstances are so bad it's safer to walk away from it all. The police aren't always on the right side in domestic violence situations. And children's services often puts kids back in bad situations in the name of 'keeping the family together.' "

That made sense, but things didn't feel clearer. There were too many possibilities. I sat for a while until I was sleepy again and dozed off.

When I woke, the sun was getting low. "How long is this drive?" I yawned, feeling slightly lightheaded.

"We have another four hours or so. I have to take smaller highways to avoid other people as much as possible. Your picture is all over the news already."

"Really?"

"Yes. Do you—do you want to hear about it?"

I considered that, still feeling queasy. "I guess."

"They found your mother and arrested a man found nearby under unclear circumstances. They are desperately searching for you."

"Who was the man they caught?" I looked at Marilyn.

"I don't know," she said, shaking her head. "They haven't released much information about him yet."

"Was, um, anyone else hurt?" *Please let Jack be okay.*

"They didn't mention anyone else."

"Do you think the man is my father?"

Marilyn frowned. "He could be, I suppose. He is a white man with brown hair. But there's no way to know yet."

Being on the news was weird. I was mortified that

all these people would know the details before I did, and felt the familiar fear in the pit of my stomach from doing something so much in the public eye.

"They're showing a short video of you jumping hurdles in jeans."

"What! They played that?" My stomach flipped again.

"Yes. They talked to someone on your track team who explained why you were in jeans. They interviewed some of your other friends, who all said good things. Everyone wants you safe." She glanced over at me with a hesitant smile.

"I can't believe the video is out there again." I covered my face with my hands, trying to calm down. I'd be the laughingstock of the whole country. It was insane.

I dropped my hands. "I can't believe I care about a stupid video when my mom was just murdered," I said, starting to cry again.

"It's going to be okay eventually, Retta," Marilyn said. "It's completely normal to be confused and distracted right now. You haven't even begun to process what's happened. That won't happen until you get where you're going, wherever that ends up being. These are going to be the hardest days of your life, but you will get through them."

"I know, but she's gone. And I hated her so much lately, and she was so mad at me." I couldn't stop. "I was a good kid for so long but not anymore. I pushed back on everything. Also, I should have been there when it happened. I snuck out and found her when I snuck back in."

"Oh!" Marilyn said. "That's awful. However, I'm

sure your mom would be happier that you weren't there. He might have hurt you, too."

A chill ran down my spine. It was true.

Marilyn continued, "That is the worst thing about losing a parent as a teenager—parents and teenagers are always in such conflict. I think it's one of the basic facts of human nature. But you must remember that she still loved you. She knew how old you were, and she went through it herself." She stopped for a moment. "Was your mom affectionate?"

"Yeah." Definitely.

"When was the last time she said she loved you or gave you a hug?"

"She used to hug me every chance she got, until I made her stop," I said quietly. "She was always touching me. I started hating it. I think the last time she said she loved me was right after one of our biggest fights ever. A few days ago, I guess."

"See, even then she knew she loved you and wanted you to know." Marilyn said it like it could only be true.

"I didn't say it back, though," I said, face in my hands.

"Don't worry—she knew. I assume you never did things to hurt her, specifically—you just did things you wanted to do that she was uncomfortable with, right? Parents know the difference."

"That's the thing—I never meant to, but I think it's my fault he found her." It was hard to admit it.

"What do you mean?" Marilyn asked, glancing over.

"There's the video for one. It doesn't have my real name anywhere, I don't think, but still. I don't look much like my mom, so I always imagined I look like my dad. Also I started doing internet searches on my mom, trying to figure out where we came from, and I requested my birth certificate from Nebraska, where my mom said I'd been born."

"You think one of those things somehow alerted him?" Marilyn asked. "I don't see how."

"I don't know." But I did know. It had to be the video. Or maybe something else, but the timing couldn't be a coincidence.

We were silent for a few minutes, and I was resting my head against the window when Marilyn started passing a car going really slow. Something about the driver seemed familiar to me, and I looked at him as we passed.

He glanced over our direction before I realized what I was doing.

I turned away, but it was too late. I didn't know him, but if he'd seen me on TV, he would recognize me. "Oh, God."

"Did that driver see you?"

"Yes."

"Okay." Marilyn's voice shook. "Let's hope he doesn't watch the news."

"He looked familiar, like this creepy guy who stared at me when we stopped for lunch earlier. I don't think it was him, but now that's two people who have seen me."

Marilyn didn't say anything, but her lips were tight.

"I should not have passed that car," she whispered.

We drove in tense silence for another hour.

"Here we are," Marilyn said, sounding calmer. She

slowed the car down.

We pulled into a small town McDonald's parking lot. Marilyn asked, "Would you like something?"

"Just a hamburger," I said. "And an apple pie. And I need the bathroom."

"Okay, there's a baseball cap in the back. Why don't you put that on and run into the bathroom. I'll leave the car unlocked so you can come back out."

I waited in the car when the thought of Jack holding my hand overwhelmed me. Just last night everything had seemed so wonderful and full of promise. And now...Mom was gone, and I might never see any of my friends again. Jack. The tears ran down my neck onto my shirt.

I wiped my eyes just as Marilyn returned and handed over two small drinks and a bag while she got in the car. "I thought you might like a pumpkin pie, too, since they just came into season. Your last ride should be here shortly."

I sniffled and nodded. "Thanks."

We waited.

Every time a car turned into the parking lot, Marilyn would take a sip from her cup.

We continued to wait. Marilyn made a phone call and had a moderately cryptic conversation. I understood the next person was on their way but was delayed.

It was almost dark when I dozed off for a bit. When I woke, nothing had changed.

After we had been there an hour and a half, another car drove in, and Marilyn took a long sip from her drink. The car parked across from us. The driver got out with a Wendy's cup and took a sip.

Marilyn rolled down her window, leaned her head

out, and said, "Are you Jamie?"

The new woman nodded. In the headlights, I could see she was middle-aged, bleached blonde, and a little worn-out looking—like she'd smoked too many cigarettes and spent too much time in the sun. But she had friendly eyes.

Chapter Eleven

Marilyn shook my hand and wished me good luck, and then I was in the car with Jamie, who gave me an update on the news. "I really loved that video of you doing the hurdles. Why were you in jeans?" She said it almost enthusiastically.

My stomach clenched when I thought about the guy finding us because of it. "Um, someone had stolen my backpack with my running clothes in it. It was the day of the tryouts, so I had no choice if I wanted on the team."

"Ah," she said, shaking her head. "That's not what the girl said on the news. She said you didn't know about the tryouts till that day, so you didn't have the right clothes."

"Which girl?"

"Skinny thing with straight brown hair. Alice—Alex—something like that."

"That was one of the girls who took my backpack."

"Well, that's the news for you—about as accurate as I am young." She laughed, then continued, "Listen, kiddo, I'm really sorry about what got you here. I truly am. But I have to warn you I'm not very good at being sad. Or serious. So please don't think any lack of respect is intended."

"Okay." It seemed an odd thing, but I was still distracted with thoughts of the video.

"I'm also sorry I was so late. What happened was pretty crazy. I made a wrong turn and didn't realize it at first, and when I was finally turning around, a tire popped! About the time I had the jack out, these nice boys rolled up in a truck and insisted on helping. They had the tire changed in minutes, but then they got all chatty." She chuckled. "Anyway, it took me quite some time to get away."

I was pretty sleepy again and yawned.

Jamie said, "We have about three and a half hours to go, so feel free to sleep if you want."

"Okay, thanks. I think I will."

****

"Retta. Retta."

I woke with someone shaking my arm lightly.

I jumped. "Huh?" I slowly recognized the last woman who'd been driving me.

"Could you scrunch down on the floor? We're about to pull into my park, and there's a boy in one of the front trailers that always watches passing cars from his porch."

I unbuckled and lowered myself onto the floor, keeping an eye on Jamie. There was a bump as we drove over something.

"Sorry, kiddo," Jamie mumbled before waving at someone out the passenger side window as the car lit up from the porch light.

After another turn, Jamie stopped the car and got out, looking all around. "Okay, it's clear. You can get up and out."

I climbed out. The trailer was small and had once been white. We walked up the cinderblock steps.

The inside seemed bigger than I had expected but

was still smaller than my own house. There was a brown pleather couch facing a TV in the tiny living room. A little table stood in the corner next to the couch with a laptop and a boxy, weird-looking typewriter on it. Jamie started to show me to the room I would stay in.

"Actually, I really have to go to the bathroom."

"Oh, sure, kiddo—this way."

Afterward, we went back to the bedroom, where Jamie showed me the dresser with some extra clothes I could wear, including long T-shirts to sleep in. "If you give me your dirty clothes, I can wash them. I am going to wash your shoes, too—they look terrible! I'll get a load started, and then we need to dye your hair."

I realized I'd left the bag of clothes in Marilyn's car. Hopefully she'd seen it.

I changed and found Jamie in the bathroom holding a small bucket with some boxes and bottles in it. She set the bucket down on the closed toilet lid and said, "Okay, let me look at you. Do you want to go bleach blonde or black?"

"Um, I never considered either." I looked in the mirror and couldn't picture myself with anything other than brown hair.

"The whole point is to make you unrecognizable and unnoticeable to the average person who might have seen your picture on TV. You have pretty fair skin, so blonde would be better, I think. Is that okay?" She moved the bucket and motioned for me to sit.

"Sure."

Jamie draped a couple of towels around my neck, over my shoulders, one for the front and one for the back.

I watched Jamie mix measured amounts of powder

and a bottle of liquid. "Why is that blue?"

"It goes on bright blue and comes off blue but magically changes your hair color. I don't know why it works, kiddo. Some chemical thing." She shrugged.

Jamie finished mixing and plopped quite a bit of it on the top of my head, spreading it around and dragging it through the length of my hair. She eventually covered all of my hair and pulled it together, piling it on top of my head.

"You look like a punk ballerina," Jamie said.

I didn't get it at first but then realized the pile of hair looked like a bun, and with my pale skin and the cream-colored T-shirt, there was quite the contrast.

"Ah," I said. "Or a reverse Smurf."

Jamie laughed and patted me on the shoulder. "We'll wait twenty-five minutes, and then you can rinse it out and see how you look."

"Do I need to stay in here?"

"No, no, come on out and watch TV with me."

A chef was making a fancy soup on a food show. I sat down on the couch, feeling like I was being swallowed by it.

"I like to watch these even though I never make any of the things they show," Jamie said, lighting a cigarette and inhaling deeply. My head jerked back at the sight of her smoking. Mom would never smoke another cigarette.

"I used to watch some of them. I was homeschooled until this year, so I watched all sorts of TV when I was home alone. My babysitter when I was really young got me started on them."

"They are fun. So many possibilities."

"Yeah."

"So, listen, I am working tonight from midnight to four, in case you get up to go to the bathroom or hear something. I do closed-captioning—you know, for TV, so I'll just be sitting here with my headphones on, typing on that thing." She pointed to the odd typewriter. "But don't talk to me. I can't be interrupted because it's all real-time."

"Oh, okay. You can do that from home?"

She nodded. "Yep."

"My mom should have done that," I said. "She would have loved never having to leave the house or leave me alone."

"It can be nice. Money's not bad, either."

We sat there until a buzzer sounded from the kitchen.

"Time to rinse!" Jamie said. "Just go wash it out in the shower. I would rinse well and then wash with shampoo twice. You can put some of that special conditioner on it and leave it for a couple minutes before rinsing again. Just make sure to rinse around your hairline and ears and everywhere. You don't want any of that gunk left on your skin. Leave it wet, and I'll braid it for you."

The idea of a shower sounded amazing to me. It sounded like a great way to wash away the last twenty-four hours. Every part of me felt grimy, and I looked at my hands and arms only to notice there were still specks of something on them, like freckles. Dirt—or blood? I grabbed a long T-shirt and towel and went back to the bathroom.

The shower started off great. All the tension poured off me until I started to cry again, thinking about Mom. I'd abandoned her. How long had she lain there alone on the kitchen floor?

About the time I'd gotten myself together, Jamie knocked on the door and asked if everything was okay.

"Yes," I shouted over the shower. "I'm about to finish."

I stepped out of the shower and wiped the condensation off the mirror. My hair wasn't as light as I'd expected, but I still looked totally different.

"Oh, nice!" Jamie said when I walked back to the living room. "It looks natural enough. Come sit here, and let me braid it for you. You won't have to do anything to it tomorrow."

"Okay." I sat down and let Jamie work on my hair. She was gentle. Mom always pulled too hard when she'd done it. That thought felt so mean, like a betrayal, that I started crying again.

Jamie tied the braid off. "There you go, kiddo. Are you going to bed now?"

I nodded and said, "Good night. Thank you for letting me stay here. And picking me up, too."

"Sure. Just my way of paying somebody back for trying to help me once." She looked off in the distance. "Good night."

I went back to the bedroom and turned the light off.

I instantly felt sick, like something was trying to push its way out of my stomach. I reached a shaking hand out to turn the light back on.

Chapter Twelve

I woke up slowly, first noticing a small window and the fake wood paneling of the walls. I closed my eyes, overwhelmed with the memory of Mom lying there on the kitchen floor.

My heart raced as I remembered running from the crazy man. And Jack saving me. Had he made it back okay? *Please let him be okay.*

I couldn't get up. A pile of bricks on my chest weighed me down.

I lay there until my heart slowed down some. I got up and walked to the dresser for some clothes, glancing in the mirror, which was a shock—my hair was so much lighter than last night, a true bleached blonde. The braid made me even more unrecognizable. I hadn't had one since I was a little kid.

I remembered Jamie had said she would wash my clothes, so I walked toward the nook between the kitchen and bathroom where I'd seen the stacked washer and dryer. I found my borrowed clothes hanging in a doorway.

I changed and sat on the couch in the living room. I flipped channels until I was faced with a picture of myself standing at the hallway of the school, looking very lost. The picture faded as the camera focused on the newscaster who continued the report, but I had trouble listening because they were showing other pictures other kids had taken with me in them, most of which I'd never seen.

I stared at the TV, the remote still in my hand resting listlessly on the couch. I'd obviously come in during the middle of the newscast, but now they were talking about Mom. They splashed up a blurry picture of her dishing what appeared to be lasagna in the cafeteria. I was queasy again. Some kids took that picture to laugh at her.

I finally paid enough attention to learn the police had someone in custody and he was in the process of being charged with the murder. The report ended. I didn't learn much, but it seemed I was safe for the moment. The queasiness started to fade, and I felt my shoulders relax. I hadn't even known they'd been tensed.

Would Jack stay quiet? He was probably okay since I hadn't seen anything about him on the news.

Jamie stumbled out of her room looking pretty rough and lit a cigarette as she sat down on the other end of the couch and said, "Mornin'."

I nodded and returned the greeting, continuing, "I saw a report on me and my mom."

"Was that weird?"

"Yeah, super weird."

Jamie looked out the window. "I know how it is. I went through a similar thing myself."

"What happened to you?"

"Oh, I'll tell you another time—you've got too much on your plate already." She continued staring out the window. She stood up and walked into the kitchen, calling, "Do you want some cereal?"

I stretched and rolled off the couch. I filled a blue

bowl with cornflakes and milk and followed Jamie back to the cramped living room.

The news had come back to my story. The man who'd been charged with Mom's murder was named Don Lytle. He'd been thrown from his car when he'd driven off the road. He had some serious injuries, but they weren't releasing the specifics. My stomach twisted at the injustice of it—why in the world did he get to survive?

He'd been found in the morning when someone stumbled across the wreck. They didn't realize he was the suspect until later in the day, after a neighbor had noticed the side door open at my house. She looked inside and found Mom. After talking to other neighbors who had seen the car parked in front of the house Saturday night, the police put two and two together and questioned the man at the hospital. He'd been sedated but was coming out of it when they got there. They placed him under arrest, but he was still at the hospital.

The news had a picture of him, an old police booking photo. He had brown eyes and short dark brown hair plus a trimmed mustache and beard. I couldn't believe how normal he looked.

****

Jamie had lots of books—a mix of fantasy and classics—and we both spent most of the day alternating between reading and watching the news cycle. I didn't hit up the internet because Jamie wouldn't let me use her work computer and didn't have a smartphone. I realized I'd left mine in the RV. The battery was still in my jeans pocket, in Marilyn's car.

I was a few chapters into *Jane Eyre* when news broke that a teenage boy was being questioned regarding my disappearance. Jack!

What were they going to do with him? What if he talked? Would they find me and all the women who'd helped me? But what if he didn't talk? What would happen?

The news wasn't very specific—and they didn't name him, but it couldn't have been anybody else—so I didn't know what was happening, but it couldn't be good.

I tried to continue reading but couldn't. I waited for each report for more news, queasier by the minute, and eventually Jamie talked me into going to bed.

She woke me just after five because the news was abuzz about a new break in the case. Mom's family had been located. *My* family.

They brought a ton of information to the table.

Mom's mom and sister were still alive. I stared at them talking on the news, uncomprehending. A slim older woman with short brown hair stood next a woman about Mom's age. The younger woman was pudgy and had long brown hair. She was the one who talked, but I truly couldn't hear.

Then the newscaster said the man in the hospital was my father.

They were showing a picture of Mom and a younger version of this man, holding me the day I was born—in Oklahoma City, not Nebraska. They both had impossibly big smiles. I had never seen Mom look anything like that. They said Mom's real name was Tracy Lytle.

I looked at Jamie, stunned. "Can it all be true? That man is my father?"

"Kiddo, life is strange." She stopped. "But it

sounds like it is. I'm sorry you were born into this mess."

My mouth hung open, and I blinked several times. "What should I do?"

"What do you want to do?"

"I have no idea." After a pause, I said, "They said my name is Frances."

Jamie looked thoughtful. "Really, names are arbitrary. You can be Frances, or you can be Retta, or you can be somebody else."

A few hours later there was a press conference with a plea from Mom's family—I still couldn't think of them as my family. Her sister and mother begged anyone with information about my whereabouts to come forward, because they wanted to bring me home.

It was confusing. They weren't really wanting *me* to come home—they were looking for baby Frances. And I didn't feel like any kind of Frances.

I wanted Mom. Even with the nasty fighting we had been doing lately, she'd still have known exactly what to do. I cried thinking of her, and my mind slipped to how scared Mom must have been.

My stomach ached at the thought of how she must have felt, worrying for me, too.

I turned to Jamie and said, "If I hadn't disobeyed her, I would have been there with her when he came."

Jamie sighed and shook her head. "That's life for you, kiddo. Sometimes it's all down to the luck of the draw."

That evening there was another plea from Mom's family for me. And there was still no further news of Jack, but he was still being mentioned, though not by name.

"Have you decided what you're going to do?"

"I don't know. What if my mom left to get away from her family, too? That's what one of the other ladies said might've happened. But what does that mean for Jack?"

"It is a possibility. It would be better for your friend if you go to the police. But why don't you think on it and decide tomorrow."

I did. I didn't know what else I could do. I watched another plea the next day, and the two women seemed nice enough. So when Jamie asked me, I said, "I guess I should go to them. I don't think I have any other real option. Do I have any other options?"

"We could possibly get you to Canada or another city here. You could go to a homeless shelter and get into foster care. We can also sometimes get you new ID papers. You could become eighteen, maybe. I'd have to check. Whatever you do, it's tough if you don't have money. And there's still the issue of your friend."

I had no choice—if I went off on my own, Jack might be in real trouble. "Will they think he killed me if I disappear?" I asked Jamie.

Jamie shrugged. "I don't know, but I doubt it. I doubt they'd have enough evidence to arrest him. Anything they have will be—what do they call it?"

I looked at her.

"Circumstantial! That's it. Since you aren't actually dead. Which is a good thing."

We watched more TV, and I considered the choices. "You know, they convict people of murders based on circumstantial evidence all the time. Even without a dead body."

"That is true." Jamie nodded. "It's always a

possibility. It would definitely be better for him if you go to your family."

"I guess I'll go to them," I decided. Once I was with them, I could safely contact Jack. I did have his email, after all. And with hope whatever trouble he was in would go away.

Jamie nodded. "That's probably best. Okay, then. We'll do that first thing tomorrow morning. It's too risky for me tonight because I'd have to drive you there in my car. In the morning I can go get a different car. But first let's talk about what you should say to the police."

****

Jamie left at seven a.m. and returned an hour later with an old Saturn. We got in and left, but not before she gave me a pair of lensless glasses. "To make you look extra different on the drive, on the off chance we get pulled over," she said.

Jamie drove for nearly two hours, and eventually she slowed and pointed down the street. "See that cream-colored building? That's the police station. If you get out and walk to it, when you go in, say who you are, and they will take care of things. I'm going to drive to the next intersection and turn around and let you out there. Go slow on your way there, and I will watch you from across the street here. When you get close, I'm going to leave."

"Okay. Is this dangerous?" Dread crept into my stomach.

"No, not really." She turned right at the intersection and then left onto a neighborhood street, and then did a U-turn before parking along the curb. She extracted a map from the glove box and pretended to study it.

My heart started speeding up. What would happen in just a few minutes?

Jamie said, "Now we're going to turn the corner, and I'll let you out." She turned onto the main road. "Glasses please." She held out her hand and stopped the car so I could get out. "And don't look back toward me, and try not to make eye contact with people on the way there. But don't act weird—just act like you're distracted by things near the ground."

I got out, heart thumping. Jamie said, "Best of luck, kiddo."

I nodded at her and said, "Thank you so much for your help."

I crept along, watching as Jamie turned left. Then I did as I was told and walked toward to the police station without turning around. About halfway there, I realized Jamie had never told me what had happened to her that was similar to my experience. For some reason that bothered me.

It took about fifteen minutes of slow walking to get to the station. The sense of dread was still there. I pushed open the heavy door and saw a handful of people sitting or moving around, but nobody looked up. I stepped up to the desk, a sour smell passing by, and waited for someone to notice me.

I waited. The station was tiny, but they seemed busy. There was one officer standing near the other side of the counter, but he had his back to me and was talking to another officer near the back of the small room. This delay would be good for Jamie. Weirdly, it was also calming me. I was back with regular people, and nothing bad was happening.

I glanced at two gray metal benches. A couple in their twenties took up one, the man holding the woman, who appeared to be crying. I considered sitting down on the other, but it was half-occupied by an older man who looked homeless, with an oversized and torn trench coat, ratty shoes, dirty pants, and a big, scraggly beard. I was pretty sure he was the source of the smell I'd noticed when I'd come in. Whatever his situation, his eyes narrowed, and he stared right at me.

I turned my head back quickly and stayed where I was. No one else was paying any attention to me yet.

"Hey, you're that girl they're looking for, aren't you?" the man said in the clearest, most well-enunciated British accent I'd ever heard.

I had the sudden urge to flee, which made no sense since I was here to tell them just that.

The cop leaning against the counter turned his head toward him and said, "That's enough, Donald. Leave the girl alone." Then he turned toward me and said, "I'll be with you in a moment, miss," before turning back around.

Donald. The man's name was Donald. He wasn't my father, but it still gave me chills. I glanced back at him, wondering why he was sitting there. He clapped his hands together and gave a giant belly laugh that was so ridiculous my fear melted away.

"Yes," he said, even louder than before, "you're definitely that missing girl. Good thing you are safe, though I am sorry for what happened to your mother. Terrible, terrible thing." He gave another hearty laugh.

I stood in place, staring at him. He was causing enough of a scene that I was pretty uncomfortable, but everyone else ignored him as if they were used to it.

After forever, the desk cop turned around and walked over to me. He still didn't react.

"Hi, my name is Retta Brooks."

"Oh, come on," he said, glancing sideways. "Don't let Donald put ideas in your head."

I stared at the officer, unsure what to do, and Donald laughed again.

The officer continued to look at me until something finally clicked, and he said, "Oh, it really is you! You dyed your hair."

I nodded. Donald was still laughing. My sense of dread dissipated with each guffaw.

I thought things would move fast, but they didn't. The officer ushered me into a small room with a table and asked me a few questions. I repeatedly said I was fine, that I'd hitchhiked, taken buses, and walked to get here, so he stopped asking even though he must have known I was lying. He explained that the other officer had contacted the Department of Human Services, and a social worker was on the way. I had to stay in this room. He apologetically offered to bring me a drink.

He returned carrying a steaming Styrofoam cup. "The social worker should be here within a couple of hours. We're pretty isolated out here in the U.P., but I'm guessing you already knew that. I also found this magazine in case you want something to read." He handed me an old issue on boating in the Great Lakes region. From that I figured out that "U.P." meant the Upper Peninsula of Michigan. I was far from home.

And far from Jack.

To keep my mind off things, I read the entire magazine but couldn't have told anyone what it said. I looked around. The walls were fake wood paneling just like Jamie's trailer, even the same color. I took a final sip of the coffee gone cold, getting a mouthful of sludgy powdered creamer and sugar.

The table was a gray speckled with tiny bits of color when I looked closely. I tore a piece off the rim of the cup and dropped it inside. I read through the magazine again.

Finally, after the cup was half its original height, and I was reading the first article upside down just to keep myself distracted, the door opened, and in walked a large, smiling woman in an animal-hair-covered black sweater and black slacks with crisp creases from being ironed but still were wrinkled. She smiled and said, "Hello, Retta. My name is Laronda Griggs."

I shook Laronda's extended hand. "Hi."

****

We pulled onto a long gravel driveway and eventually parked in front of a small, weathered, two-story farm house of the foster family they had found on short notice.

"Well, here we are," she said. "This is where you will stay until your aunt comes to pick you up. Helena is a very nice woman. She doesn't have any other foster children with her right now, so it will be just you."

I nodded. "Here we are."

I followed her up to the porch. A white-haired woman came to the door after Laronda knocked.

"Hello, Retta," she said as she opened the door. "I'm Helena. Please come in." She backed up and held the door wide open for us.

I stepped in and looked around. We were in the kitchen, which had a small round table with two chairs and dull sage wallpaper decorated with little flowers peeling in several spots. A clear glass bowl full of plastic sunflowers sat near the center of the table.

I could see into the next room, which had a baby blue couch with three cats sleeping on it.

Someone was talking to me. "What?"

Helena asked, "Did you have any things with you?"

"Oh, no. Nothing."

She nodded. "Let me show you where you will sleep, and then you can stay there or come into the living room and watch TV." Helena started up the stairs next to the kitchen, and I trailed her upstairs. Laronda was right behind us.

The room was painted a muted yellow, and the small bed had a poofy white bedspread. It was inviting, though I wasn't tired.

I sat on the bed and the comforter deflated. I could hear the stairs creaking as Helena and Laronda went back down. I sat there. Just sat, not even thinking.

****

I'd been with Helena for three days, and we'd hardly spoken. She was nice, but I didn't feel like chatting. I'd had to talk to two Iowa police officers who came up to take my statement regarding what happened the night of the murder. I had to describe finding Mom and running away from the man.

It was when they asked me where Jack had taken me that my heart began racing. I didn't know what I should say. "We ran into a woman in a parking lot, and she gave me a ride. Jack had to get home, and I had to get away."

They pressed more, but I stuck to that version. "He's not in trouble, is he? If he hadn't been there to help me, I don't know what would have happened."

Ultimately they didn't seem to care too much. How or why I got away wasn't their main interest—that was the murder.

Now they were gone, and Laronda was here again, and she insisted on talking. "Do you know anything about your family yet? Samantha and your two cousins?"

"No. I only saw my aunt and her mother on TV."

They were waiting on a shelter care hearing, which would happen the following week, before I would be sent to live with my aunt. Samantha would be visiting the next day, and all the adults hoped I'd be in Oklahoma within a couple weeks. I wavered between not caring and feeling a sense of dread, wondering if I should have seen what else Jamie could have come up with.

"She has two kids, a boy named Frankie and a girl named Tracy. Frankie is ten and Tracy is nine. I've talked to Samantha on the phone, and she is very excited to see you again."

"That's nice," I said flatly, feeling nothing at all.

"She is divorced, so it will be just the four of you. I don't know what her job is, exactly, but I believe she is some kind of chemist. She works for the Oklahoma State Bureau of Investigation. Like the FBI, but for the state."

Maybe my aunt just wanted me to babysit all the time. Why wouldn't Mom have tried to stayed in contact with them if they were so great? Had I done the right thing?

But there was Jack. My heart contracted; he was so far away. The only thing I could think to say was, "This is going to be weird."

"Yes, it will be. It will also be difficult. You're going to be dealing with a new family, a new city, a new school, and more. But there will be a lot of people there to help you adjust."

How could anyone help someone adjust to a brand new family after their mom had been murdered? And what if there really had been a reason Mom hadn't kept in touch with them?

Chapter Thirteen

Helena woke me up about in the morning and left me alone to prepare for Aunt Samantha's first visit. I brushed my teeth and got dressed and sat on the unmade bed. I waited. My mind alternated between blank and the memory of Mom, lying there on the floor.

Helena came back upstairs and said Samantha had called and would be there in about half an hour. Laronda was already there.

Helena sat on the bed with me and asked, "How are you feeling? Are you ready for this?"

I was quiet and then said, "I honestly don't know. It's just so weird."

Helena patted me on the knee. "Yes, it is. Samantha sounds nice and also very anxious to meet you. These are all good signs."

I nodded. But why did Mom really leave? Why had she told me they were all dead?

"Okay, I will leave you up here. Try to come down soon. I'll be serving sandwiches for lunch, but if you want something for breakfast, come down sooner rather than later. Okay?"

"Yeah, okay."

I still didn't feel hungry. I sat for a while, not sure how much time had passed, until car tires crunched on the gravel outside.

I closed my eyes and stood up. I chewed on my

thumbnails, something I hadn't done since I was little. The front door opened, and I sat back on the bed.

Helena talked, and the new woman—my aunt—answered. She had a voice that sounded a lot like Mom's, kind of low, but she had a hint of a southern accent Mom never had.

Someone was coming upstairs. Helena stepped into the doorway. "Retta, can you come downstairs now? Samantha is here."

"Okay." I followed Helena downstairs, one slow step at a time.

I recognized Samantha as the pudgy woman from the news. She wore jeans and a sweater with wide blue and gray stripes and had light brown hair in a single long braid. Strands of hair had escaped the braid and framed her face.

"Frances, I'm so glad you're okay!" she said, tearing up. "You're so tall!" She approached me, and I flinched.

Samantha backed off. "I'm just so…I don't know how to express how happy I am to get to see you again. We all thought we'd never see either of you…" Her voice thickened, and she continued, "I still can't believe Tracy is gone. We'd always hoped…" She wiped her eyes. "I'm so sorry you had to go through that. It must have been awful."

"It is." I didn't have anything to say to this woman. She was a stranger.

Helena said, "Would you like to sit in the living room?" She pointed, and we sat on the floral couch. Helena left the three of us alone.

"You still have blonde hair," Samantha said.

"I bleached it a few days ago."

"Oh." Samantha stared at me without saying anything more, a surprised look on her face.

"What?" I finally said.

"I'm sorry. It's just, you look so much like Don did when I first met him." Her face colored.

I turned toward the window and didn't say anything. How could this woman compare me to the man who had murdered Mom?

"I'm so sorry; I shouldn't have said that." She grimaced and shook her head. "Did you know my kids are named after you and your mom? My daughter is Tracy, and my son is named Francis—spelled with an 'i'—but we decided to call him Frankie in case we ever got you back."

"Well, you didn't need to worry because I am not going by that name." I knew this was not a nice thing to say, but I couldn't muster any kindness for this annoying woman. I still couldn't believe she'd compared me to Don.

"Ah, right. That's okay. I know you go by 'Retta' now. The kids are both very excited to meet you."

I forced myself to nod. I looked at the pictures on the wall, which I hadn't really noticed. They must be Helena's kids at different ages, a girl and two boys, posed doing various things. One showed a boy in a baseball uniform holding a bat, and the two others both had shots with soccer balls. What would it have been like if I'd grown up where pictures like this covered the walls?

Samantha asked, "So can you tell me a little about yourself?"

It seemed a reasonable question, but I could not answer it simply because I had no idea what I was like now. It was like I knew nothing about myself. I couldn't even really say, "My name is Retta," could I? It wasn't even true. Plus, I knew what the old Retta was like, but I was not that Retta.

But I should say something. "I like languages. And running. I study a lot. I watch some TV but not much anymore."

Samantha nodded. "I saw your video."

I didn't know what to say. Again the video—the one that probably brought Don to us. I glanced at Samantha. The woman reminded me of Mom, if Mom had been inflated and had brown hair. They were the same height and had the same nose I'd always wanted. "Oh," I finally said.

Samantha smiled weakly, which is when I noticed her blue fingernail polish, which made her look younger.

There was more awkward nothing-talk for another half hour, and then Helena came into the room and said lunch was ready. We moved to the kitchen and ate in silence. Laronda tried to get a conversation started a few times, with no luck. I looked down toward the table and could see out of the corner of my eye that Samantha studied her hands, which were clasped together on the table. She'd run out of things to ask, and I wasn't volunteering anything.

****

I spent the next week in a fog, not doing anything other than lying on the bed except for the time I had to speak with the prosecutor so they could file the indictment. That had been pretty much a rerun of my statement to the police. On Wednesday, I went with Laronda and Helena to the court hearing, where the judge ordered me released to Samantha's custody. It was weird to be talked about like a prisoner. Regardless, I would be going to Oklahoma.

Samantha returned two days later. When I was going out the door, Helena hugged me and said, "Just so you know, you will be fine. I've known a lot of kids and seen many really cruddy families in my time. But you are a sharp one, and it's clear you have a decent family ready to welcome you. Just don't rush the grieving process. It will take time. Don't be afraid to cry, and it will be good to talk about your mom even though it will be hard. I know you're going to land on your feet eventually."

I nodded. How could Helena know?

Once we were in the car, Samantha said, "It's going to take about forty-five minutes to get to the tiny little airport we'll be flying out of. We have to drop off the car before we get there, but they'll drive us out to the airport."

I didn't say anything. The idea of flying seemed weird.

"It's a funny airport—barely more than a field," Samantha said, laughing and glancing over at me staring out the window. "But we're lucky because your grandparents chartered a plane for us so we can avoid the press as much as possible."

Grandparents? The idea that I had those was strange. They'd always been dead.

We were silent for the rest of the drive. The place looked even more rural than Buckley had been. Just fields and a tiny town.

Samantha pulled the car into a gas station and filled the tank. She parked the car and said, "This is where we get out. Let's go inside."

I sank into an orange vinyl-covered chair. Why was I so tired all of a sudden?

It was an effort to stand up, but I managed it. The man picked up Samantha's bag, and I followed the two of them out to an old Mustang, where I squeezed into the back with both bags.

It took only about five minutes to get to the airport, and Samantha hadn't been exaggerating—it was just a building and what looked like a long driveway.

Soon we were heading south. I knew I should be taking in my first experience of flying, but I was numb and also nervous about what I would face in Oklahoma.

I remembered Jack, feeling guilty that I hadn't thought of him more often. What was he doing? It was just after nine—he was in French. Without me. My heart ached, and I wondered if he was lost to me forever, too.

Part Two: Chapter Fourteen

I woke up in a moment of peace before remembering. The blood. Mom. Everything.

It couldn't be real, could it?

But it was.

****

I woke with a start. Where was I?

Oh. Still at my aunt's. The sun was up, and I needed the bathroom. I stumbled down the hall, glad not to run into anybody. I got back in bed and slept.

****

I woke. I slept. I lost track of everything.

There were dreams, frequently featuring the kitchen. Mom was always alive in these dreams. She was usually cooking something elaborate—something she'd never done in real life—with things coming out of and going into the oven, and multiple pots on the stove. In a particularly odd dream, I found Mom pulling the freshly baked Converse out of the oven, rancid smoke coming off them, the plastic emblem and shoelaces melted into puddles of goo. The fumes of burning plastic, visibly wafting off the mess, made me gag.

Once, I woke from one of these dreams and found a little girl standing in the open doorway holding a tray with a bowl of something that looked like oatmeal and some water sloshing around in a glass. Her eyes were wide and her mouth hung open. She crept in and set the tray on the nightstand I hadn't even noticed was there.

"Hi," the girl said before scurrying out. I had already turned away from her.

****

Mom was serving a fancy meal at our dining room table for Jack, Rachel, Lily, and me. Strangely, there was no place setting for Mom—then I realized that was my fault because I'd been the one to set the table.

I woke feeling guilty.

It was dark. And very, very quiet.

I could barely make out a lamp next to me and reached over to turn it on. An explosion of light made me slam my eyes shut, and the image of Mom lying dead painted itself against my eyelids. I opened them and replaced the image with that of the room. The strange room in a house in a city I would now have to call home.

A plate with a half-eaten peanut butter and honey sandwich rested on the nightstand. I vaguely remembered a boy bringing this tray. Sometimes it was the girl, sometimes the boy. I also remembered eating some of the sandwich. I couldn't taste it. A glass of water stood next to the sandwich. I was parched, so I took a sip.

The water was horrible, with a chemical aftertaste. Nothing like the water we had in Iowa.

But I was so worn out I forced myself to drink it. Running would be out of the question if I couldn't swallow a sip of water.

I slept again.

****

I woke to find that it was dark again. Of course the

image of Mom was there in my mind, but I had to pee, despite my lips and tongue feeling like tree bark. I stood up, wobbly and weak.

I stepped into the dark hall and started toward the bathroom. As soon as my back was to the pitch-black hallway, it was like someone was right behind me. Where was he? He must still be in jail. Heart pounding, I crept sideways down the hall, the whole time imagining that Mom must have been even more scared. Probably all the time, even before the man was in our house. The worst part was getting past the two open bedroom doors, because the banister was opposite them and obviously anybody could be coming up the stairs.

Just before I stepped into the bathroom, something brushed against my leg, and I gasped and my heart almost stopped. I looked down and barely made out a gray and white cat snaking around and between my feet. It must have slinked out of one of the bedrooms.

"Okay, okay," I whispered, pushing past it and feeling my racing heart slow a tad. When I turned to shut the door, it was standing in the hall staring at me with its expressionless face, creeping me out.

There was a nightlight in the bathroom, but I still checked behind the shower curtain. Nobody.

When I opened the door to go back out, I looked for the cat, but it was nowhere. As I walked slowly back, I was overwhelmed with exhaustion. I slid to the floor between the first two bedrooms, sitting there waiting to feel better, glad my eyes had adjusted to the darkness.

A rustling came from one of the bedrooms, and I looked up, heart racing again. A little boy in red pajamas stood next to me.

He whispered loudly, "Frances? What are you doing?"

I blinked, trying to think of something to say.

"My name is Retta. And I'm sitting down."

"Do you feel better now? Mom says you are sick."

"I got tired."

"Oh." He stared at me for a moment before whispering, "I'm going to the bathroom." He stepped past me, twisting his skinny neck to stare back at me all the way there.

After he made it back into his room, he popped his head out the doorway and said, "I'm glad you moved here. Now I have a cousin!" He disappeared into the room.

I sat there a couple more minutes, trying to think of the name of the boy. I should know it. I had to use the banister for help getting up and slid along the wall back to my room.

Where had the man been hiding when he'd been waiting for me?

****

It was light out, and I was awake.

"Retta, sweetie, it's time to go."

This floated through the door.

I'd already been told earlier and was wearing a black dress and shoes they'd given me. The dress didn't fit perfectly, but it was better than the cargo pants and T-shirt I'd arrived in.

I sat on the edge of the bed, looking at the carpet, which was worn down and a color I couldn't figure out. Tan, maybe.

There was another knock.

It was time to go. Time to say goodbye to Mom.

Chapter Fifteen

Finally I woke and couldn't sleep anymore.

Where was I? Really?

In a house with people who thought they knew me, while everyone I cared about was either dead or several states away. Thinking about it all made me dizzy, almost like I was floating away from reality without the strength to hold on.

I closed my eyes and told myself I'd go running again. I'd feel the ground. As soon as I had some energy.

I sat on the edge of the bed and looked around. The bedspread was a blue and green plaid print that matched a guy's shirt on a sagging, yellowed Pearl Jam poster. A squat white dresser stood to the right of the bed next to a white bookshelf built in to the corner; another bookshelf on the wall at the foot of the bed, which took up nearly the whole wall. Neither overflowed with books, but there were quite a few between the two of them.

It felt sort of good to just sit there. Everything was new. Nothing reminded me of my real home. Nothing except the pictures in my mind.

I couldn't sleep when the dreams changed. Now they always ended the same. With Mom lying in her own blood, all alone in the kitchen. I'd wake up sweating and terrified. And I'd see the image of Don they'd shown on the news. He was still in jail, right?

****

I didn't know what to do with myself. My back ached from spending so much time lying in bed, and I didn't even know how long I'd been doing that.

Nobody bothered me, and it seemed I was free to do anything but didn't know what that should be. Lying there with my eyes closed was the worst, because the backs of my eyelids were the perfect canvas for the horrible pictures of Mom.

But then a faraway memory percolated back up. Jack.

What was he doing? He must have seen the story on TV and known I was okay. How much trouble had he gotten into when he got back?

What was happening at school? What about the cross country team? What did they think? What about Coach Olson?

Daylight infused the room, but I had no idea what time it was. I lay there for some time, concentrating on feeling the bed and memorizing the patterns on the ceiling.

Maybe I'd go downstairs and see if there was something to eat. They would bring me food again, but I was hungry now. And I wanted to run again.

I got up and started down the stairs, holding on to the banister for support because my legs weren't working right. A squeaky bottom step gave me away.

"Frances?" I heard from another room. "Retta?"

I froze. An older woman I recognized from the memorial service walked into the foyer from the kitchen.

"You're up! How are you doing? Are you okay?"

The woman had a warm smile under that familiar snub nose and dark brown hair trimmed short.

I stared at her.

"Oh, honey, do you remember who I am?"

"You're my mom's mom."

"I'm sorry, I should have said. Of course you won't recognize me as easily as I know you. Anyway, how are you doing right now?"

"I feel okay right now. But is there something I can eat?"

"Definitely! I can make you something. Grilled cheese? We have some tomato soup if you'd like that." Her hands flew around as she talked.

I was surprised—that was exactly what I wanted. It's what Mom would have made me in these circumstances. "That sounds good."

"Here, come with me into the kitchen." She gently took my elbow and led me to the table. "Have a seat, and I'll make it for you." She pulled a pan out.

"Whose room am I sleeping in?" I asked.

"It's Samantha's old room." She buttered two slices of bread. "But it's complicated, because this is the house Tracy and Samantha grew up in, and most everything in there was Tracy's first." She opened the fridge and grabbed slices of cheese, which she stuck on the bread before putting the sandwich in the pan. "Would you like green chiles on your sandwich?"

I blinked in surprise. "Yes." Just like Mom did grilled cheese.

"Tracy gave Samantha all her posters when she moved out of the dorm. Samantha got into all that same music, too, but after Tracy left, we put all her stuff in that room to remember her." Her voice cracked. "We can take the posters down if you want. But we thought it might be comforting to you."

"It's okay." It was kind of weird. It looked like a teenager's room.

"Good." She cleared her throat and started cranking open a can of soup. Two cats came racing in and looked up expectantly.

"Oh, kitties, this isn't for you!" the woman said, throwing her hands up. Then she poured the soup into a pan and turned toward me. "Milk or water?"

"Oh, water."

"Just like Tracy. Samantha wants hers creamy."

I didn't know what to think. This was too weird. Watching this lady make my favorite comfort food made me miss Mom even more than I already did all the time I was awake.

The woman said, "Honestly, these cats are incorrigible. Have you met them?"

My heart sped up as I remembered the encounter with the cat. "I saw the gray one. I think it was a couple nights ago."

"That's Wes. He's the shy one. The other one is Giles." Something about the names seemed familiar, but I couldn't place it.

She got some cat treats out of another cabinet. They gobbled them up, and then Giles lunged at Wes for no apparent reason, and off they went.

"Giles can be so mean." She sighed and turned back to flip the sandwich and stir the soup.

"Anyway, where was I? Al and I moved into the condo several years ago and let Samantha and her husband—ex-husband—buy the house for the remaining payments. Al passed last year." She stirred the soup more before pouring it into a bowl. "Croutons?"

"Sure, thanks." Mom did that, too.

"Here you go, Fran—er, Retta," she said. "I'm sorry, that's going to be hard for me. I've thought of you as Frances for your whole life. We just missed you so much, dear."

I took in a spoonful. It was good. The woman was talking more. I knew I should think of her as my grandmother, but I just didn't feel that. She put a plate with the grilled cheese on it next to the soup, and I took a bite of it. Perfect, just like Mom's. This must have been where she'd learned it. In this very kitchen. Tears threatened.

I fought them off.

As I finished the sandwich, the woman—my grandmother—was saying something. "What?"

"Nevermind, dear. Nothing. I'll ask you another time."

I got up. "I think I'm going back upstairs. Thank you for lunch."

"Okay. I'll be down here reading if you want to chat or need anything. I mean it—don't hesitate if you need anything, sweetie."

****

I lay on the bed, staring at the textured ceiling again. I'd managed to fall asleep after lunch but had woken sharply from another nasty dream, and now the sun was low. Almost anything could be seen in the ceiling if you looked long enough. The streaks of sharp light coming in through the blinds added to the possibilities. I was trying to keep myself from thinking about Mom but having a hard time of it.

149

I remembered how mad I'd been at her and all the times I'd screamed accusations at her. She *had* been hiding something, and I'd meddled in things and caused that man to find us. It had to be my fault, somehow. It couldn't be a coincidence, not with the timing.

Panic descended, and my heart sped up. I ran down the pitch-black street with him behind me again. I felt worse and worse. Queasiness took over, and sweat covered my forehead and arms.

Jack. He'd been the one to save me that night. I had to talk to him. I had to talk to him...

How could I be so dense? I started down the dark stairs, checking behind myself several times as I descended. When I reached the bottom, Samantha called, "Retta?" My fear eased.

"Yeah," I managed.

"We're in the kitchen. Are you hungry?"

I walked toward the voice and found Samantha and the boy and girl, all sitting at a small kitchen table looking expectantly at me. There was a bowl of green beans on top of a blue tablecloth, and Samantha was in the process of dishing some sort of casserole onto one of the kids' plates.

Samantha pointed at the empty seat opposite her and said, "Come on and sit down, Retta."

"Uh, actually, I was wondering if you had a computer I could use? I want to email a friend of mine."

"Oh, sure! I'm sorry I didn't think to offer before!" She pushed the chair back. "Follow me."

I trailed her into the room across from the kitchen on the other side of the stairs. A desktop computer sat next to a TV with a small black pleather couch and a couple of recliners aimed toward the TV.

"The password's 'chemistry,' so you can log on any time." She added, "When you're done, feel free to come eat with us if you're hungry." She was obviously trying to be nice, but I didn't care. I was already opening the browser.

I had a ton of email, most of it junk. It's kind of weird that all sorts of horrible things can be happening to you, but you'll still be getting spam. I found several from Jack. I scrolled through to the oldest one, from the Monday morning after it happened. It simply said:

Where are you?

He kept emailing, about once a day, asking how I was, saying he'd seen me on the news. The one he sent yesterday just said:

Please email as soon as you can!

I felt so weird—excited that he was desperate to hear from me but also nervous because I wasn't sure what to say. I wanted to talk about how much I missed him, because suddenly I missed him more than anything I could think of, anything at all. I'd do anything to hear his voice again, hear him say something funny. But I didn't think I should say that. We'd held hands all night before I left, and my heart expanded at the memory of the way he touched my face, but that was like a lifetime ago. I decided to be cautious.

Hi Jack,

I finally have access to email again. I don't have a cell phone.

What happened after I saw you last?

Retta

Send.

I waited.

I opened up a new tab on the browser and typed "Retta Brooks" into the search. There were 170,000 results. That seemed crazy. A search for "Frances Lytle" yielded almost as many.

I couldn't face clicking on any of them, which was fine because when I checked my email again, I already had a reply from Jack.

Retta! TG you're OK! I guess you're OK? How is your new family? I can't believe you had a whole secret identity and didn't know it.

He must have been watching the news. I saw he was on GChat just as he IMed me.

jaxing94: retta!

runningretta: hi jack

jaxing94: omg im so glad ur ok

runningretta: yeah it's been crazy, but im ok now

jaxing94: people here cant stop talking about u, even quentin and those guys. kayla and jules made a big production of asking me if id heard from u when the principal was standing there

My face flushed with embarrassment and then anger. Those backpack-stealing jerks. And pretending to be my friend so they could be on TV...

runningretta: ugh

jaxing94: so how are u doing? and u know i never got to say it properly, but im really sorry for what happened to ur mom, and that u had to find her

runningretta: im ok. thx. i keep having weird dreams about her. and i cant stop thinking about seeing her. i dont know how i feel about my family. they seem ok

I frowned. At first, I couldn't easily explain how I felt, but then I hit on what it was.

runningretta: i dont feel any connection to them but they think they know me

jaxing94: that sounds really weird. and hard

runningretta: i know. so what happened to you that night? and after?

jaxing94: i just drove back home

runningretta: did you know that hed crashed? i thought wed just outrun him

jaxing94: i didnt know but i thought maybe. but then i saw the car there, wrecked. so when i got back, my parents were sitting up, about to call the police. they were so mad. theyd only just noticed i wasnt there or they would have already called them. i thought i was in the clear

runningretta: did you tell them what happened?

jaxing94: not at first. but the cops were frantically looking for u sunday. they couldnt find u so they thought u ran off on ur own. but eventually they figured out id helped u

Had they found out about the network? I couldn't blame Jack if he'd given up the little information he had. He wasn't exactly trained to withstand interrogation. What would happen if the police figured out how I got away? Would they care?

runningretta: so what happened to u? i was really worried when i saw they were talking to u. i knew it had to be u

jaxing94: yeah, it was me :) it wasnt a big deal. they talked to me several times. they searched my truck and i guess there was some blood in it from your shoes. and hands. they didnt really know what to do with me. now its ok because they know it was not your blood

How was that not a big deal? But I couldn't handle

it. I closed my eyes and imagined what it would be like if I were still back there with Mom and my friends. Jack. I was half a world away. I just couldn't bear it.

runningretta: jack, i have to go
jaxing94: ok, ill look for you on here later!

A couple tears escaped when I opened my eyes, but I was determined to not cry. I stood up when the little girl—my cousin—came running in and said, "Do you want some ice cream?"

Something about the girl reminded me of something, but I couldn't place it. Whatever it was, I didn't like it.

"No." I added, "Thanks."

A cat followed me as I headed up the stairs, and I had to check a couple times to make sure he was the only one. Don must still be in jail. Wes tried to come in when I opened the bedroom door, but I shut it before he could squeeze past me. I didn't get cats.

Jack sounded happy to be back in touch. I lay on the bed, knowing I wouldn't be able to sleep, and remembered how he'd held on when we'd hugged goodbye. A deep ache started in the center of my chest. How could I stand not being able to see him?

Chapter Sixteen

I looked through the bookshelves in the room I was staying in. There was mostly sci-fi and fantasy. Mom had always read it, and I'd never understood why. I'd tried a book or two, but I couldn't get through them. She had always laughed and told me it was no worse than the dystopian or vampire stuff I read.

My grandmother had told me this room was full of Mom's stuff, so that must mean that the books were hers. I wondered when Mom had gotten into medical thrillers since I didn't see any. There was one high shelf with only a few books on it, making it look like they were prominent in some way. I pulled a handful off the shelf and threw them on the bed.

I wandered over to the CDs. More Pearl Jam, Nirvana, and other old bands. I recognized many of them, but not all. Nothing that looked remotely country, thank goodness. Maybe Mom's dislike was real.

I pulled out one of the CDs and stuck it in the player. It was one I hadn't heard of—Mother Love Bone. I pressed play, lowered the volume, and sat on the bed. This must be something Mom had done. Lounged around and listened to this band.

I picked up a book off the bed—*Ender's Game*—and read the back. Invading aliens were not really my thing, but this was Mom's book. She must have liked it, so I started reading.

It started off a little slow, and twenty-five pages into the book, it claimed that women had "evolved" to be physically and mentally inferior to men. I threw the book onto the desk. I didn't need that kind of anti-women crap now, so I listened to the rest of the CD while staring at the ceiling.

After the player went silent, I noticed I was chewing on my left thumb nail, which was down to the quick and matched the other one. I picked up another book—one called *Illusion*. It was a thick paperback with thin pages, and sci-fi or fantasy—I couldn't quite tell. The book also didn't sound amazing, but at least it was by a woman. Plus, the cover was sort of awesome. It showed a teenage girl in rags standing in a doorway with a wrought iron gate barely open on either side of her. The gate's metal work was shaped like butterfly wings, making the girl look like a fairy rather than the dirty and half-starved beggar she probably was. Then there was some guy on the back holding a metallic sphere that didn't look at all like something that belonged in a fantasy book.

This book also started a bit slow, but soon I'd read fifty pages, and then a hundred, two hundred, and then I was halfway done. The house was dead quiet. It must have been very early morning.

I needed to go to the bathroom but couldn't bear the thought of the dark hall. Walking past the top of the stairs made me feel so exposed. Instead of going, I closed my eyes and tried to sleep, dozing off for a bit before starting awake from yet another nightmare. I shook my head to erase the image and started reading again.

Then I couldn't wait any longer. It was still dark,

but there was a tiny bit of light poking in with the dawn. I walked into the hall. My heart still raced as I slid down the wall toward the bathroom, not sure I'd make it. I checked behind the shower curtain again, glad to find the tub empty. The walk back to my room was nerve-wracking, and I didn't relax until I was back in the bed after checking the closet.

Soon, the kids were up and moving around. The little girl offered to bring breakfast up, but I refused it, so she left. I was glad when she was gone. I still didn't like her for some reason. Finally, the front door closed a few times, the car started up and backed out, and everything was quiet.

I might as well finish the book and pick another. It was doing an okay job of keeping the pictures at bay.

****

I managed to doze again. When I next woke, I had one coherent thought as soon as my pulse slowed and I cleared the horrific picture of Mom's body from my mind: running. I'd lost track of time, but it must have been at least three weeks since I'd last run. That was more than enough to lose both strength and stamina, and I didn't want it to get any worse.

I went downstairs, hoping the grandmother would be there, while the gray cat—Wes—trailed behind me. What was with that thing?

"Retta, is that you?"

"Yes." I walked into the living room where my grandmother was sitting. "Do you know if there might be some shorts and a smaller T-shirt around? I need to go for a run."

"Oh," she said, appearing thoughtful with her hand to her chin. "I am not sure. We can look." She walked into the downstairs bedroom and started poking through a bottom drawer of Samantha's dresser. "Samantha used to be thinner and keeps some of her old clothes here just in case, but I don't see anything small enough for you. I thought she might have something with a drawstring. Looks like she doesn't."

"Okay."

"Would you like to go clothes shopping?" she asked. "You really could use something else to wear, couldn't you?"

I didn't want to go. But I did want to go running, and having more clothes would be good. I'd spent my whole time here in oversized T-shirts and too-big flannel pajama bottoms I had to hold onto whenever I walked around. At least Helena had bought me a couple packages of underwear. If we left now, I'd still have time to run before it was dark. Jack was still in school, anyway, and there was nothing for me to do until he was home so we could chat.

"Okay," I said.

"Let me get your other clothes."

I changed into the cargo pants again. My grandmother was sitting in the living room working in a puzzle book when I got back downstairs. "Ready?"

As we got in the car, she asked, "Where do you want to go?"

I said, "I don't care. We always shopped at Walmart."

"There's a Walmart nearby, plus some shoe stores. You could use a new pair of running shoes, right? Since you love running so much?"

"Yeah, that would be nice." I almost smiled. "I just need a couple pairs of shorts and shirts for running.

Plus some socks. And some jeans and shirts for normal stuff. Plus some pajamas."

"Okay, we can start at the Walmart. But there are other places if you want to go there, too. There's a Ross not far, and we could always go to Dillard's. I don't mind."

It all sounded exhausting. "Walmart's fine."

As soon as we got there, my grandmother got a cart and headed straight toward the Juniors section.

"Actually, I'd like to get the exercise clothes first, if that's okay. I don't need to try them on."

"Sure, whatever you need, honey."

I picked a couple pairs of shorts, the same exact ones Mom had bought me a few months ago, checking the price to make sure it was still okay. I threw both pairs into the cart. I found the short-sleeve wicking shirts I liked, and tossed one solid red and another green and yellow striped one into the cart.

I picked a couple sports bras off the shelf and looked at my grandmother, who was glancing off to the side. "Um. Hi?" I said, holding them up. "Are these okay?"

She laughed lightly. "You know, the kids call me Nana. You can call me that, too, if you want. Or Grandma. Or even Nancy, if you're more comfortable with that."

I hadn't thought about what I would ever call my own grandmother. But it was just a name, right? "Okay, Nana. I can call you that."

Nana nodded at the bras and said, "You know, you can get more than this if you need it."

"I know; I am going to get jeans and stuff."

"No, I mean more workout gear. Samantha only

does laundry once a week, and if you exercise as much as I think you do, you could use more. I mean, you could do your own laundry if you want. But we can afford more clothes for you."

"Oh. Mom never had much money."

"Right, I understand." She looked very sad. "It breaks my heart how you two had to live for so long."

I could think of nothing to say to that at first. It'd seemed okay at the time. "Well, she didn't make much money." I grabbed more of everything.

Nana shook her head. "Did you know what she was doing when she left here?"

"No." I tossed a couple packs of underwear into the cart.

"She was in medical school."

"What?" I was so stunned I had to lean on the cart for support. "She went to college?"

"Of course she went to college," Nana said, laughing for a moment before her face fell. "I'm sorry—that was insensitive. I know she had to be a totally different person when she left. But she was always such an achiever. Did you know she was a National Merit Scholar?"

"Really?" I knew only that that was when kids took the PSAT in their junior year. If they did well enough, they could get scholarships.

"Oklahoma gives out full scholarships to go to any school in the state. Samantha missed that one but still got a full scholarship from her ACT score."

"Oh." I was still holding onto the cart. "Why didn't she do something like that in Iowa? At least be a nurse or something?" I made myself let go of the cart and walked back toward the Juniors section as Nana followed.

"My guess is that her new identity didn't come with a degree. Plus, she explained to us that they generally advise people to do completely different things with their new identities."

"You knew she was leaving?" I found several pairs of jeans and some T-shirts to try on, throwing them over the side of the cart. I tried to stay calm, but my heart was ramping up.

"Yes, she was extremely careful about letting us know without giving us any details about the group that helped her, where she was going, who she would be, or anything. It happened pretty quickly. The hardest time of our lives." She sighed.

Nana continued, "It was good she hadn't told us anything, because Don came around after she left and threatened—Samantha, me, and Al—trying to find out what had happened. It helped that we didn't know. He had a knife. If our neighbor hadn't shown up..." She looked away.

This conversation was too surreal and made my stomach flip. But I could tell Nana wanted to finish telling me. "Didn't he just come back?"

"No, because he was arrested later that night after stabbing someone in a bar fight."

"Did he just get out of prison before coming...to Iowa?"

"He'd been out for a while. Several months. He was in and out of prison over the years. He's a violent man." She shuddered.

"Oh. I'm going to go try these on now," I managed, feeling boxed in. I made it back to the changing room, sat down on the little bench, and put my head in my hands. The world spun. Images of Mom returned like a tidal wave. And all the talk about Don. I still guessed I'd somehow started him on our trail.

I sat there for quite a while before I managed to calm down. Then I didn't have time to try everything on, so I threw it all in the cart. Walmart always took returns. I could just try them on at home.

We picked up other odds and ends. When we checked out, I was stunned at the amount—over four hundred dollars—and the fact that Nana didn't even flinch.

As soon as we got in the car, Nana said, "Would you like a new cell phone?"

It was like I was back with Mom, getting my new phone a few months ago. An image of Mom lying dead in the kitchen splayed across the windshield in front of me. I inhaled deeply.

"Are you okay?" Nana asked.

"Yeah." My stomach roiled. But I did want a new phone. I could talk to Jack. Hear his voice.

"So would you like a phone?"

"Yes. Can I get one that does email?"

We got a new smartphone, and soon I'd picked a couple pairs of shoes to try on at the sporting goods store.

"Um, Nana, I like them both, but these feel a bit better, but they're one hundred and nine dollars. The others are seventy-nine dollars."

"Oh, go for it. If it's a better shoe, it's better for your feet."

"Thank you." This was so different from how I was raised. The extravagance made me uncomfortable. But the shoes were awesome. It'd be like running on a cloud.

On the way home, I started when I glanced up and noticed a street sign reading *Garth Brooks Blvd.* Hadn't Jack mentioned him? Some big country star? I couldn't get away from country. The thoughts of Jack and country music made me half-laugh.

Once we were back at the house, I thanked Nana again and went upstairs to change into my new running clothes. I let Nana know I was going for a run.

I started off at a walk, but I was impatient to fly again. I sped up to a jog for a couple minutes and then a run. The abject weakness evaporated. The neighborhood was bigger than the one I'd grown up in, and I kept track so I could just reverse the run. It was hot and humid for October. I wondered if it would slow me down after I'd gotten back into running.

A sign for a park entrance caught my attention, and I found it led to a large expanse of mostly treeless land with several trails snaking all over. I was able to run the length of two of them and focus on the running. But it took me back to the feeling I always had when I ran in Iowa—like I was doing something I shouldn't, something I had to hide from somebody.

I was about to run one of the trails again when I felt someone's gaze on me. I spun around, but there was no one. Nothing out of the ordinary.

Plus, it didn't make any sense. Don was still in Iowa. Who would be watching me? But it had spooked me enough to send me back onto the neighborhood streets, where I ran for another quarter hour.

As I headed back to the house, a school bus passed me and stopped. While I ran past it, one of the kids waved enthusiastically. I recognized Tracy and half-lifted my arm in a wave, but kept going. Just a couple more blocks.

Nana greeted me as I opened the front door. "How was your run?"

"Good." I was glad to be back in the house. I hadn't shaken the sense of being watched. But I was also exhausted.

"Why don't you sit down here until the kids get home? It should be any minute."

I edged toward the stairs. "I think I'm going to go up. I want to have a shower."

"Okay, come back down and have cookies with the kids if you feel like it."

I sat on the bed to set up my phone. I also had to check the exact date. It was October eleventh, a Tuesday. The thing had happened three Saturdays ago. So I had been here since about Friday. I couldn't remember exactly how long I was at Jamie's. And that other woman's—Helena.

I checked my email.

Nothing from Jack, but I emailed him my new number.

When I got back from the shower, there was a text message from Jack.

—*Cool! heres my number—*

It made my heart swell.

Chapter Seventeen

On Friday, I lay on the bed listening to a Pearl Jam CD. The orange one. I'd heard them before, but the first song was pretty heavy, and so was the next one. I soon found that I liked the sound of the whole album. I knew Mom had, too.

After it ended, I fell asleep and woke to the sound of someone knocking, somehow escaping any terrible dreams for the first time. Was that it? Were they gone now? There was another knock.

"Yeah?"

"Hi, Retta," Samantha said, tentatively. "Can I come in?" She wore another baggy sweater.

"Okay." Like I had any real choice. I sat up.

She sat on the desk chair sideways so she faced me. "So, Retta, there are a few things I need to talk to you about. The first has to do with school." She paused like she was waiting for a reaction.

I didn't have one.

Samantha continued. "You could start school here if you wanted."

"At the high school?" It hadn't occurred to me that I'd have to go to school again, and the idea of starting all over with other kids—other kids who might steal my backpack or do something worse—sounded terrible.

Samantha nodded. "That's not the only possibility, though."

The weight in my stomach lightened a tiny bit. "What are the other options?"

"I called your school in Iowa, and they are willing to let you finish the semester there, by doing your work from here. You'd have to start here in January, though."

Relief washed over me. "That sounds okay. So I would just study on my own until January?"

"Yes," Samantha said. "After that, you'd either need to go to the high school, or there is one other possibility."

"What?" I was starting to feel boxed in again.

"Tracy homeschooled you until this year, didn't she?"

Tracy? Oh, right. Mom. "Yeah."

"Nana said she could homeschool you if you don't want to go to the high school. But we both think you would be better off going to the high school. You could join the running team." She picked at some loose fabric on the back of the chair.

"Cross country is only in the fall. Track and field is in the spring."

"Oh, well, wouldn't you want to do that?"

"I guess. Maybe. I don't know." I had no idea what I wanted to do and lay back on the bed.

Neither of us said anything for a moment.

Finally, I said, "Can I just decide later? About spring?"

"Of course!" Samantha said. Her smile was just like Mom's rare one, and seeing it hurt. "I just wanted you to have it in your mind. I don't want to put pressure on you, but I think it will be good for you to get back to regular life."

I was quiet, and Samantha continued, "But you do

need to decide what you want to do about this semester soon."

I sat up again. "I'll finish through my old school. It will be easy for me since I studied on my own for so long, anyway."

"Okay," Samantha said. "That's what I figured. I'll call them tomorrow to get all the details. We'll have to buy the books this week. Nana will take you."

"Okay."

"Then there's the second thing I needed to talk to you about." She pulled on the loose fabric again, and I noticed her purple nail polish was chipped.

"Yeah?"

"We made an appointment for you to see a therapist next Wednesday."

"A therapist?" I bit my lip. I hadn't thought about that, either. I didn't like the idea of talking about things. What was the point?

"Yes."

"I don't want to see a therapist."

"It's at eleven. Nana will take you." She sounded almost apologetic. "I really think this will be good for you."

"Okay." I didn't care, after all.

"And there's one more thing." A dark look passed over Samantha's face.

"Yeah?" I said.

"Mom?"

I looked up to see the little girl in the doorway.

Samantha saw her and smiled. "Hold on a second, honey."

She turned back to me. "Your other grandparents have said they would like to see you."

"Uh, Don's parents? They want to meet me?" One more thing I hadn't thought of.

"Well," Samantha said, "they knew you when you were a baby. But yes, they want to see you again."

I glanced at her and saw she was staring at the floor.

My stomach churned. "I...don't feel like it. Do I really have to? Now?"

"No, but it might be good if you did soon. I..." Samantha stopped.

I didn't know what to say. I chewed on my lip. The idea of having to meet Don's parents was horrifying.

"I'll leave you to your music," Samantha said, patting the bed as she left the room. When she got to the girl, she put her hand on her shoulder.

The girl looked up. "I love you, Mom."

"I love you, too."

They disappeared, and a wave of envy hit me.

But then my brain tracked back to the more immediate concern. What would Don's parents say to me? What would I say to them? Would they try to defend Don, tell me about him?

I texted Jack.

—*hey, give me a call if you have time*—

My phone rang a moment later.

"Hi, Jack." Just saying his name made me feel all fuzzy.

"How are you?" he asked. I'd never noticed his voice before. It was smooth and low. I could hear him smiling.

My whole body relaxed. "I'm okay."

"How are you...settling in?" he asked.

"Well, it's still super weird. I think they're trying

too hard. One of the kids bugs me."

"Which one?"

"The girl," I said.

"Why?"

"No idea. Just...she reminds me of something. I don't know."

"Huh."

"So," I said, "they are all concerned with me getting back to normal life, because apparently that's what you do when someone's mom just got murdered."

"That's..." I could picture his grimace.

"Yeah, I know. They said I have to finish school. But they said I can finish there. In Iowa."

"Really?" He perked up a bit. "You'd come back?"

That made me smile again. "From here, I mean."

"Oh."

"So I was curious about whatever happened to our project."

"Oh. That." Jack laughed. "What a mess. I'm in a 'group' by myself now. She told me I could join another group, but I said I'd rather stick with our original plan." He paused. "I liked it. We worked it out so that I just have to do the half we'd already decided I'd do. But are you saying you'd be back in?"

"I guess maybe. I need to find out the details. Why don't you talk to her tomorrow and see if that's okay?"

"Yeah."

"Cool," I said after a pause.

"Great."

I didn't know what to say next, so I was quiet until I panicked and said, "Okay, I guess I better go."

"Right," he said. "I'll let you know what she says."

I hung up, frustrated for not thinking of a way to

keep him on the phone longer.

****

I woke early Saturday morning and dressed for a run. I had been thinking about running a marathon or at least a half-marathon. There was one here in April, and I'd need to do proper training for it.

Samantha was reading in the living room, her arm draped across Tracy's shoulders while the girl played with a tablet, all nestled against her mom.

"Hi," I said, looking away from the scene.

"Morning." Samantha smiled at me. "Are you going running?"

"Yeah."

"Good for you," Samantha said, shaking her head. "You're a better person than I am. There's cereal on the table if you want some. Milk's in the fridge."

"Okay. So I don't want to meet Don's parents right now." Or ever, really.

Samantha nodded grimly. "I don't blame you, but you may have to meet with them eventually. They can be pretty persistent."

"Okay," I said. "I'm going to go run now. I might be gone a while, more than an hour, so don't worry."

I did a warm-up lap around the neighborhood and then headed off to the park. If it ever rained, this might not work so well because the trails were dirt. I'd have to wear my older shoes.

My run was good even if it was humid out. I spent the first part of the run thinking about Jack. What would have happened if I hadn't had to leave Iowa when I did? What would happen now? I wanted to think of him as my boyfriend—already sort of did, really— but everyone knew long-distance relationships like this were kind of pointless. How often would we see each other? If only there were a way for us to live closer to each other.

I also started wondering about what things were like for Mom when we first left. I hadn't thought about what she was going to tell me. Would she really have revealed our situation? Or was she just going to tell me where we'd lived along the way, without the reason behind it? There was a burn in my stomach that was my desire to know.

I wrapped up the run at about five miles and still felt as good as new physically, if emotionally run-down.

On the walk back from the park, I passed an old blue sedan parked on the street several houses down, which was odd since the house it was in front of had an empty driveway. I didn't see anyone inside as I went past. When I stepped up to the front door of the house, I heard Samantha on the phone through the open window in the living room. I stopped to listen.

"No, Becky, I did not tell her to say no." A pause. "I understand. Yes, I know you chartered the plane." Her voice was tense. "It was good of you to do something nice for your granddaughter given the situation *your son* put her in." Another pause. "Mm-hmm."

I opened the front door while Samantha talked again. "She hasn't—look, I have to go. I will let you know." The phone beeped like she'd hung up.

Samantha came out into the hall as I was about to head upstairs. "I just talked to your other grandparents and let them know you won't be seeing them right away."

"Okay." It was nice of Samantha to stand up for me.

"I'm not happy about it, but I think it might be easier for you in the long run if you get this out of the way. Just think about it." She sighed and looked away.

****

Sunday night, we went over to Nana's. I didn't get a tour, but it was a smallish condo, one- or two-bedroom, I guessed. We were standing in the cramped living room with its cushy paisley loveseat behind a glass-topped coffee table.

Nana said, "Samantha and I are going to finish dinner. Why don't you three watch TV?"

Frankie turned the TV on, but Tracy pulled a drawer out at the bottom of the coffee table and extracted a photo album.

"Look, Retta," she said. "This has all the baby photos of you. And lots of pictures of Aunt Tracy. They wore funny clothes."

I sat down on the loveseat with Tracy on one side and Frankie on the other. Tracy put the album, an old-fashioned blue hardbound book with sticky pages and plastic sheeting over the pictures, in my lap and opened it to the first page. Wheel of Fortune played in the background, but it sounded miles away because of what I saw.

The first pictures were all of Mom on what looked like a college campus. "Where is this?"

"This is when Aunt Tracy first went to college," Tracy said. "At OU. Some of her friends took them."

I looked at Mom when she was just a few years older than I was now. There were several shots of her around the campus, not doing anything specific. A couple pictures showed her with groups of people, maybe at a concert.

"Can I turn the page?" Tracy asked.

"Hold on a second," I said, still stunned by how happy Mom had been. And how young. And alive. I'd never seen her look anything like that. Like she wasn't worried about anything.

I turned the page. This one had several more pictures of Mom with various people, including an unrecognizable young and slim Samantha, if what the little girl said was true.

Frankie leaned in and pointed to one of Mom leaned over laughing while standing next to a guy wearing jeans and a plaid shirt open over a black T-shirt. "That's Don," he whispered.

"Really?" I looked closer, but I could not make this picture connect with the image I had of the man that came into my house and murdered Mom. He had a scruffy goatee in the photo.

"That was before he turned bad," Frankie continued, still whispering.

There were more shots of Mom, and in these, she had started to dress differently, wearing plaid and jeans and black boots, like Don. I turned the page to see a few pictures from the wedding.

"Turn the page!" Tracy said. "These are my favorites!"

I did, and the first thing I saw was one taken from the side showing Mom very pregnant and looking off into the distance, hand on her belly. But what caught my attention was that she had on the blue Doc Martens.

I gasped, and my hand covered my mouth.

Nana yelled from the kitchen, "Dinner!"

Tracy and Frankie went running.

I sat there holding the album, my hand still covering my mouth. I missed Mom, but I also was kind of mad that she kept all this secret. She'd always seemed so bland, but she wasn't—she'd a whole rich life before it all went to crap. And she had been about to tell me everything. I wanted to cry.

I took my phone out and snapped pictures of the album pages and some close-ups of the more interesting photos.

Was this why she'd held onto the boots? To remember she'd had a happy life once? I just had to know who Mom really had been. And where we'd been.

"You coming, Retta?" Nana asked, her head poking out the side of the doorway.

"Yeah." I closed the album and left it on the table.

As I walked into the kitchen, Tracy and Frankie were both staring at their plates looking very glum and Samantha was finishing saying something to them, "—to be sensitive."

Nana was sitting down and said, "Honey, they didn't know. I don't think it was wrong, either. Retta, did you enjoy the album? You were the cutest first grandbaby ever!" She winked at Frankie and Tracy.

"I didn't actually get that far. I was looking at my mom. I had no idea she was ever…wild."

Nana laughed as she started serving a chicken casserole. Bowls of carrots and green beans were passed around.

Samantha studied me. I didn't give her any clues.

Nana said, "What was that music called that you two were so into?"

"Grunge, Mom," Samantha said, sighing.

"Grunge, that's right. I never can remember."

Somehow this admission seemed to ease the tension a little.

Samantha said, "Yeah, she got into grunge. It was what she and...he first had in common. Around here, not very many people were really into it the way they were." She paused, apparently thinking. "Then I copied her. We called all the fair-weather fans 'poseurs.' Because we were just so real ourselves." She shook her head, looking wistful.

"You were into it, too?" I asked.

"Yeah, I pretty much did everything she did. It drove her completely crazy."

"So, uh," I said, "I was wondering about this picture." I found the one of Mom pregnant and wearing the boots and held my phone up for Samantha.

Samantha laughed. "She was so happy then," she said, shaking her head and starting to frown.

"No, I'm actually wondering about the boots."

"The boots?" Samantha looked closer. "Oh, the boots." She smiled again. "Docs were the single most important grunge fashion marker, at least around here. There was a little store on Campus Corner—that was the little block just north of campus that had a few restaurants and shops everyone went to—and she bought those boots there her first semester with her leftover scholarship money." She laughed. "She thought she was rich, she had so much money left after tuition and room and board. Mom and Dad practically had a heart attack when they saw the boots."

She looked at Nana, who rolled her eyes.

"But that was just the first, because they almost

died again when she dyed her hair blue to match the boots," Samantha said, grinning.

My eyes must have bugged out. How was that even possible?

"Yeah, I know. It was pretty awesome. What makes you ask?" Samantha said.

I shrugged, barely managing, "Nothing."

Samantha looked at me, probably guessing that wasn't true. "Well, I don't know what ever happened to them, because I never saw them after she left."

I just nodded.

"Did you know who you were named after, Retta?" Nana asked.

"No, I have no idea. Do you mean my original name?"

"Yes, 'Frances,' " she said. "It was the name of the daughter of that one fellow—what was his name—Ken or something? The one who ended his life?"

"Mom, it's Kurt Cobain. And Courtney Love. They had a daughter named Frances Bean Cobain, which we all thought was cool. She's grown now. So that's where it came from."

"Hmm." Being named after some tragic rock star's child was weird. "What about 'Loretta'?"

Both Nana and Samantha shook their heads. "No idea on that one," Samantha said. "The only thing I can think is it's the last thing she really would have named you."

"It may not have been her choice," Nana said.

All of this talk about Mom started to make me feel strange. For all my life, Mom had always been just mine—there had been nobody else. But now all these people knew more about her than I did. I had been there only for the ruined part of Mom's life. I had to admit I was envious.

I ate in silence for the rest of the meal. Frankie and Tracy finally had a chance to talk, and they took advantage of it. I kept wondering what Mom would have told me "soon."

As everyone finished up, Nana said, "So you'll be working on high school again, right, Retta?"

I nodded but didn't say anything.

"I'm sure it will be good to get back to normal life."

Why did they keep saying that?

Chapter Eighteen

The next day, I got spooked again during my morning run. I kept going but couldn't shake the feeling of someone watching me. And then the empty sedan was still parked where it had been before. Maybe the two things were related.

But no. Must just be PTSD or whatever.

Then, after a quick shower, I discovered the closet. I'd gone in there to put my new clothes away, and had found a treasure trove of old clothes taking up one half the space. I guessed it must be what Mom had left behind since they said this was all her stuff.

I found a green and blue plaid flannel and put it on over my T-shirt. It felt nice, even though it smelled old. A little musty.

There were plenty of other shirts in there—flannel, band T-shirts, various black things that looked sort of goth but not quite, and a couple of weird velvet tops. I spotted another pair of black Doc Martens. Boots, but not as tall as the blue ones.

Grief rolled over me, and I had to step out of the closet and shut the door. I lay back on the bed and closed my eyes, crying for a while. Was this who Mom had been? It was weird to be looking through her stuff without her being just around the corner, waiting to explain herself.

When the feeling of longing waned, I sat up and

pulled my phone out. Every time I looked at the pictures from the album, I was more fascinated. I still couldn't imagine Mom being that person. The tears came again. It was so unfair.

To have that all ripped away by…what, exactly?

What had she fled from? Don, but why did it happen? How could somebody go from being the man in the pictures to who he was now?

And why had Mom been so distrustful of the police? I considered asking Samantha, but the idea of talking about Mom with anyone still seemed impossible. I might lose total control and break down. How would all these people deal with that?

I fired up the computer downstairs. I was going to try to figure something out about Mom. I couldn't answer all of my questions, but surely I could find something.

While the computer booted up, I rested my fingers on the keyboard. Once we'd left, she had her new identity. So any place we lived was probably under the same name, right? Unless she had gotten another new identity. Unlikely. It seemed hard to do.

The familiar colorful window appeared on the screen, and then I was able to log in. I fired up the browser. Typed in "Jenny Brooks."

There was a ton of results. Most about the murder, so I skipped those. I followed the other links one by one. Some were for various long-dead Jennifer Brookses. Most were for social media sites. Obviously Mom didn't have one of those. There also was apparently a country singer by that name. I couldn't get away from country.

I added "Buckley, Iowa" to the search and soon

had dozens of links to white-pages-type sites. My heart started pounding. This was it. I clicked on one and scrolled until I found her. Jennifer Brooks, age forty. She was the only one listed in Buckley. Buckley, Iowa; Des Moines, Iowa; Lincoln, Nebraska; Omaha, Nebraska.

This should have felt like a huge revelation, but it didn't. The newspapers I'd found were from Des Moines, so I already knew that much. That must have been where we'd been immediately before Buckley. So the list was probably in reverse chronological order.

Why didn't this make me feel better? It was what I wanted to know, wasn't it?

It wasn't enough.

****

The bedroom door swung open while I was reading another of Mom's books, trying not to obsess about where we'd lived, and the white cat stood in the doorway. I must have failed to shut the door properly. The cat gazed at me with his yellow eyes like he was thinking of coming over but decided against it. The door was naturally left wide open, but I was too worn out to go shut it.

A little later, I glanced up from the book to see the little boy standing there. "What are you doing?" he asked.

I blinked. "Reading."

"What's it about?" He stepped in until he stood right by the bed, eyes on the book.

"Well, these people, they go to Mars. But it's hard to live there, and there's a lot of stress and disagreement. It's hard on everybody."

"Oh."

We were both quiet for a moment, then Frankie said, "I like to read, too. Tracy doesn't."

"Oh, yeah? What do you like to read?"

His eyes lit up. "Warriors and Harry Potter. And Percy Jackson. And what's it called...the series about bad events—unfortunate events."

"I don't know what any of those are except Harry Potter."

"Warriors is all about these cats who are warriors!" His voice had gone high and fast. "They live in the forest, and they eat mice for real! And they fight the other clans sometimes. And Percy Jackson is a, uh— what do you call it—a demi-god? And he has to fight bad guys all the time to save the world. And the other one is so many books—thirteen!—and really, really funny. All these terrible things happen to these kids."

"That does sound funny," I said, giving him a sideways smirk.

He laughed and said, "Hold on," before running out of the room.

When he came back a moment later, he carried a short stack of books. "This is the first of all my favorite series. You should read them!"

I took them from him and set them on the nightstand, pulling the Harry Potter book out and handing it back. "I already read all of these, so I don't need it. But I will keep the rest, and I'll read them. Maybe not right away but eventually, okay?"

He nodded, obviously excited.

"Does your mom read?"

He shook his head. "Only the paper."

"Okay, well, that's too bad," I said. "I don't think it counts. But I'd like to get back to my book now."

"Okay," Frankie said, smiling and turning to walk out just as the white cat returned. "Giles!" he said and picked him up. The cat's feet dangled as Frankie walked out.

I felt weird. Sort of happy. The kid's excitement over having somebody to share his love of books with was sweet, but it also made my heart ache; that bond was something I'd had with Mom. It was one of the few things between us that had been real.

Where in Des Moines had we lived? A house? An apartment? I needed to know. But I wasn't sure how to figure this out. Reading her book distracted me and made me feel better.

I got up and shut the door.

A few pages later, there was a knock.

I sighed. "Yeah?"

"Can I come in?" said a small voice. The little girl.

I sighed. "Okay."

She opened the door and stood in the doorway. "What are you doing?"

"Reading." I glanced at her over the top of the book but didn't put it down.

"Do you want to play Barbies?" Tracy asked while looking at the floor.

"Not really."

"We have a Wii," she said, leaning forward slightly so her long blonde hair fell off her shoulders. "There's a horse game if you want to play that."

"Maybe another time." I put the book face down on the bed.

"We also have bowling."

"Listen, I really just want to read."

Tracy's eyes were sad above the family nose, but

she left, leaving the door ajar.

I sat there, trying to figure out what bugged me about the girl. She did make me think of myself at that age. But I didn't know why it mattered.

I continued reading until my phone rang. It was a number I didn't recognize but with an Iowa area code.

"Retta! It's Rachel! I hope it's okay—Jack gave me your number."

"Oh, hi, how are you?" I put the book down again. I couldn't believe I hadn't thought about Rachel or my other friends once since getting here. That was horrible.

"I'm fine. The question is, how are you?" She sounded very happy to be talking to me again, which was nice.

"I guess I'm okay. Things are pretty weird."

"I'm really sorry about your mom. I can't believe it happened."

"Thanks." I was abstractly glad Rachel had called, but I had nothing to say to her. I didn't feel like just chatting right now.

"So…how is your new family? Are they nice?"

"Sure, I guess. It's pretty weird to live with so many people, especially people who aren't paranoid about everything." I was lying back and staring at the ceiling.

"I bet."

"They bought me a bunch of new clothes, because I didn't have any when I got here." I laughed. "Actually, by the time I got here, I was wearing cargo pants and a monster truck T-shirt. It was different."

"Huh. Not your choice, I guess," Rachel said. "So I'm curious…what happened when you left?"

"Oh, you mean how I got to Michigan?" I asked,

closing my eyes.

"Yeah."

"Well, I'm not supposed to talk about it. I just got help from some people." I paused before adding, "Sorry."

"Oh, okay," Rachel said, following quickly with, "It's so crazy."

"Yeah."

We were silent for a moment, then Rachel said, "Okay, well, I guess I'll let you go. But now you've got my number, so give me a call some time. Seriously. I don't want to lose touch with you. You should get on Facebook so we can keep up!"

"Yeah, I will. Talk to you later," I said and hung up, glad to be off the phone. Then I felt guilty about that.

Talking to Rachel made my mind wander to Jack. His hand on my face. What it might be like to kiss him. I shivered and lay there, unmoving.

Samantha poked her head around the door. "Hi, Retta—oh, that shirt! I haven't seen it in ages! Did you find it in the closet?"

I nodded, not bothering to ask if wearing the flannel was okay.

"Neat. We're set up to receive most of your school assignments tomorrow with some more coming later. There are some exams to do, too, but I found out we can get those proctored. Once we have the assignments, let's sit down and make a schedule, and then you can show me your progress as we go along. We can mail stuff off—or I think we can scan and email—every week."

"Okay." I didn't care one way or another.

"Great." Samantha looked like she wanted to say more, but she got up to leave. "Dinner's in about half an hour."

"Okay."

Footsteps moved away from the room, but they stopped and started again until there was another knock on the door. "Retta?" It was Samantha again. The door opened.

"There is something else," Samantha said, a grimace on her face. She came in and sat on the bed.

"What?"

"Did you—are you aware that you are expected to testify in Don's trial? As a witness?"

Chapter Nineteen

My heart nearly stopped. "No! Why do they need me?" The idea of sitting in a courtroom full of people and talking about what happened was terrifying.

"Because you are the one who...found her. And because he chased after you. I've been in contact with the prosecutor. They would like to speak to you again." She raised her eyebrows.

I gaped at Samantha, my mind a swirl of emotions, all dark and scary.

"I know this has to be hard, but it's really important to the case."

"What am I supposed to say?"

Samantha nodded, almost as if to herself. "I think you just tell the truth. Say what happened."

"I don't understand why. I already gave a statement to the police and talked to the prosecutor when I was still in Michigan." I chewed on my lip while my stomach roiled.

Samantha looked away. "Yes, I know. I'm truly sorry—I tried to talk them out of it, but they say they need your testimony. They want to talk to you about the trial and how it will work. Then we may also have to go to Iowa for a deposition first."

I lay back on the bed and covered my face with my hands. "This is crazy."

"I know it is. I am going to have to call them back

to set up a time for a phone call."

"Okay, whatever. I want him to go away for life, so I guess I have to cooperate." But what would it be like, seeing him in person?

My mind settled on a new thought. "He is still in jail, right?" What if he was the one watching me?

Samantha shook her head. "I thought you knew. He's been bailed out. But you know he's in a wheelchair, right?"

What? I nodded. I knew about the wheelchair. But he was out?

"Why do you ask?"

Should I say? Or would they just worry too much about me? "Sometimes when I'm out running, it feels like someone's watching."

"Honey, Don's living in a rehab home while he learns to be more mobile. They'd let us know if he disappeared from the home. He can't be here."

Okay. It must all be in my head.

Samantha didn't say anything for a moment. "So I'll let you know when I talk to the prosecutor again. I think it's for the best, even though it will be hard." The bed shifted, and soon the door clicked shut.

I got up, tossed the book that was clearly not getting read today onto the floor, and pulled the Docs out of the closet. The leather was creased and stretched everywhere, and there were scuff marks on the insides of the heels, like with the blue ones. I blew years' worth of dust off them and put them on. They fit nicely, just like the blue ones had.

I went downstairs and sat at the computer. Jack wasn't logged in on Gmail so I stared at the screen, fingers on the keyboard. I typed in Mom's name and cities again. I found some voter records, but it wasn't her because one Jennifer Brooks had come from California and the other from Oregon. Mom came from nowhere. It was like she'd materialized in Omaha at twenty-five. Then there was really no evidence of her there except for the city name.

Wait. Would somebody have an actual address for her? I began clicking through every stupid link, and after about twenty of them, I hit the jackpot. There it was—an address on Dayton Street in Omaha. I mapped it—an apartment complex. I didn't have the unit number, but the street view showed a run-down building facing the street. Maybe that had been ours?

This was where we'd lived when I was two, for at least a while. What had Mom done while we were there? Had she worked? What did she do with me during that time?

I leaned back in the chair. I still didn't feel better, even though I now knew more. Not relieved like I'd hoped. It didn't change anything.

What must Mom have thought when she saw the place for the first time? She was probably still freaking out—I had trouble imagining her doing something as bold as escaping that way. I'd done it, but it was under terrifying circumstances, and there'd been no time to think.

But maybe she'd felt the same way? Don was obviously dangerous. She was probably not paying much attention to the quality of the place when we got there. Worrying he already knew where they were and was coming.

I typed "don lytle" into Google and hit Enter. There were a ton of results. I started at the top. Most were about Mom's murder rather than about Don specifically. The only explanation for the murder itself was that he was angry at Mom for leaving him and taking me. The article said he might have blamed her for everything wrong in his life.

How could he? He was the one who'd ruined *her* life. And killed her!

A cat brushed up against my leg just as the computer pinged. The noise brought me out of the darkness and made me smile.

jaxing94: hey, retta, hows it goin

runningretta: fine, how r u

jaxing94: not bad

jaxing94: i found out im actually going to be close to okla in nov cuz were visiting my grandparents in kansas

runningretta: oh thats cool. my grandparents also live in kansas

jaxing94: really? do you visit them

runningretta: not so far. its dons parents

jaxing94: oh

runningretta: yeah. i have to meet them this saturday

jaxing94: really?

runningretta: i really don't want to. i mean, what kind of people could have raised someone like him?

jaxing94: yeah. but maybe theyll be okay

runningretta: i guess

jaxing94: if they are and you end up ever visiting them, maybe i could drive down to see you? if i am at my grandparents?

My heart squeezed.

runningretta: yeah, maybe, i dont know whats

going to happen, but it sounds cool to me

jaxing94: awesome

runningretta: so get this. i have to testify in dons trial

jaxing94: what!

runningretta: i know. i cant imagine seeing him. ill have to be in the same room as him. how can i do that?

jaxing94: you shouldnt have to do that if you dont want to

runningretta: i do want him to go away for life though. i also found out i have to go back to iowa to a deposition even before the trial

Frankie came into the room and said it was time for dinner.

runningretta: dinners ready and im hungry so ill talk to you later

jaxing94: bye

On the way to the kitchen a couple minutes later, I glanced at a cabinet with a bunch of DVDs. Right in the middle was the entire collection of *Buffy* and *Angel*. How weird. Samantha, too? A family thing, even though the shows hadn't started until after Mom left.

Once I was in the kitchen, Samantha's gaze fell on the shoes, and her expression turned quizzical, but she said nothing.

****

Saturday morning I got up with my alarm at eight. I was planning to do eight miles before I had to meet Don's parents later that morning. I'd agreed to "get it out of the way," as Samantha had put it.

This would be my first time going over five miles, but it was part of my marathon training, and I was excited about it. I got dressed and ate a banana before grabbing a water bottle—I needed more water here than I had on my runs in Iowa—and was out the door before eight-thirty.

The run started off well. This time, I didn't feel like there were eyes on me, so it must have been in my head. Everything was fine.

I'd spent most of the week digging on the internet for Mom. I'd found addresses for Des Moines and Lincoln, too. In Lincoln, we'd lived in one of those horrible motels, the kind you see on crime shows full of drug dealers and prostitutes. I couldn't believe it. At least Des Moines was a nicer apartment complex. "Roaring Springs."

But I was stuck. Now what?

It finally hit me. I'd call the places! Duh. I raced back to the house, a couple miles short, only to find a Chrysler with Kansas plates parked in the driveway. I opened the front door, not sure what to expect inside.

"There she is!" Samantha said as soon as I stepped in.

An older woman rushed in from the living room, followed by a man and Samantha, who wore a strained expression.

"Frances!" the woman exclaimed, barreling toward me with her arms spread for a hug.

I backed up a tad just as Samantha said, "She goes by Retta now."

"Of course, Retta," the thin woman with silver hair said, dropping her arms. "How are you, Retta? You were running?"

"Yeah, I did. I'm sorry, I thought I'd have time to shower before you got here." I was sweating again despite having cooled off on the way back.

"Yes, we were so anxious to get here that we left early. Well, why don't you go have your shower," the woman said, awkwardly patting me on the shoulder.

When I got back downstairs, they were all sitting in the living room. Samantha was telling them about the classes I was taking.

"Ah, Retta," Samantha said with an unnatural smile. "I was telling Bob and Becky about how you don't have a lot of clothes yet, and they offered to take you shopping today if you're up for it."

I stared at them, uncertain. I could use more clothes, sure. But from them? Then again, if I was going to spend time with them, maybe shopping would be easiest. "Okay." I paused. "What am I supposed to call you?"

"Honey, you can call us whatever you want. What do you call your other grandmother?"

"Nana."

Becky said, "You can just call us Grandma and Grandpa if you want. We don't have any other grandchildren."

I nodded. "Okay." I glanced at Grandpa, a thin man, tall and clearly serious. He was mostly bald, but his remaining gray hair was trimmed short.

"We thought we could sit here and chat for a bit, then go out for lunch and shopping after," Grandma said.

The chatting involved Grandma asking a bunch of questions about my life and me answering them with as few words as possible. I just wanted to get the phone numbers off the internet and dial them. But eventually, Grandma said it was time to leave for lunch. "How does barbecue sound?"

"Fine."

"Good, Samantha says there's one across from a Kohl's if you want to go there."

"That sounds fine." This was just to get this out of the way.

****

After they dropped me off, Samantha was cleaning up dinner. I stopped in the doorway to the kitchen. I'd found the numbers on my phone, but both apartments were closed for the weekend now. I still could call the motel once I was upstairs, though, and I couldn't wait.

"Wow," Samantha said, motioning to all the bags in my hands. "They really did take you shopping, huh? Did you eat dinner?"

I nodded and walked over toward the stairs.

Samantha followed behind. "So how was it?" She sounded cautious.

"It was fine." I stood at the bottom of the stairs.

Samantha said, "What did you do?" She dried her hands on a dish towel she held and smiled weakly at me. "Come talk to me while I load the dishwasher."

I looked up the stairs as I dropped my bags next to them and followed her back into the kitchen. "We just went shopping and out to lunch and dinner, basically."

"That's nice," she said as she started putting the plates in the dishwasher. "What did you get?"

I leaned against the doorframe. "Some new clothes, some CDs, some books. A new laptop."

"Oh, wow. That was..." She paused. "Nice of them." She had her back to me.

"Yeah, I guess. They seemed to like it," I said, playing with the sleeve on my flannel shirt, which had a small rip at the seam. I needed to know something. "Is it true they were the ones who chartered the plane?"

Samantha turned around and looked at me, eyebrows raised. "Did they mention that to you?"

"No, I overheard you talking on the phone once," I said.

"Oh, I thought..." She shook her head and looked down. "I'm sorry. They're not my favorite people. You have to forgive me." She brought her head back up, but I didn't say anything. "Anyway, yes, they're the ones who did that."

"They seem kind of like people who can buy their way through anything."

Samantha exhaled. "I suppose they are. Do they make you uncomfortable? Did you feel safe with them?"

"They were okay. Though she—Grandma—sure can talk a lot." I started to back up.

Samantha laughed and said, "You know, I think those might have been the exact words your mom used when she first met her. Minus the 'Grandma' part." She poured soap into the dishwasher and shut the door before starting it, leaning against the counter and frowning. "I really miss my sister."

"But—" I said, stopping. I wasn't sure if I should continue, but I wanted to know. "She was gone this whole time. Doesn't that make it easier?"

"No," Samantha snapped, her face coloring. She took a breath and looked away. "We always held out hope that she would be able to come back. Now she can't."

Before I could think of something to say—this was the first time I'd seen her sort of lose her cool with me—tears were welling in her eyes.

Seeing her cry about Mom brought it all back for me, too. Soon we stood there crying together.

"They tried to apologize to me," I said. "For Mom. For Don."

Samantha's face darkened, and after a moment, she wiped her eyes with the back of her hand and said, "Well, aren't we a pair."

I nodded, still thinking I had more of a right to be upset. Then I remembered what they'd said. "By the way, they told me they want to come to church with us tomorrow before they leave. I told them I didn't think you went to church, but they found that hard to believe."

"Oh, yeah, we don't. I'll give them a call."

"Okay, thanks," I said. "I guess I'll go upstairs." My phone beckoned me.

"Good night."

"Night."

I took the stairs two at a time and dropped my bags just inside the door.

I sat on the bed and dialed the motel.

"Sunshine Motel," a gravelly, bored man's voice answered.

"Um, hi, how long have you worked there?"

"What? Why? Who is this?"

Okay, I should have had a plan here. "Sorry. I just need to know something. About fourteen years ago a woman with a little girl stayed there for a while. I'm just wondering if you remember anything about them."

He snorted. "Fourteen years ago? A woman and a little girl? That's not much to go on, princess."

My heart nearly stopped, and I dropped the phone. Princess? That's what he'd shouted at me that night.

When I picked it back up, he was saying, "...you want to know anyway?"

"How long have you worked there, then?" I asked.

"I told you. Two years. Not long enough to remember your mystery woman and child."

"Is there anyone—?"

There was a ding in the background. "Goodbye," he said.

The call ended, and I let the phone fall and crashed back on the bed. And sobbed.

How was I going to find anything out?

Okay. I sat up to think. I could call back tomorrow and get someone else. I wiped my eyes and got the bags.

I unwrapped the new Principal Pike CD and put it in the player. I went into the closet, intending to organize it a bit so I could put my new clothes away. Soon I was digging through some boxes on the floor of the closet, hoping to find more interesting shoes, when I stumbled across a scrapbook.

It wasn't some super-girly, frou-frou mess of a thing, thank goodness. Instead the plain green cover had *Trace* written on it in block letters with a black sharpie with + *Don* tagged underneath. Inside, there were concert tickets and pictures taped to white pages without any real adornments other than some handwritten explanations for some of the pictures.

But this, this was not like the photo albums I'd seen at Nana's. This was way more personal. No, I knew without a doubt that Mom had made this herself.

I sat with it on the bed and opened it to the first page, Principal Pike singing in the background.

A picture of a band playing in what looked like a

small parking lot covered the top of the page. It wasn't a very good picture, and there appeared to be a dumpster in the background. Then there was another picture of a girl with long blonde hair standing in front of the set with a guy who was wearing a bass and had his arm around her, his eyes scrunched and mouth open like he was yelling. Between the two pictures was written *First Nixons show! Gas station parking lot, no less...*

There were loads of ticket stubs in there: Alice In Chains, Pearl Jam, Nirvana, Nine Inch Nails, Smashing Pumpkins, Concrete Blonde, The Dead Milkmen, Def Leppard, Metallica, White Zombie, Principal Pike, Aerosmith twice, The Nixons several times, The Flaming Lips twice. There were also handwritten set lists for some Nixons shows—apparently Mom had been obsessed with that band, whoever they were.

There were quite a few pictures of Mom, Don, Samantha, who was thin enough I didn't realize it was her for several pictures, and some other people, but they were almost always in parking lots. Frequently they were holding up or wearing T-shirts for the camera and smiling ridiculously. Don seemed to favor that particular hand sign where you make a fist but point your index and pinky fingers up, like horns.

In some of the pictures, Mom had this crazy, shoulder-length, electric-blue hair. It was astonishing, and my mouth stretched wide.

Why were they always outside in these photos? Maybe they didn't want to take those big film cameras with them to a concert. But wouldn't they want to get pictures of the show? It seemed weird.

And who took the pictures? Must have been

friends. Mom sure had plenty of them. She hadn't had a single friend in Iowa, a thought that filled me with black sadness.

I flipped another page and found a ratty piece of lined notebook paper that had been folded into eighths and then unfolded and taped to the page. Mom had written *Principal Pike—There Was a Time* at the top and written out the rest, which I recognized as one of the songs I'd heard on the album currently playing. The lyrics were all in green ink except for some lines written over a second time in black:

You think about it...all the time
You remember it...you're all mine
I'm losing it fast, not slow
There was a time, you knew my soul
There was a time, I had control
Try and fake it, I can't do it
I'm losing it fast, not slow
I got one behind my back just for you
Can you feel it?
There was a time, you knew my soul
There was a time, I had control
You think your eyes are open and mine are closed
But I see everything you do
There was a time, you knew my soul
There was a time, I had control
There was a time, I had control
There was a time, I had a soul

I shuddered. I turned the page, but it was empty, as was the next and the next. That was it. There was nothing more.

Chapter Twenty

Monday morning, I woke up early without the alarm, immediately thinking of calling the places. But it was only six, so I got ready for a run and went out. I finished up and grabbed some peanut butter toast and milk to take upstairs. I scarfed that down.

The first apartment opened at seven.

"Roaring Springs, how can I help you?"

This time I was ready. "Hi, I'm calling with an odd question. Did you happen to work there fourteen years ago or so?"

"Me?" She laughed. "I was in middle school fourteen years ago."

"Oh." My heart dropped.

"Besides, this isn't the same place at all. The old one was condemned and knocked down like ten years ago."

Oh, no. "So would you know anyone who worked at the old one? Who was around back then?"

"No chance. Different management companies. The old one folded, too."

I grimaced, and my stomach pinched. Nothing.

"Why're you asking, anyway?" She sounded genuinely curious.

"I'm just trying to find out what happened with me and my mom back then."

"Okay..."

"Anyway. Thanks." I hung up abruptly, because I couldn't handle it anymore.

I got in the shower, where I couldn't tell if I was crying or not, for all the water running down my face. But the time I got out, my hands and feet were wrinkled. I tried to read but couldn't concentrate. Finally, my phone said it was eight, when the other office opened.

That call was equally fruitless. It was the same complex with the same name for over two decades, but had new management, too. I asked for the old company's name, but they'd gone out of business.

I stretched out on the bed, hands behind my head, and tried to wait until ten. I'd decided that would be the best time to call the motel. I lasted until nine forty-five.

"Sunshine Motel." This time it was a woman's cigarette voice.

I explained myself and my request.

"Fourteen years ago, you say?"

"Yes." Suddenly I was hopeful.

"My brother ran this place back then," she said.

"Really?" burst out of me. This was it, a breakthrough!

"He passed on a couple years ago."

"Oh." Shattered.

She coughed. "But his wife used to help out a lot. She might know something."

There was hope again.

"But she's in Africa right now." She paused. "Living it up with her new rich husband."

"When will she be back?" Surely she'd know something.

"I'm not sure. Give me your number, and I'll have

her call you."

I gave it to her, and she said, "Okay, she'll call you. Probably will be at least a week."

A whole week. I'd die.

But I knew she'd remember something. She had to.

****

Dr. Iravani was a middle-aged woman with curly black hair and a roundish face. She had a hint of an accent as she greeted me and introduced herself, but I couldn't guess from where.

Not that it mattered.

I sensed myself being inspected as we sat down. I wore the Docs, black fishnets, short jean cutoffs, and a maroon, velvet, sleeveless shirt under a black jacket with decorative metal studs. I had no idea what impression all that might give to a therapist and didn't really care.

The fishnets were actually sort of uncomfortable because they dug into my skin, but I liked the way they looked, so I'd worn them anyway. I especially liked the couple of rips, one on the left knee and one on the right thigh just below the shorts hem.

"So, Retta, why don't you tell me a little about yourself."

I blinked. "Well, I don't know what there is to say. I'm fifteen, and I used to live in Iowa, but now I live here."

Dr. Iravani smiled a tiny bit. "I'm sure there's more to you than that. What do you like to do?"

"I guess I like to read." Saying that brought up the memory of sitting with Mom when I was little, reading together, which overwhelmed me so much that I had to close my eyes, which then brought up the image of

Mom's body lying on the kitchen floor and made me dizzy. I opened my eyes to see Dr. Iravani and the dark plaid loveseat she was sitting on, and the brown desk next to it with the classic green banker's desk lamp.

"What else?"

I shrugged. "I like languages."

"Really?" Dr. Iravani cocked her head. "That's interesting. Do you speak any, besides English, of course?"

"Spanish," I said in a monotone. "I am okay in French and German. I'm going to study languages in college. And Chinese."

"That's interesting. Why Chinese?"

"Lots of people speak it," I said, shrugging again.

"Very true. Anything else?" Dr. Iravani asked.

"I'm a runner." I played with the fishnet tear on my left knee.

"Oh, that's nice. Exercise is good for you in so many ways." She paused, possibly waiting for me to volunteer something else. "Now why don't you tell me why you are here today."

That surprised me. And annoyed me. Didn't this lady watch the news? Didn't they tell her when they made the appointment?

"Well, my aunt made me come." I shifted on the couch.

"Okay. And you don't want to talk about why?"

"Not really, no."

Dr. Iravani nodded. "That's fine. But I will always be straight with you. So I do know what you've been through. It's a lot for you to be dealing with, isn't it?"

I shrugged.

"Who are you living with now?"

"My aunt."

The therapist nodded, holding her pen to her lip. "It's good that you're with family." She picked up a clipboard and said, "I have a series of questions to ask you. Is that okay with you?"

"What happens if I say no?"

"I hope you don't. I want to help you, and this will enable me to do that."

I looked at the wall. A very pale blue. What choice was there?

She proceeded to ask all sorts of crap, going way back. But the more recent stuff was of more interest, clearly. No, I didn't sleep particularly well. No, there was not a known history of mental illness in my family—even though my biological father had to be not right in the head. No, I didn't do drugs.

After all the questions, Dr. Iravani explained the therapy. It would take place over the next few months, twice a week at first, but would not last forever. Each week we'd work on a new set of skills to help me move forward.

I didn't see what this lady could do to change anything, but I said, "Okay," whenever it was time.

Nana looked up at me as I came out of the office door, and she smiled in her comfortable way with soft eyes. "Ready?"

I nodded. I paid no attention while we picked up the textbooks I needed for my classes, but I did notice the stack of them was way bigger than I remembered.

When I got home, I went for another run, and it felt particularly good to shake all that therapy talk out of my system. A blonde woman with a ponytail said hi to me on the trail, and I felt okay about it. Even the sight of the blue car parked on the street didn't make me nervous this time. It was just a car. It had all been in my head.

****

That evening, I sat on my bed with my phone in my hand. I'd been about to send Jack a text about the therapist. But a line I'd read in the scrapbook—and heard yesterday—flashed across my mind: "But I see everything you do" and I felt sick to my stomach. Was that what Jack had done? Looked at me, even when I didn't know?

But no, this was Jack—he couldn't be like that, could he?

Could he? Now it seemed entirely possible. Mom had married somebody like that and must have not known.

I was jolted out of my thoughts by a knock on the door.

Samantha poked her head in and said, "How did your session with your counselor go today?"

"It was fine," I said, distracted by thoughts of Jack.

"Did you feel comfortable with her?" She was still standing in the doorway.

"Sure." Jack couldn't be a bad guy.

"Okay, good." She paused. "There was something else I needed to talk to you about. Can I come in?"

When I nodded, my stomach jumpy again, Samantha sat down at the end of the bed and said, "You will tell me if you aren't comfortable with her, right? We can find someone else if we need to."

"Okay." What now?

"Okay, so the other thing. This might be tough." She stopped and took a breath. "We need to get your old house back to the landlord, which means we need to decide what to do with everything in the house."

I was taken aback. The old house. This was another part of my life I hadn't thought about since it happened, except in the dreams. I blinked.

Samantha continued. "They want it empty by the middle of November."

"Oh."

"Do you want to come with me to go through stuff and bring back some of it?"

My heart nearly stopped. "What? Are you going to throw it all out?" I managed.

"No. But I don't know what to do. I thought I would donate most of it, but I want to bring some of Tracy's things back here, and of course anything you want."

"Oh." My stomach calmed slightly.

"Do you want to come with me?" Samantha reached out like she might touch my arm but then dropped her hand. She'd painted her nails purple this time, which was so at odds with her dumpy mom look.

"When?"

"In three weeks. I'm going to take a few days off work."

"Oh," I said, still reeling a bit at the idea of my old house. Everything...still there.

"I thought it might work out—you could visit your friends. The boy who helped you—Jack."

But actually going into that house again... "Will it look like...?"

"Oh, I think I know what you're worried about," Samantha said, looking relieved. She put her hand in front of me on the bedspread. "It has been cleaned up already. Who could bear it?" She shook her head and turned away, before looking at me again. "I still can't believe what happened there. If you don't want to go, I'll understand. I can pack up your room. I just find myself wanting to be the one to pack up my sister's house, so I am going to go regardless."

I nodded. I should, too. "I'll go." I'd regret it if I didn't. Plus, I'd get to see Jack again. Then I remembered what I'd been thinking about before, and my stomach lurched.

No, it was okay. It was fine.

Samantha looked at the stereo like she'd just noticed it was on. "Is this Bush? I haven't heard this in ages!"

"I've been listening to the CDs in here. This is all my mom's stuff, right?"

"Mostly. She wasn't a huge fan of Bush—that was more me, but she liked some of their singles."

I nodded.

"So we're ordering pizza tonight. What kind do you like?"

"I don't really care. Whatever's fine." I walked over to the CD player.

"I am going to get a couple of mediums, one pepperoni and one ham and pineapple, if that works."

"It's fine," I said as I changed the CD mid-song.

"Okay," Samantha said, a hurt expression on her face as she shut the door.

****

After dinner Thursday night, Samantha had the kids helping clear the table, and she looked at me and asked me if I'd put plastic wrap on the casserole dish and put it in the fridge. Afterward, I went into the

206

bathroom for a minute, and when I came out, the three of them were in the den getting ready to play the Wii.

"Come join us, Retta," Samantha said while the console fired up.

I stared at the scene. Both Tracy and Frankie were looking at me expectantly.

I couldn't. I'd be an interloper. I shook my head and took the stairs to my room, working on homework for a bit. When I came down for a glass of water, they were all laughing, and I glanced in there as Tracy wrapped her arms around Samantha's waist, who hugged her back.

"I'm going to get you back, Tracy. You can't punch your mom in the face and get away with it, even if it is a game."

Frankie fell on the sofa in hysterics. "You're so bad at this, Mom!"

Samantha ruffled his hair as Tracy joined him on the couch. "I'm not bad. You two are just good. I could whoop both your behinds at Super Mario Bros. any day."

Frankie laughed again and then noticed me watching.

I turned just as Samantha and Tracy saw me.

"Do you want to play?" Tracy asked.

As I poured the water, I called, "No, thanks."

But it wasn't fair. Why couldn't I have had that growing up? I knew Mom had always loved me, but we'd never had fun. Not that I could remember, at least.

Chapter Twenty-One

As I got out of the shower after an afternoon run, I heard the kids coming in downstairs. Frankie would be upstairs to talk to me any minute. This morning, I'd told him I'd finished one of his books last night. The one about cats that lived in the forest and were clan warriors. I left the door open and lay down to read some of *The Scarlet Letter* for school, a book I was not enjoying at all.

I found it was often that way with classics. Mom had said the same thing—sometimes however great a book was supposed to be, it could be boring, or sexist, or racist, and she couldn't even finish it.

Mom. Lying on the kitchen floor, in the dark, with the knife.

I started crying and closed my eyes, trying to remember the tricks Dr. Iravani had been teaching me to deal with this. She called it thought interruption or something like that. Basically, you told yourself to stop thinking about it and then thought about something else. It wasn't working.

"Retta!" Frankie stood in the doorway.

I opened my eyes.

"Oh," he said. "Are you sad again?"

"I'm okay." Actual interruption was way better.

"So did you like it?" He walked in with Tracy right behind him. They sat on the floor.

"Yeah, it was pretty good." I sniffed and wiped my nose. I actually had enjoyed it more than I'd expected.

"What did you think about Tigerclaw?" Frankie asked.

"Well, he's a really bad guy," I said. "Killing those other cats just because he wanted power."

"Yeah! And what he did to Ravenpaw!" He picked up Wes and put him in his lap.

"I know, poor Ravenpaw. So innocent and getting badmouthed like that. And people—er, cats—just believing it because somebody told them."

"It made me so mad!"

Tracy reached over to pet the cat and whispered, "Hi, Wes," before turning back to watch me.

"Me, too," I said. "People can be so gullible!"

"You mean cats," Frankie said.

"Oh, yeah," I said, laughing. "Cats."

"Do you want to read the next book?" he asked with wide eyes.

"How many are there?"

"Six."

"Wow, that's a lot," I said with a sigh. "You can give it to me, and I will read it when I can."

He was clearly excited by this and jumped up, the cat falling out of his lap, and left the room with Tracy trailing behind him.

Wes stood in the middle of the room, yawned, stretched, and watched me. I looked back. He apparently read something into this exchange, because he bounded over and onto the bed, curling up in the corner and going to sleep, as if he belonged. As if I did.

I left him alone and tried to make my way through more of *The Scarlet Letter* before dinner.

****

"So have you figured out who to get the Jeans video from yet?" I said into the phone, lying on my bed with my eyes closed. I had a smile on my face just because I was talking to Jack. I'd decided I was being ridiculous about him. He was a decent guy. Surely.

"Well, actually," he said, "about that..."

"What?"

"I always meant to tell you, but you were freaked out at first, so I didn't...I'm the one who put the video together. Jason asked me to."

"What?" My eyes popped open. "Did Rachel give you the footage?"

"What? No, Jason and Sarah."

I'd always wondered who it had been. I knew them only through cross country. They were always nice to me.

But Jack was the one who'd edited the video, and he hadn't told me? Why had he kept it secret? That was just...that was just not okay. A new hole opened in my chest.

"Jack, I have to go."

"Retta, are you mad? I don't know why I didn't tell you earlier; it was stupid, just—"

"I'll talk to you later." I hit the end call button.

The line "But I see everything you do" flitted across my mind again. I wasn't an expert on video-making, but I knew enough to know that he'd have had to study me—to stare intently at me moving frame by frame, probably in slow motion, watching those clips over and over—while he'd pieced that video together.

And it wasn't just that. Jack had admitted to watching me long before he'd ever even met me. In fact, he'd said he'd been watching me since he'd first seen me, when I was four or whenever. That was creepy. He wasn't sneaking into my bedroom to watch me sleep at night, but it definitely registered on the creep scale.

And wasn't he always a bit enthusiastic about things, always sort of expecting me to go along with them? Like trying to arrange to visit me in Kansas? Almost like he couldn't control himself? "There was a time I had control."

I already had a text from him.

—*im sorry. please dont be mad. it was stupid, so stupid, i know*—

But I was mad at him.

Wes was curled up at the foot of the bed, and I leaned over and touched him on the back. He lifted his head sleepily, and I jerked my hand back. Then I reached forward again and tried petting him. He stretched and rolled over onto his side. I kept petting him, liking the feel of the silky fur under my fingers. My tense shoulders relaxed as he started purring.

****

The next two weeks were cruddy and awkward ones. First, I hadn't heard from the motel lady. I'd called the motel back a few times before I'd gotten the lady I originally talked to. She told me she wasn't back. So I was high-strung about that.

I dutifully went to my therapy sessions, doing the bare minimum to keep Dr. Iravani from getting too annoyed with me. The rest of the time—when I wasn't running—I tried to study, having to struggle to make myself do everything, even French and German. Plus, here I was again, studying languages without the benefit of being able to practice speaking them just like before. I'd told Dr. Iravani I could speak Spanish, when speaking it was kind of hard. Slow.

I also worked with Jack on our project.

That was where most of the awkwardness lay. I couldn't shake the bad feeling. I didn't trust him anymore, and he seemed confused that I wouldn't forgive him. He tried to explain himself. He hadn't told me he'd made the video at first because he panicked at my reaction; then he meant to tell me but hadn't, and it had kept on that way.

I never called him. We'd only talked once on the phone, when I'd accidentally answered. We usually just IMed or emailed to discuss the project. But after two weeks of this, it must have been obvious to him that something was different.

If I was being honest, I was curious how Jack would behave once we were in Iowa. I had never managed to unmake our plans to meet. Because maybe he wasn't a bad guy...maybe he would show that. If only the creep radar would stop sending out alerts.

*****

I finished another IM session with Jack. We'd sent each other drafts of our blog posts and discussed them. Jack had talked about my upcoming visit in just three days. He seemed to be under the impression that I was over my anger by now. Samantha had wanted to meet him—for more than a minute—so the plan for Saturday night was for Jack to go out to dinner with Samantha and me, and then he and I would go to a movie with Rachel and some of the others.

But now it was time to try the motel again. It had been three days since I'd last called, and I'd gotten some grumpy guy who had no idea what I was talking about.

"Sunshine Motel." Good. It was the smoker lady again.

"Hello. Is she back yet?"

"Huh? Oh! You know, she is. Got back a couple days ago, I think."

I could hear my pulse in my ears.

"Give me ten minutes and call me back, okay?"

As antsy as I was, I still appreciated that she was being so nice. I'd actually ended up chatting with her earlier, telling her about our background.

My phone rang three and a half minutes later. A Nebraska number, not the motel.

"Hello?" I almost didn't recognize my own voice, it was so desperate.

"I heard you've been trying to get in touch with me. It's a big mystery." The woman sounded suspicious, but she had a southern accent, which made her less intimidating.

Still, I was out of words. This was it. If she didn't know, I wouldn't have any more hope.

"What is it you're looking for?"

I cleared my throat. "My name is Retta Brooks." I explained about how we'd lived there back then for at least a little while.

"Oh, honey," she said dismissively. "I couldn't possibly remember. That was so long ago. Do you know how many people went through that dump?"

"She would probably have been wearing blue boots."

"Doesn't ring any bells."

"Please—you're my last chance." It was like the

desperation was oozing out of the phone and running down my arm.

"I'm sorry. I don't have anything for you."

"Oh." I'd never felt so hopeless in my life. "Could you—um—call me if you do think of something?"

"I can. But I won't remember anything."

Two matching tears raced each other down my cheeks. I lay back for a while until I couldn't stand it.

I grabbed Mom's scrapbook off the nightstand and flipped through it one more time. After landing on the last page, I looked at the lyrics again; they sent another chill down my spine. At least I wouldn't be alone with Jack.

There was one other thing I would do. Something I'd been putting off—or saving, really—since finding the scrapbook: turning the closet upside down to see if there was anything else that could tell me something about Mom. I had been silently imploring the universe to make it so, which was why I'd been waiting. Because what if there wasn't?

It was true I hadn't asked Samantha anything about Mom. Samantha seemed to understand that I couldn't talk about any of it. Or at all. Dr. Iravani said it was pretty normal at this stage for me to take any thought of Mom and turn it into the horrific image I had seen in the kitchen that night. Supposedly, we were still working on it.

It's what I pictured right now. I flipped the scrapbook open to an early page and saw Mom smiling and holding up a Smashing Pumpkins T-shirt. I stared at the picture for a while.

I headed into the closet and began meticulously picking through everything, organizing a bit as I went.

My previous searches had left the closet in disarray.

An hour of searching yielded only a single shoebox with several packets of photos. I flipped through them. There was nothing new.

I lay back on the bed and cried some more. I hadn't gone through all of them yet, but I knew that was it. Nothing more. How could I ever know who Mom truly was?

Maybe it was time to talk to Samantha.

Chapter Twenty-Two

I stood at the front door of my house in Iowa. Samantha was next to me, the house key in her shaking hand.

"Are you ready?" she asked me.

No. "Yeah."

Samantha unlocked the door. Right away, I noticed the locks had been changed, even before she pushed the door open. I couldn't help but feel the horror of the last time I had done that here.

A faint scent of bleach wafted out. Without even stepping inside, I could see the house looked all wrong. Everything was there, but nothing was as it should be. Two of the dining room chairs were at the ends of the table instead of squeezed into the sides, the table next to the front door was in the wrong spot, and a stack of papers was bizarrely perched on the couch. The throw that normally sat on the back of the couch—or bunched up in the corner of it—was instead folded up on the armchair, which had been shifted at least a foot from where it should be.

My hand flew to my mouth, and tears streamed down my cheeks. Samantha put her arm around me and pulled me in tight, and I didn't resist. It didn't register until later, but she also was crying.

She took a step in, pulling me with her. I glanced toward the kitchen.

She wiped her eyes and said, "Wait here for a minute. I'm going to walk around and check things out."

I nodded, not moving.

Samantha went into the kitchen and returned, saying, "It's clean, but the linoleum has been removed. You don't have to go in there." She walked into the living room.

I felt like I did have to go into the kitchen, so I did, tears still flowing. There were splotches on the concrete floor that were lighter in color than the rest of the floor, like they had been bleached, rather than darker like I'd expected. But there it was, covering the area where Mom had lain all alone for hours—almost a day. My stomach roiled, and I hurried back out to stand near the front door for some air. Samantha hadn't recognized it for what it was. The upstairs floorboards squeaked, and my heart lurched again, but of course it was just Samantha.

Samantha came back downstairs and said, "Okay, we can go up there. It's okay." Then she put her arm on my shoulder and said, "How are you doing? Do you think you can do this, or do you want to go back to the inn?"

I sniffed. I couldn't explain how I felt, but I needed to do this. For Mom. For all the hell I'd put Mom through during those last few months. "I can do it." I hadn't been upstairs since before it happened. Don had been up there more recently.

"Okay, sweetie," Samantha said, squeezing my shoulder. "Just let me know if you need to leave."

****

We packed until Samantha asked, "Do you know

any good places around here for lunch?"

I had to think. "There're a couple diners in town."

We drove downtown and took a table at the first one we came to. A few people looked at me like they knew who I was, but nobody said anything, and there were no high school kids there. Our server brought me pot roast and Samantha a chef salad.

"This place is cute and has perfect diner food. Did you come here often?"

"I've never been here. Mom hated me to be out in public except when absolutely necessary. It was only in the last couple years or so that she even let me go clothes shopping with her."

"That must have been so hard on you." She shook her head. "Also, it sounds nothing like my sister as I knew her."

"When I was little, we joked we were hermits, and when I was about eight, I ran across the term 'hermetic seal' and told Mom those were seals like us. She cracked up."

Samantha shook with laughter and said, "That's one of the best things about having kids, honestly—they say some of the funniest things you've ever heard." She took a bite of her salad.

"But you know what," I said, "that's an odd memory that sticks out more than for how funny it was. You know how she was always so tense—or I guess you don't know. She was always so paranoid, so worried about doing things that might be seen by a lot of people. And just nervous. And tense. But that time, when she was laughing, I think that must have been the first time I remember seeing her totally relax her guard. It's weird." I couldn't resist smiling before trying my pot roast.

"I can't imagine having to live like that," Samantha said, shaking her head again. "And on top of being scared for herself and for you, she tried to protect you from her own paranoia, I suppose."

I nodded and finished chewing. "As much as she could, I guess. It would have been better if she hadn't had to run away in the first place."

"I know," Samantha said grimly.

I asked, "What was Don like before they were going out?" Samantha had given me a bit of their history when I'd asked a few days ago, but there were some holes.

"Well, I was still in high school, so I didn't hang out with them too much then, but I went to a few concerts with them. He was quiet, a thoughtful sort. Smart. He was on scholarship in the engineering school and worked to keep his grades up, I know. It was one of the things your mom liked about him." She stopped to eat some of her salad.

"And you were a freshman in Mom's junior year, and that was when he disappeared, right?" I asked.

"Yes. He left after their sophomore year to go home for the summer, and she didn't see him until she started her senior year. He'd been one of her best friends, and then nothing for over a year." She exhaled. "We should have known it was a bigger deal than he said."

What had happened, I'd learned before, was that the first week he'd been home, he and his younger sister had been in a car accident, and she'd been killed.

"I think when she saw him again that year, it was the happiest day of her life," Samantha mused, resting her chin in her hand. "He was obviously broken, and Tracy swooped in to help fix him."

I had to close my eyes and concentrate to will away the image of Mom on the kitchen floor that had come into my mind. Really, it had been there since they'd been in the house, but the more they talked about Mom and Don, the more real it felt.

"Then what was he like?" I asked.

"It was odd, even at the time. He was more…animated. Boisterous, even. And he started drinking a lot more. Nobody thought much about it at the time, but it ended up being part of the problem. But he seemed pretty sweet with Tracy." She was looking over my shoulder. "At first," she finally added.

"What do you mean?"

"He was overly involved in her life. Wanting to talk to her all the time, wanting to know where she was. We didn't recognize it for what it was." She paused. "Or, I sort of did, but I figured it was up to her. I never said anything like I should have. Until after you were born." She put her head in her hands and took a deep breath. She obviously felt guilty about it.

I bit my lip. "Do you know why Mom hated the police so much?"

"Oh. Yes, I do," Samantha said, recovering. "They were at their apartment numerous times but never did anything. In those days, the police often had a hands-off attitude about domestic violence. It was up to individual officers to decide what to do." She added, "Things are a little better now."

I didn't know how to feel, so I said nothing.

Samantha said. "I know she worried that somehow you'd end up with him, if something happened to her. It terrified her. I think he might have threatened you. I'm not sure, but Tracy said something once."

I stared at the table.

"It won't happen, Retta."

I nodded, relieved.

Samantha said, "You ready?" She paid, and we left and went back to the house, spending the next few hours packing.

After finishing bringing down the boxes we'd packed in my room, we sat on the couch.

"Are you excited to see Jack again?" Samantha asked. "I'm surprised you didn't want to see him sooner."

"Yeah, uh, this was good enough. I guess I wanted to make sure to get some of the packing done first."

"What, aren't you excited to see him?" she asked.

"I guess." I was both dreading it and looking forward to it, which made no sense. At least Samantha would be there in case it got weird. I wanted to believe he was an okay guy. He'd been so good to me. There was just the one big lie...

Samantha looked at me with a confused frown before getting up and going into the kitchen. "I'm going to work in here until it's time to leave," she called.

****

We pulled up in the long drive of the Singh farm.

Samantha laughed. "That's not what I expected to see after this driveway," she said, pointing at the Prius.

"I know. It's his mom's car. They won't be what you expect either. Don't be surprised."

"Okay, I won't. Are we going to go in?"

"I don't think so."

"Why don't you go up to the door and wave me

over if they need to meet me."

I shuffled to the door. Jack opened it before I could ring the bell. He grinned at me, then he seemed to notice what I wore—a ratty Nirvana concert T-shirt, jeans, and the black Docs. He looked perplexed for a second, but the expression passed, and his goofy smile returned, which made me do the same thing. Seeing him wasn't as bad as I thought it might be—it actually felt kind of nice. Sort of familiar, even safe, as if that made sense. He was still cute. Then I wasn't sure again.

"Hello, Retta, how are you doing, sweetie?" Janie asked.

"I'm good, thank you," I said.

Janie stepped off the porch and gave me a sudden hug that lasted a long time while I hugged her back.

"I'm so sorry about your mom," she said, squeezing me again before letting go.

When she stepped away, Jack was standing right behind her, and he hugged me, too. He smelled like Iowa—kind of earthy, but it was comforting.

Janie waved at Samantha, who rolled the window down, waved, and shouted in a friendly voice, "Hello!"

Jack stood there looking at me, obviously happy.

"Well, off you two go." Janie gave him a light push on the back to get him moving, and all three of us walked to the car.

When we got there, Jack got in the back seat, and Samantha said, "I'm so sorry; I should have come up to the door instead of making you walk out here. I'm Samantha." She stuck her hand out.

Janie smiled, shook her hand, and introduced herself. "Don't worry about it. So you are going out to dinner, then a movie?"

Samantha nodded. "I'm taking them to dinner, and then I'll drop them at the theater where they're meeting their friends."

"We'll get a ride home from Rachel," Jack said.

"Sounds good to me. It was nice meeting you, Samantha, and good seeing you again, Retta." Janie waved us off from the porch.

We went to a small Italian place in town. I sat down first in the booth, but when Jack slid in next to me, he sat close. I scooted up next to the wall, still not sure what to do. He gave me a funny look with narrowed eyes, but I didn't know what he was thinking.

Nobody said anything, so Samantha started in with questions. "So, Jack, you are a senior. What are your plans for next year?"

"I'm going to go to Iowa State to major in Agricultural Engineering and International Agriculture." He sounded like he was already looking forward to going.

"Wow, you seem like someone who knows what he wants! Good for you." Samantha was obviously impressed.

"Yeah, I love farming. But I think there are lots of things that can be done better."

"Nice. What about the international part?"

"Yeah, that's a second major. I want to go to India, or maybe somewhere else in the Peace Corps."

"I'm impressed."

I felt unmoored. I hadn't known he wanted to go away. Why hadn't I known that about him? Also, if he was dangerously obsessed with me, would he plan to go away? At this precise moment I didn't like the idea of him wanting to leave.

"What about you, Retta?" Samantha said. "I've never asked you about your long-term plans. I just know you're serious about your studies."

"I guess I still want to be a translator or interpreter," I said. "I can sort of speak French and German, and I know Spanish pretty well. I want to study Chinese and Japanese in college."

"Nice, there should be good job prospects there. That's really neat. I always liked languages even though I was no good at them." She laughed.

Jack touched my arm. It was nice, and I didn't flinch. He said, "You should learn Punjabi so you can impress my dad—by speaking it better than I do. He'll forget how much you're corrupting me."

We all laughed.

He surprised me by taking my hand, on the seat, sending what felt like an electric jolt down my legs into the floor. I jumped but left my hand in his.

I wondered if I should move it—Was he a creep, or not? Was he, was he, was he?—but I didn't really want to move it, so I didn't.

After dinner, Samantha dropped us off in front of the little downtown theater, where I saw Rachel and the others already waiting.

As soon as we got out, I heard my name being called, and several friends ran over to greet us. Rachel and Lily each gave me a hug, and everyone asked how I was doing. A couple of them gave my shirt odd looks, but nobody said anything about it.

I glanced over and saw a blue sedan that looked familiar cruise past us slowly. My heart sped up. Was it the same one? What could it be doing here? I tried to see the license plate, but it was too dark to see where it was from, though I could tell it wasn't an Iowa plate.

Jack touched my arm, and I jerked. "You okay, Retta?"

"Oh. Yeah." I looked at his concerned face and then at everyone else watching me. When I glanced back toward the street, the car was gone.

I was just being paranoid. It was nothing. There had to be plenty of blue sedans around. And Don couldn't be driving a regular car. He was in a wheelchair, and they would let Samantha know if he left the rehab center.

I had been worried that being in the dark theater might freak me out, but I felt okay with the others there. Plus, my fear of the dark was getting better, anyway.

During the superhero flick, Jack took my hand again, and I didn't resist. But as he held it, he ran his thumb along the back of my hand. I got annoyed at how comfortable he seemed. Had he forgotten how mad I was about the video?

Had *I* forgotten how angry I was at him?

I slipped my hand out without moving my eyes from the screen, sensing his head turn toward me.

"You okay?" he leaned over and whispered.

"Yeah, I'm good." I was hanging out with friends and happy to be there. It was a little like I'd never left. Except for one big difference.

Chapter Twenty-Three

While I bagged clothes, I couldn't stop thinking about Jack. I was so confused, now that we were apart again. It did help me keep my mind off Mom, which was good since I held Mom's clothes in my hands.

Samantha hadn't yet found a charity that could pick up this week, but she was waiting on a call back from one that might do it.

We bagged for a while until Samantha said, "Do you think you would mind if I brought some of her stuff home to use?"

"Like what?"

"Well, I like her comforter, for one." She stopped. "It looks just like one she would have chosen."

I shrugged. "I don't think I care." I hadn't thought there was anything special about it, and I looked at it again. It was colorful and kind of cool, with wobbly stripes running the length of the bed.

We were quiet a moment longer, and then I said, "I guess she had good taste in comforters. She picked mine out, too."

Samantha smiled and said, "Hear, hear, for good taste in comforters." We both laughed.

Samantha wiped a tear from each eye. "My poor sister. You have no idea how...amazing she was when she was young. I can't believe what she did here. She always had such dreams, and I know working in a cafeteria wasn't one of them."

"I still have trouble imagining her being this person you knew," I said. "It's weird. She was always my mom the lunch lady. I mean, looking through her closet and photo book have helped, and obviously so has you telling me more about her. But she was a totally, completely different person here."

"It just makes me sad you never got to know the person she was. You would have liked her. I already know she adored you." Samantha looked off behind me.

It made me sad, too. Like barbed wire squeezing my heart.

I blinked. "One thing that didn't change was her interest in music. She taught me to be picky. But I never heard her play any grunge."

She didn't look at me. "That sounds like her. I'm excited to see her music collection, to see what she got into. If that's not weird."

"Oh, well, it's all in iTunes now. I know her passwords, so I can get into it. It's on her laptop."

"Of course," Samantha said. "I still buy CDs, like an old lady."

"She did, too, until a couple years ago when I convinced her to sell the CDs when they were still worth something. They gradually went to the shop where she buys her books as she ripped them."

"So did she still read a lot? I know you picked up the reading bug."

"Yeah, she read a lot of sci-fi and fantasy. And medical thrillers."

"Medical thrillers? She never used to read those. Huh." Samantha looked thoughtful. "I guess because of med school. What about you? What do you read?"

"I always read more...just regular stuff."

"No paranormal romance for you?" Samantha grinned.

"Well, sometimes. Not very often." This made me think of Jack, and confusion circled me again. Samantha must have seen the look on my face, but she didn't say anything else.

We continued working in the closet.

"Oh, my God!" Samantha exclaimed.

"What?"

"The boots!"

"Oh, yeah." I blushed. I should have told Samantha about them. "I knew they were here."

"Ah," she said. "Why didn't you say something?"

"I don't know." I truly didn't.

"We're taking these for sure."

"Okay." I was already looking forward to wearing them.

We finished the rest of the bagging. Samantha said, "Let's each grab one and head downstairs and take a break."

After dropping the bags, we sat on the couch for about ten minutes before I got antsy and stood up and said, "I'm going to start packing up her books."

After a couple more hours, I finished boxing the last of the books, having filled ten more boxes. I sat down on the couch, looking around. I couldn't believe it—we were almost done. There were bags and boxes all over, some to keep and some to donate. Samantha was finishing up in the kitchen. I should help, but the idea of going back in the kitchen was just...no. I couldn't.

I went upstairs, making noise on the stairs so

Samantha wouldn't wonder where I was. In my bedroom, I dug some of my old running clothes out of the box we'd packed them in and changed. I called to Samantha on my way out to let her know I was going.

For the first time ever, I'd be running these streets without having to sneak around.

I did a quick jog around the neighborhood to warm up and then headed out onto the main road.

Running here was different from running in Oklahoma. It was cooler despite the bright early afternoon sun. I could see nothing but fields, farms, and curving gray lines snaking off into the distance.

Sweat dripped into my eyes, and I wiped it away. When I dropped my hand back down, a car was up ahead and coming toward me. It seemed to be moving slower than most others out here. The driver was looking down at something in the car, so I edged over farther on the gravel shoulder and wished it was wider.

As it got closer, I could see the car was blue. My stomach lurched.

No, it couldn't be.

I squinted to see the driver and felt my feet pound the ground in half time with my heart. The sun glinted off the metal on the car, but the driver was a woman with big hair. I spotted a Nebraska front license plate as the car approached, faster now. As it blew past, I glanced nervously at the driver, who kept her head facing straight ahead.

I stopped and leaned on my knees while trying to slow my heart back to a normal running pace. It was nothing. Just a coincidence. It wasn't Don. Still, it had killed my desire to run.

It had to be nothing. There still were lots of blue

sedans out there.

****

Samantha smiled at me from the kitchen doorway when I came in the front door.

"Good timing. I just finished in here. How was your run?"

I still hadn't calmed down after the car incident. "Fine."

She narrowed her eyes. "Are you okay? You look spooked."

"I..." I wasn't sure if I should say something, but she was still looking at me, obviously concerned. "I thought I saw a blue car I've been seeing in your neighborhood a lot."

"The one parked on the street?"

I nodded.

"Rumor has it that one of the renters has a cousin staying. I wouldn't worry about it. I'm sure it's a coincidence."

I frowned. But she was probably right.

"Okay?"

"Yeah."

"Great. I found someone to come and pick up everything tomorrow, but I looked at what we want to take back, and it won't fit in the car. So I found a U-Haul rental that has a trailer we can take, but we have to go pick it up now."

My first instinct was to stay behind, but I did not want to stay in the house alone. "Okay," I said, getting up and then following Samantha down the stairs.

"I want to leave the day after tomorrow," Samantha continued. "Do you want to call Jack and see if he can come out to dinner with us tonight?"

Did I? Maybe I'd try again. "Okay." I pulled out my phone and saw I'd missed a call from him. I texted to see if he wanted to go.

He replied right away. —*Yes.*—

We headed into town. "There's also a realtor coming by tomorrow. The landlord asked me to show her around."

I nodded.

Samantha continued, "As soon as they have picked up all the donations, we'll pack the trailer. We can park it in the garage overnight so nobody will break into it. I figure we might as well fill the trailer up as much as possible so we don't have too much in the car."

I heard but didn't respond. The scenery of my town flew by—fields and mailboxes—yet I felt like I was such an outsider that it was almost as if I'd never existed here.

"Does that sound good to you?"

"Sure, fine," I said, without looking away from the window.

We turned into a gas station that always had a few U-Hauls, and Samantha pulled through past the pumps. She turned the car off and started to get out.

"Do you want to stay in the car?"

"Yeah."

Almost as soon as Samantha had walked off, Jack called. "Hey, what time are we going to dinner?"

"We are picking up the trailer now. I guess we can swing by on the way back to the house to pick you up. Samantha wants to put it in the garage and leave it there so we can load it tomorrow."

"Cool."

After a few minutes, Samantha returned and

backed the car up to a trailer. A guy hooked it up for her before she got back in.

"Are we going to pick Jack up now?" I asked.

"He's on the way, so sure."

We drove over with the empty trailer bouncing the whole way. Samantha parked, and I started toward the door, but Jack was outside before I got there.

As soon as he was in the car, he said, "You can drive around the house so you don't have to turn this thing completely around."

"Oh," Samantha said. "I hadn't thought of that." She needed to back up a bit in order to get onto the track that led around the house and started backing up.

"Hold up!" Jack yelled. She slammed the brakes.

"Have you driven a trailer before?" he asked.

"Just over here."

"There're some tricks to it. First, you have to be careful not to jackknife. That's when you turn too tight and the front of the trailer hits the bumper. Then, to turn the trailer in one direction, you turn the car in the opposite direction."

"Oh...the guy who rented it said something about that, but I didn't think it would be that hard and didn't really pay attention."

This was pretty funny, but I managed not to laugh.

"Also, go really slow. It's always safest."

"Okay." She turned the steering wheel the other way and started creeping back, and the trailer started moving in the right direction so she could go forward, and she easily followed the track around the house, and down the drive, and onto the main road.

"Well, that was difficult," she said.

"Yeah, it's counterintuitive," Jack said.

"Thank you for your help." We were moving along, trailer bouncing again, and soon turned into the neighborhood. Samantha slowed down as we neared the house, looking at the driveway. "Wow, this is going to be a lot harder than I thought," she said, putting her hand on her chin. "No wonder people always leave trailers on the street."

"You want the trailer in the garage, right?" Jack asked.

"Yeah."

"If you want, I could do it for you."

Samantha tapped on the steering wheel a few times. "Okay." She put the car in park and got out.

Jack got in the driver's seat and said to Samantha, "No problem. Why don't you get out and stand in front of the garage to help guide me in. If I look off track, stop me."

She nodded and walked up the driveway.

He rolled down the window and shouted to her that we were going to do a loop around the neighborhood. I'd been enjoying the whole exchange more than I ought to have. It was kind of…hot to see him so good at something, even if it wasn't a particularly appealing thing.

Eventually he pulled up against the curb, several feet past the edge of the driveway, and started backing up. He managed to get the trailer onto the driveway in one smooth motion, and it was in the garage in a couple minutes, safely detached from the car and stowed away.

"That was amazing, Jack," Samantha said, shaking her head.

He shrugged and grinned sheepishly. "Practice. Lots of it. I've always had to help around the farm."

"All right, let's go to dinner."

Jack took my hand—and this time I let him—until we reached the car, and Samantha started it up. "Where are we going?" she asked.

"We could do the Mexican place downtown," he said.

The whole episode had relaxed me enough that this time, I let him keep hold of my hand.

****

The following day, Samantha and I got to the house early. I began loading the trailer while she worked on making sure the donation bags were clearly marked.

I started with the books since they were the heaviest boxes. It felt so weird to be doing it. Several times I had to stop and sit down because I realized this was the last time I would see this house. Mom was gone. But normally people get to remember a dead person based on how they knew them. I wasn't getting that. I would lose the mom I'd grown up with, again. Mom's memory was getting a replacement—the one my new family knew—but her old one would truly be gone, unless I worked hard to keep it all on my own.

I stepped out of the trailer and spotted the boxes of books in the corner of the garage. I'd forgotten about them. About the secrets they might hold. One more chance!

I opened up the first one and began flipping through the paperbacks. Naturally, they smelled like old books, which was comforting, but not enough to calm me down. I was almost frenzied as I searched.

I was in the second box when Samantha came out.

"What are you doing?" She sounded curious, not

judgmental.

"I'm...trying to find something." I looked away.

But since she'd stopped me, the futility of it all struck me.

"Are you okay?" She looked concerned again.

"Fine."

"If you're sure, I'm going to go back in and finish up. The realtor should be here soon. But if you need me for anything, please come get me, okay?"

Now I was despondent again. I'd found nothing and that wasn't likely to change. Mom was just a woman—she wasn't a spy or undercover or anything exotic. I would find no secret papers or stash of weapons. I started loading the rest of the book boxes into the trailer. I'd go through them anyway, once we got back to Oklahoma. But there'd be nothing.

I was repositioning some boxes in the trailer when the doorbell rang and I heard Samantha let someone in. I kept working on loading while Samantha showed the woman—the realtor—around. I was in the garage when they got to the kitchen. I heard the woman ask Samantha, "Is this where it happened?"

Samantha said it was, and the woman said, "It's so awful. I don't understand why things like that have to happen."

The lady was right—it was awful. And things like that don't *have* to happen. They just do. Because some men think if they can't have what they want, no one should.

I sat on a stack of boxes and cried for Mom. And for everything Mom had given up, and for my own old life, and the fact that that old life had sucked so much, but most of all I cried because now I didn't want to have to leave Jack behind again. My heart was being twisted and pulled, twisted and stretched, gradually pulled out of me, but in painful slow-motion.

They were probably going to come into the garage any minute now, and I couldn't bear the thought of having to meet that woman. I climbed out of the trailer and ran out the garage door and into the backyard and kept going.

Chapter Twenty-Four

After I returned from Iowa, I camped out in my
room. I read more of Mom's books, listened to more of
Mom's music, wore more of Mom's clothes. In a way, I
felt closer to her than I ever had. Going to Iowa had
been the right thing to do. Even though I had gone
through the boxes once we were back. There was
nothing. I was still desperate to think of something else.

The biggest problem was Jack. Since getting back,
my unease had returned. He had suggested I get my
GED and go to Iowa State next year, at the same time
he did. Was that being controlling? I decided being
around him must have clouded my judgment. All that
ridiculous handholding. And what was so impressive
about being able to drive a trailer, anyway?

I got up early on the Sunday before Thanksgiving
and left on my long run. I'd been invited to Don's
parents for the holiday and was trying to decide if I
should go or not.

I could ask them stuff about Don. Would they
answer my questions? I didn't know them well enough,
but it could be worth trying.

But what if I didn't like their answers? Was it
better to not know? Would they try to get me to contact
Don? I didn't want to do that.

God, this was not helping me to clear my head at
all.

I concentrated on my feet and looking at my surroundings. I mostly ran on the trails near the house, so it was a wide expanse of grass and dirt, with a few trees in the distance. The trees I could see were some pretty spectacular reds, though. Fall seemed more yellow and orange in Iowa from what I remembered. Here the colors were bolder.

The blue car was nowhere to be seen. I'd been hoping it would be there, and I'd see that it didn't have Nebraska plates. But I wasn't feeling watched, which was both a relief and concerning since maybe the woman just wasn't there at the moment. But why would some woman from Nebraska be stalking me? It didn't make any sense.

Frankie was in front of the house riding his bike in circles when I walked back up.

"Hi Retta! Did you finish *The Lightning Thief* yet?"

"I did. I finished it last night."

"Did you like it?" He'd stopped circling and followed me onto the driveway.

"It was pretty good. Different from what I expected. I know some Greek mythology from studying it, and so it was interesting."

"Really?"

Tracy ran outside, slamming the front door and grabbing her bike off the front sidewalk.

She looked at me and stopped, holding her bike halfway off the ground, and quietly said, "Frankie, let's go riding."

Frankie waved at me, and the kids sped off.

I was glad Tracy hadn't said anything to me. I felt bad about that but only a little.

When I went inside, Samantha was in the sitting room.

"Hi," I said. "I've decided to go to Don's parents for Thanksgiving after all." I needed to find out more about Don, and talking to them was probably going to be the only way.

"Ah, okay," Samantha said with a clear frown. "If that's what you want. We'll plan it without you. We'll miss you, though." She paused. "When's your marathon?"

"Not for a while. April 29th."

"That's so neat."

"Yeah, I'm pretty excited." One nice thing about visiting the grandparents was that they had a ranch, so I hoped I'd be able to do some running on grass again. Then in January I'd have to start at the high school here, so maybe I would join the track team. It would be all about sprinting, but I hoped I could get some help from the coach on marathon training.

****

That night, we were over at Nana's for dinner, eating a nice spinach and broccoli quiche that even the kids liked. During a lull in the conversation, Samantha glanced at me and said, "Mom, Retta has decided to spend Thanksgiving with her other grandparents."

"What?" Nana exclaimed, putting her fork down loudly.

"Mom…"

"No, Retta," Nana said, looking right at me, "you can't. They can't tear this family apart yet again."

"Mom!" Samantha said.

Nana broke eye contact, and I didn't know where to look, so I glanced at the kids who were both staring at their plates. I did the same.

Nana pushed her chair back, stood up, and walked away from the table. Samantha followed her out of the kitchen, leaving the three of us still looking at our food and not moving.

Frankie whispered, "She never gets mad." Neither Tracy nor I replied.

I strained my ears to try to hear what Samantha and Nana were saying. I caught snippets, but they were informative: Samantha said, "honor her wishes," and Nana said, "you tiptoe around her;" Samantha mentioned the word "counselor" and then "her family, too."

Tracy took another quiet bite of quiche, and Frankie followed suit.

When they came back in, I looked up and could see Nana's red face straining to be calm. There seemed a simple solution to the problem. I said, "Look, it's okay—I'll just tell them I can't come for Thanksgiving. I'll go the next week."

Samantha still looked mad, but Nana's face softened, and she said, "Would you?"

"Mom," Samantha said, "what did we talk about?"

"She volunteered," Nana said.

"Really, Samantha," I said. "It's okay. I was going then because that's when they invited me. I can go another time."

"Not Christmas," Nana said.

"Okay, not Christmas," I said. The idea hadn't occurred to me. I couldn't imagine spending my first Christmas without Mom with the parents of the reason I didn't have one anymore. We'd never done much for Thanksgiving, but Christmas was special.

"Fine," Samantha said, frowning. She sat down. "Frankie, do you want more quiche?"

"Yes, please." They all watched her put another piece on his plate. "Thank you," he said.

Tracy said, "Mom, can I please have another one, too?"

As Samantha served the second piece, she gave a forced smile and said, "Gee, Mom, we've got them 'pleasing' and 'thanking' all over the place."

Nana laughed uneasily. Her hand shook as she cut a piece of quiche off with her fork.

****

Thanksgiving at Nana's was nice, though at first I didn't get what the big deal had been. Holiday meals didn't seem like a big deal. Mom and I hadn't had any other family, after all. That realization made me appreciate it. *Mom*, I thought, *we're finally doing a family Thanksgiving. Wish you were here.*

I went to Don's parents the following Sunday. The visit wasn't bad. I spent most of the week reading books from Mom's shelf that I'd brought with me, plus some homework. The weather was nice and cool, and I got in several long runs. I also considered the Jack problem more, although I was so deeply ambivalent that my thinking did not clear things up at all.

Grandma did most of the talking, but she also did a lot of cooking, which was pretty great. It turned out she was an amazing cook. Being there made me realize I'd never really had good food. I had paella, prime rib, pasta carbonara, and home-smoked salmon. Grandma might have been showing off, but she could certainly cook.

But being there wasn't without problems. In the

end, I got shy about asking questions. There were a few photos of a young Don around. There were also baby pictures of me and one picture of Don and Mom standing together holding me. It made me long for something, but I didn't even know what. A better Don? Why did things go bad?

There were also pictures of an awkward but smiling brown-haired girl—Don's younger sister, who had been sixteen when she'd been killed in the car wreck.

"You look just like her," Grandma had said, looking off behind me. Based on the pictures, she wasn't wrong.

Grandpa just pursed his lips and straightened his newspaper.

"What was her name?" I asked.

"Maxine," Grandma said. "We called her Max."

I nodded.

"You're a lot like her. She was sporty, too." Her eyes teared up, so I looked away.

At the end of the week, they drove me back to my house, and Grandma and Grandpa walked me to the door. I stiffened when I saw Grandma coming in for a hug, but I didn't resist.

After the awkward hug, Grandma said, "Thanks so much for spending the week with us. You have no idea how much it means to both of us."

Grandpa nodded and patted me on the shoulder.

Chapter Twenty-Five

December ended. I hadn't seen the blue car again and figured I must have imagined the whole thing. Or at least the significance of it.

But I hadn't thought of anything else I could do to find out about Mom, and me, moving around, and I was pretty down. The dreams had improved, but they were back. Dr. Iravani seemed worried, but what could she do? What could anyone do?

With January came news that Don's case was proceeding. Samantha and I would have to go back to Iowa for it in early March. I was terrified—Don would be there. But still, my immediate concern was school starting up. How much would the kids at school know about me? How would they act?

I picked my clothes out for the first day, aiming for conflict avoidance. I wasn't even going to wear makeup. I didn't have any now, anyway. But that should get the right message across—I'm not even trying, so please leave me alone.

I draped a pair of jeans and a simple green long-sleeve T-shirt over my desk chair. Then I grabbed a flannel shirt to wear over it and made sure I had all I needed crammed in my backpack. It was the same one I'd had in Iowa, and I could still see the tire marks.

With everything ready, I lay on the bed and dragged ever-present Wes into my lap. When Samantha had taken me to register for school last week, she had produced my birth certificate. I'd insisted on looking at it, holding it. "Frances Maxine Lytle" it said. Maxine. I hadn't even known my own middle name.

I wondered if I should start going by "Frances." I was starting to feel like "Retta" didn't fit me anymore. Retta was the old shut-in girl doomed by circumstance, but things were different now. Not really better, just different.

The next morning, I rode the bus to school, noting the sign at the main entrance announcing the home of the Millers, which was a pretty hilarious school mascot. Who did they compete with? The Cobblers? Tinkers? Tailors? But it was also a much bigger campus than my last school. There was a big stadium behind the school.

After a few days, it was weird being back in school; I couldn't feel more different than I had when I'd started back in Iowa. Mostly I just felt meh, but some of it was a real hassle. They were using different textbooks in all my classes, French and German conflicted so I had to go down a level in German or take Spanish again—I chose Spanish to get some practice speaking it, and they were reading different books in English.

I had known all this when I registered, but coming to school and being in classes made things more frustrating.

Also, people recognized me on the first day. They stared and whispered.

I'd just sat down in English and felt the kids all eyeing me. People were still coming in when a guy sitting two rows over and up a couple seats said, "Hey, I saw you on TV."

At first I thought I'd misunderstood him because he did have one of the strongest southern accents I'd heard here, but he looked at me like he expected a reply. Some of the other kids' eyes went wide at the statement, and somebody said, "Luke!" I'd heard him right.

"Yeah, I was on TV," I said.

"Was that cool?" he asked, ignoring everyone else.

"Um, given the circumstances...no?"

"Too bad."

"Yeah." I shook my head. What the hell?

Nobody else in the class made eye contact with me or said anything to him or even to me afterward, so he was probably important in some way. He looked like the type of high school boy who played football—tall, muscular, broad shoulders.

The cafeteria situation was the same as my old school—too many kids, not enough places to sit. I'd gone through the line and bought a slice of pizza and some fries since they were both easy to carry, plus a skim milk, and ended up eating while strolling around outside. There had been a few empty spots at tables, but I didn't know if they belonged to somebody. I planned to keep an eye on the open spots for this week and then decide where I could safely sit. It wasn't that cold.

Math class was very similar to the one I'd had in Iowa, so I didn't have any catch-up work to do. But after class Wednesday in my second week, I had to go up to speak to the teacher, whose name I couldn't remember. I stared at the floor while he talked to another student.

When he was finally free, I said, "Hi, I didn't manage to get the homework done for today. Can I turn it in tomorrow?"

He was a younger guy, blond and kind of cute, but also a tad shorter than me. I forced a smile. He simply said, "Okay, since you're new—this once you can. But in the future, I don't take late homework. You can turn it in with the Thursday homework."

"Thank you. I really appreciate it."

My next class was on the other side of the campus, and I didn't feel like rushing, so I didn't arrive until just after the bell. I had to go all the way to the front to sit down, which was annoying. I focused on ignoring everybody staring at me.

This was French, the other class I had homework in that I hadn't done, so I also had to talk to the teacher after class.

"Madame Leibniz? I was not able to get the homework done and—"

"Mademoiselle Brooks, à ce niveau, nous parlons uniquement en français."

"Ah…okay." I was only allowed to speak in French now. Great. "Uh, *je n'avais pas en*, uh, *le temps de terminer le…travail. Puis-je le*, um, *remettre …demain?"* I was pretty sure I said I hadn't finished it and asked if I could turn it in tomorrow. Speaking in French was a million times harder than reading and writing it.

"Oui, puisque vous aviez une telle période difficile. Rendez-le vendredi, s'il vous plaît."

"Okay, *merci beaucoup.*" I hadn't caught the part in the middle, but Madame Leibniz told me I had until Friday to turn it in. I left to head over to the cafeteria for another walkaround lunch.

****

I spotted a couple of places to sit in the cafeteria that seemed promising. On Wednesday and Thursday they were either empty or had different people in them. Still, on Friday, I grabbed a burrito and some salsa, plus my milk, and left the cafeteria. But I wanted the salsa on the burrito, which was difficult to do standing up, so I decided to find a place out of sight where I could sit. I went behind the cafeteria, where I could see a back door and a picnic table, and not far beyond that, a dumpster walled in with tall fencing. There was also a fair amount of noise coming from an exhaust pipe on the roof.

A woman dressed all in grungy white was sitting at the picnic table surrounded by smoke pouring off her cigarette. "What are you doing back here?"

"Just walking," I said. I continued past the picnic table, feeling the woman's eyes on me. I walked past the trash area and saw there was one long wall with grass up to it. I sat down and leaned against the building and began to eat the burrito. Once I finished it and the milk, I pulled out my phone to check the time. I had thirty minutes left.

I was exhausted since I'd been up late again. I'd started to get into my new book just before midnight, so I was up until after two again. I mentally kicked myself for not bringing it with me, as I was sitting here with time to kill and nothing to read or do. I leaned my head back and closed my eyes.

Something was tapping my foot and saying something.

"What? Hi," I said to the brown-uniformed man standing in front of me. Must be a janitor.

"Are you Retta?" he asked.

"Yes," I said, stretching and standing up. "What time is it?"

"Twelve forty. They have been looking for you."

"Oh." I was surprised. That meant fifth period was just ending. I'd missed a whole class.

"Let me walk you to the office."

"Okay, sure," I said, shrugging. What did it matter?

****

"So the principal called me today," Samantha said after she got home from work that night. She was standing in my bedroom doorway.

"Yeah?" I said, petting Wes, who was curled up next to my hip on the bed.

"They are concerned. Obviously, missing class is a problem, but they were surprised you were able to fall asleep with all the noise behind the cafeteria. They also said you didn't turn in any of your homework this week." She leaned her head against the doorframe.

I nodded.

"So what's going on? Are you having trouble sleeping?"

"You mean, because of…no, whenever I go to bed, I sleep fine." This wasn't necessarily true, but the dreams had stopped coming so often again.

"How is your therapy going? I thought it was going well?" Samantha asked.

"It's fine."

Samantha sighed. "Retta…I thought you cared a lot about school. Is being there so hard?"

"I don't know. I guess it is. It's just different from how I spent most of my life."

"So what about not doing your homework? Are you planning to start doing that?"

"I don't know," I said, shrugging. "I didn't plan to not do it. It just happened."

Samantha closed her eyes for a moment. "I know you want to go to college."

"Yeah."

"Well, you can't fail your junior year and go," she said with a slightly raised voice, before lowering it again. "You'll need to start working. Especially since you were homeschooled."

"I know."

"Do you not like the new school?" Samantha sat at the foot of the bed.

I pulled my feet up to make more room. "No, it's fine. Better than Iowa. So far no one has stolen my backpack and driven over it."

"That happened there?"

"Yeah. It was why I was running hurdles in jeans in that video. They took my bag with my shorts in it."

Samantha shook her head. "Teenagers," she said under her breath.

"I know, right? Teenagers." I made a big show of rolling my eyes.

Samantha blinked. "So you don't like school. What is your plan to get yourself to start working again?"

"I have no idea," I said flatly. My legs were heavy, glued to the bed.

Samantha said, "Maybe if you can find something to look forward to with it, it will make school more tolerable. What about joining the running team here?"

"I already missed the cross country season."

"It's that short?" Her eyebrows shot up. "They don't still train?"

"I guess they probably still train. Maybe I could

sign up for track, if there's still time. I don't know." I shrugged.

"That sounds worth pursuing."

"Yeah, I guess."

Samantha sighed and was quiet for a moment. "Please let me know if there's something I can do to help you feel better."

I wondered what that could possibly be.

Chapter Twenty-Six

I didn't know why I couldn't get myself to start doing my homework. The first problem was that something about the school was demotivating. I didn't feel like I was a part of it, or of anything, really. Whenever I tried to do any work, thoughts of the deposition distracted me. If I didn't get my act together, Samantha would be on my case. And truthfully, I knew I'd regret screwing up my grades later.

But before that could happen, it was time for the deposition. Samantha and I flew to Des Moines. Don's lawyer was based there, and it was where Don was also living because the hospital where he was doing his rehab was there. The prosecutor had agreed to travel.

On the flight in, Samantha said, "Retta, I've been reading about depositions. I know Greg told you to expect anything, but I'm not sure if either of us grasped what that meant." Greg Milford was the prosecutor on the case, and I'd spoken to him a few times.

Samantha continued after a pause. "It sounds like they can be pretty brutal. Apparently the lawyers can ask about almost anything. There are no objections like at trial."

"What's there to ask? I found her. He did it." I'd been trying not to think about it at all.

So when we walked into the conference room in the law office on the seventeenth floor of a downtown skyscraper, I gasped at the sight of Don sitting there calmly in his wheelchair. His face stretched when he smiled after he saw me, and he said, "Hi, Frances, I'm so glad to finally get a chance to see you." His lawyer leaned over and whispered something in his ear, and a dark look passed over Don's face.

My mouth dropped open as my heart started racing. I backed into the hall. I'd known he'd be here but hadn't realized what that would feel like. It felt just like the terror of running from him.

No words made it to my lips, but my eyes were wide, and Samantha held me tightly by the arm while we stood in the doorway until one of the other men, standing in front of a chair across from Don, said, "Ms. Brooks, Ms. Simpson, thank you for coming. I'm Greg Milford. I know we've spoken on the phone several times, but it's good to finally meet you." The prosecutor followed his greeting with an extended hand, which I stepped in to shake, if weakly.

The two men on the other side of the table to Don's right both stood and introduced themselves and extended their hands. I completely missed their names. One was short and bald from age, with just wisps of white hair remaining, while the other was a much younger blond guy with strangely rosy cheeks.

"Here, have a seat," Milford said. He motioned to two of the three remaining seats, all across from Don and his lawyers. Then he pointed out a woman sitting at the end of the table. "This is Ms. Li, who will be recording the proceedings today." The middle-aged woman had one of those weird typewriters like Jamie's.

I rolled the chair out and sat, leaving my hands on the armrests. Don was watching me when I stole a glance at him. He was clean-shaven, and his dark brown hair was longer than in the booking photo I'd seen. If I'd passed him on the street, I wouldn't have thought twice about him. He looked perfectly normal.

Everyone was looking at me. I'd missed something. "What?"

There was one more man who I hadn't noticed at first. He said the deposition would begin. Ms. Li started typing as he continued speaking. He told me he was an officer of the court, gave his address and the date. I had to take an oath to speak only the truth during the deposition. It was perjury to lie. My stomach fluttered, and the fact that this might be worse than I'd been expecting started to sink in.

Samantha's hand squeezed my arm through the oath and remained there. Okay, maybe it wouldn't be that bad. I'd already been honest and thorough in my statement to the police and my conversations with Greg.

The rosy-cheeked lawyer smiled at me while shuffling a stack of papers and pulling out a few sheets, which he set next to his legal pad already covered with notes. He started with some legal mumbo-jumbo, but I didn't pay full attention except when he said my name—Frances Maxine Lytle—and spelled out the last name. Then he asked me to state my name for the record, and I had to parrot back this still unfamiliar name. He asked me a few questions about where I lived and my school situation.

He turned to a blank sheet on the legal pad before smiling again and looking up at me. "Now we just have a few questions about what you've previously stated."

"Okay," I said, looking only at him, though he was

right next to Don, so it was impossible not to see him, too.

"Let's talk about the day your mother died," the lawyer said. *Died*? I thought, but the lawyer continued before I could process that. "You said you had sneaked out. Why was that?"

"What do you mean?"

"Why did you sneak out? Why didn't you just tell your mother where you were going?"

Samantha squeezed my arm again. "Because my mom wouldn't let me do anything with other people. Because she was so paranoid about me being seen out, and she didn't trust my friends."

"I see. Why was that?"

I stared at him, stomach stirring again. "Because she was afraid he would find us."

"Who?"

"Him. Don." I tried not to look his direction, but his face darkened anyway. The bald lawyer leaned forward and wrote something on his own legal pad.

The younger lawyer nodded. "Why didn't she trust your friends?"

"I don't know," I said, brow furrowing. "She was just always overprotective." Samantha's grip was firm.

"Did she regularly overreact to things you did?"

Of course she overreacted, but didn't all moms, probably? "Maybe sometimes."

The questioning lawyer wrote furiously on his legal pad. Then he said, "So you're saying that she sometimes acted irrationally with regards to you."

"Irrationally?" I said frowning. "I don't think—" Greg Milford had told me before they would try to see if I would get angry or defensive, because it would make me an untrustworthy witness in the jury's eyes. I took a deep breath. "No, I didn't say that."

"Okay, that's fine," the lawyer said, looking up and smiling at me yet again. "Did your mother have a boyfriend?"

I tensed. What did that have to do with anything? Don leaned forward to hear my answer. "No. She never left the house except to go to the store or work."

"Did she drink or do illegal drugs of any type?"

"No!"

"Okay, let's change track a bit," he said, pulling out another sheet of paper. "What did you do while you were out that day? The day your mother died."

That was easy at least. "I went horseback riding with a friend and then hung out with him and other friends outside until eleven or so."

He pulled out a sheet of paper from the stack and glanced at it. "This friend you mentioned is Joginder Singh also of Buckley, Iowa, correct?"

I nodded.

"Could you speak your answer for the record?" He motioned to the transcriber.

"Yes," she said. "The friend I went riding with was Jack, or Joginder Singh."

"Okay, great. Is he your boyfriend?"

I flushed as Don's eyes narrowed. "No, not really."

The man nodded while the older lawyer wrote something on his pad and pushed it over for him to see. "Was he then?"

"No," I said as the urge to cry from remembering holding hands with him all night came over me. I'd been so happy, all while Don was stabbing Mom.

The lawyer cleared his throat. "Were you having

sex with him?"

I jerked back and blushed again. "No! I said he wasn't my boyfriend!"

"Okay," the lawyer said. "How long were you alone with Jack that day?"

My heart was still racing from the last question. What was this they were doing? "I don't know," I managed. "It was when we were riding. I guess a couple hours."

Don leaned back, and the lawyer wrote on his pad. "And then you spent the rest of the evening with the other kids?"

"Yeah."

"Did you go back to your house with Jack that afternoon?"

"What?" I felt sick. I knew what they were doing now. How could they?

"Did you and Jack go to your house the afternoon your mother died?"

"No!" My heart was about to beat its way out of my chest.

"Okay," he said. "Did you resent your mother for not letting you hang out with your friends?"

I closed my eyes, wanting to scream. I bit my lip—hard—before regaining control and answering. "Yes, I didn't like it. But I did not go back to the house. I didn't kill my mom."

The bald lawyer leaned over and whispered something to the younger one, who then asked, "What did you do after riding, when you were hanging out with your other friends?"

I tensed up more, thinking about what they'd be asking soon. About finding Mom. "Just sat around a fire and talked."

"Did you drink any alcohol?"

I frowned. "No."

"Did you do any illegal drugs?" Don leaned forward again.

I bit my lip again as I remembered the pipe getting passed around. I was glad I'd skipped it. "No."

He looked at his legal pad. "Are you sure?"

"Yes, I'm sure," I said, wanting to scream it but keeping my voice level.

"Okay," he said, writing something down. "Now we're going to change the topic. After you found your mother, why didn't you call the police?"

I stared at him, willing my mouth to stay closed until I was ready. "Because he was chasing me."

"For the record, who do you mean by 'he'?"

"Him. Don." I pointed at him, trying and failing to avoid his eyes which were boring into mine.

The lawyer nodded. Don leaned over and whispered something in his ear, and he nodded again, curtly. "Are you sure he was chasing you?"

I blinked. What were they trying to pull here? "I ran, and he ran after me. Then I got in Jack's truck, and he drove after us and even rammed the back bumper. I think that qualifies as chasing."

"Okay," he said, pulling out another sheet from his stack. "Still, why didn't you call the police once you thought you were safe?"

This one did make Mom sound crazy. She wasn't crazy—she was right. But they were going to act like she was. I took a breath. "My mom never trusted the police. I didn't know why until recently. But she made me promise to call someone else if anything ever happened to her."

He nodded again, looking up. I hated his smile. "Who are the people you stayed with while you were missing?"

"I don't know their real names."

"But you must know where you were. Where did you stay?"

"I was mostly in the car." Samantha's grip was tight on my arm again.

"You were gone for several days. Where did you stay when you weren't in the car?"

"I don't know." I wouldn't say.

"Try to describe where you were," the lawyer said. Don was looking at me intently, and my stomach was having fits.

After a pause, I said, "We drove from Iowa to Michigan. I stayed with a woman in Michigan near the town where I finally went to the police station."

He nodded, shuffling some papers. He asked a few more questions, but I'd managed to avoid giving anything away. Still I had to fight myself to stay in control, but it seemed like the worst of it was over. Or at the very least I had gotten used to it.

When it was over and they were out of there, Samantha was still gripping my hand. "That was horrible," she said quietly. I just nodded in reply, not sure what else there was to say.

Chapter Twenty-Seven

A week after getting back, I was walking down the school hall one morning feeling a little sorry for myself because it was my birthday. I anticipated the end of the day. We were supposed to go out for a birthday dinner. Out of the blue, a girl ran into my shoulder hard enough that it made me crash against a bank of lockers, and I faced a group of expertly made-up girls. One said, "Watch where you're going, freak."

Something snapped in me, and I launched off the locker and slammed my palms into the girl's shoulders, sending her sprawling onto the thin carpet. All three girls gasped like they were appalled and couldn't wait for me to get in trouble, which I did, less than sixty seconds later.

I was more surprised by all of it than anyone else, really.

"Young lady, we cannot condone this kind of behavior, regardless of the words people use against you." That was the principal.

"But she slammed me into the locker first."

"It was an accident!" claimed the girl who'd shoved me. Her posse all wagged their pretty blonde heads.

I faced the girls. "Of course you say that."

Once we were back in his office, the principal tented his hands and said, "Retta, you know you cannot physically lash out at people. I have no choice but to suspend you for three days."

"Okay. I'm devastated." I looked away and shrugged.

He sighed. "Go sit outside my office."

I was getting pretty good at making people sigh lately.

When Nana got there to pick me up, she looked worried. I tried to smile at her, but it came out all wrong, more like a grimace.

Nana just watched me with a wrinkled brow as I went upstairs to my room to change for a run. It might be my last chance for a while, if they made me stop. I didn't know what they'd do.

****

I ran so long that my legs were like wet spaghetti as I made my way off the last trail.

"Hi," a woman called just as I neared the park entrance.

I looked up and stopped. A woman with big wavy blonde hair waved from maybe twenty feet away. She had on a miniskirt and didn't look at all like she belonged in a park. And she seemed familiar somehow.

"Would you at least talk to him?" The woman's eyes glowed.

"Who?" I said, skin tingling with growing fear. Something wasn't right here.

"Your father. He just wants to know what happened."

My stomach caved in, and I clutched my belly as my pulse quickened. The woman stood in front of the exit, but I could probably make it around her.

"What are you talking about?" I asked.

"Come on." The woman motioned to me.

"Leave me alone," I said with a venom that surprised me. I marched toward and around the woman and headed out onto the sidewalk.

She trotted to keep up with me as I headed toward the house, an impressive feat in her heels. "Come on, Frances."

"Who are you?"

"It doesn't matter." The woman was breathless. "What matters is who you are and what you did."

I started jogging away from this crazy woman. What was she talking about?

I continued alone until a large gray van materialized next to me, pulling to a stop just in front of me. By the time I stopped, I was right next to the open sliding door, and the mystery woman reached out from inside to grip my arm.

I yelled before jerking back. In the split second when I extricated myself, I saw over the woman's shoulder that Don was behind the wheel. I took off as fast as I could toward the house, heart on fire.

I threw open the front door so hard it crashed against the wall. I turned around to close it and saw the van in front of the house.

"Retta!" Nana called. "What happened?"

"It's Don! He's here!" I slammed the door and turned the lock shut.

"What? That's not possible!" She was standing in the foyer with a crossword puzzle in her hand.

"It is possible, because it's happening. And there's a woman with him. We have to call the police!"

Nana ran back into the den and picked up the phone. She started dialing when there was a loud pounding on the front door, where I still stood.

"I know you're in there!" The woman's words were muffled but clear enough.

I backed up toward the stairs. I heard Nana yelling into the phone.

The woman's fist slammed against the door. "I know what you did, and you will pay, you little bitch!"

Chapter Twenty-Eight

I held onto the bannister and stared at the front door.

"Open this door!" The doorknob jiggled.

Nana came racing back in, phone in hand. "They're on their way." She looked at the door. Her hand shook as she held the phone to her ear. "She's still here. She's banging on the door like she wants to tear it down."

"Frances, you have to admit what you did!"

My stomach swirled.

A horn honked outside. The pounding stopped for a second before starting back up. The horn sounded again, a constant wail this time. The woman stopped hitting the door, and the horn stopped soon afterward.

It was eerily quiet until the sound of squealing tires filled the foyer.

Nana and I looked at each other. Her eyes were wide. "I think they left," she said into the phone.

I went to the den to look out the window. There was no van in front of the house. It appeared to be truly gone.

A few terrifying minutes later, a police car pulled up, and an officer knocked on the door. "It's a cop," I confirmed from the den. Nana opened the door.

He followed her into the den, and Nana put the phone back in its cradle. The officer nodded and asked for details of what happened. When I described the van, he called it into the station and then asked me to continue.

This was much better. There was a man with a gun on my side. That may not have made Mom feel safe, but it did me.

****

Samantha came home a couple hours after the cop got there with the two kids in tow. The school bus had been diverted from the neighborhood, and all the parents had to pick their kids up at the school. The first thing she did upon entering was squeeze my shoulder, though it looked like she'd considered coming in for a hug.

"I'm so sorry. I'm so glad you're okay." Samantha shook her head. "I can't believe this happened. We should have been informed that he'd left the home this morning."

She sent the kids up to their rooms while the three of us sat in the den. The tension in the room was palpable, and I still felt ill.

The officer stood by. We could hear occasional noises from his radio, but it was hard to say what they were saying.

Eventually, he came in from the foyer and said Don and the woman had been found. They were en route to the police station.

I closed my eyes and exhaled. Nana put her hand to her mouth and said, "Thank goodness." Samantha was wringing her hands.

We had frozen meals for a quick and very quiet supper.

I was reading in my room when Samantha came in a bit later, after an ominous knock on the door, and sat on the bed. I stared at her hands with their now green nail polish, again chipped.

I finally had to ask about it. "Samantha, why do you paint your nails?"

Her eyes widened. "What?"

I motioned toward her hands.

She held them out and looked at her nails. "It reminds me of your mom," she said in a thick voice. "She always wore fun colors, so it's my way of always remembering her."

Oh. I hadn't been expecting that, and it made my stomach hurt. Maybe she did miss her almost as much as me.

She didn't say anything for a moment and took a deep breath.

"But Retta, I'm so sorry about what happened with Don. And I'm sorry it had to happen on your birthday. We'll do something to celebrate this weekend. But what is going on with school?" She obviously meant in the big picture.

"I don't know." This was absolutely true.

"Really? Is this who you are?"

My heart started racing all on its own. "I don't know who I am!" I shouted, surprising even myself.

"What do you mean?" Samantha asked in a level voice.

"I mean," I said, quieter, "that I don't know who I am. Who am I? You tell me. Because I don't know."

Samantha's face softened. "Retta, you are an amazing person. You are smart, talented, driven, and resilient. Why are you suddenly reacting like this?"

"I don't know!" I was on the verge of tears and didn't know why.

"Can I give you a hug? I think you really need one."

"No." I pinched the comforter and rubbed the fabric between my fingers.

Samantha got up and sat next to me and gave me a tight hug. I jerked away, but she didn't let go, and I gave up and just lost it, sobbing. I missed Mom so much, the way she used to hold me, even when I hadn't wanted her to anymore. I hadn't known how much I treasured that until it was gone.

Samantha didn't let go until I peeled myself away.

"I'll tell you what, Retta," she said, still holding onto my shoulders. "Why don't we do this. Nana would let you stay with her for a few days. It's away from here. No kids. No school."

Something clicked in my mind. "Actually, I have another idea. Maybe I could go back to the other grandparents." I added, "That's even farther away from everything." I could get some of my questions about Don answered. He'd be locked up for a while now. Maybe they would know who that crazy woman was.

A shadow fell over Samantha's face, but I knew she wouldn't say no, as much as she might want to.

Chapter Twenty-Nine

Grandma cooked more great stuff for me. Cajun shrimp and grits, chicken tikka masala. But I had let slip to Jack that I was there, and by chance he was coming down to Kansas with his mom for the weekend, so now he planned to make the two and a half hour drive down to visit me on Saturday. I hadn't been able to figure out a way to weasel out of it and wasn't sure if I wanted to, anyway. Everything had been dragging on as before, with him not giving up on me like I thought he might, and sometimes wished he would. We only chatted every few days now.

I was in my room when I heard a car in front of the house. I looked out the window and saw Jack in his mom's Prius. My heart did a weird jump thing that seemed to be both nerves and excitement.

He hugged me when he first got out of the car, and despite my uncertainty it made my pulse speed up. My doubts seemed to dissipate as fast as rubbing alcohol from a wound. Was I so shallow that just seeing him made my brain go all stupid? What was it?

Jack was tentative and didn't say anything except, "Hi." He did not reach for my hand while we wandered over to look at my grandparents' horses, which made me sad.

"Have you ever thought of riding again?" Jack asked. "You seemed to take to it pretty quickly."

Nausea filled my stomach. "No. We were riding when it happened. We were laughing and joking around when my mom was being murdered."

Jack blanched. "God, you're right. I'm so sorry. I'm an idiot."

"It's okay," I said, the nausea fading faster than I expected. We were quiet for several moments, leaning on the fence overlooking the pasture.

Finally, Jack asked, "So how have you been, Retta, really?"

I shrugged. "Okay. The thing with Don was scary and horrible, but then it was over. I got in some trouble at school, though. That's why I ended up here."

"Oh yeah? What happened?"

"This girl pushed me against a locker and called me a freak, and then I threw her onto the ground." I felt the rush of the thrill it had given me all over again.

"No way!" He looked over at me with wide eyes. "That's sort of awesome."

"I know. Even my shrink thought it was a small breakthrough. Maybe not the right reaction, but a reaction."

He laughed. "Nice."

I missed his hand. Mine felt lonely. But both of his were up on the fence.

We were silent for a long while.

"Do you want to walk?" Jack finally asked.

We meandered a bit, not talking very much. I got the nerve to reach for his hand. It was a bit clumsy, and I'd obviously caught him off guard, but I glanced at him as a big smile lit up his face, so I knew he'd been worried about the way I'd been treating him. And now he felt better about it.

What was I doing? I wished I knew.

****

Jack left at about four, and I read for a while until we sat down to dinner.

"So your boyfriend is cute, Retta," Grandma said.

"He's not my boyfriend. He's only a friend." I took a bite of my potatoes.

"Oh, he seems keen on you."

After I finished chewing, I said, "Yeah. I'm just not sure about him."

"Why not? He's a very well-behaved boy."

Grandpa was heads down in his veal, apparently staying out of this conversation.

"I don't know, I guess I think he's too into me."

Grandma laughed. "I wouldn't expect to hear that from someone your age. What makes you say that?"

"I don't know, it's just a feeling." I didn't think I'd tell them—they were the parents of the whole reason I'd thought of it.

"Well, you have to trust your instincts, honey."

"Yeah." I almost snorted. Good instincts didn't run in my gene line.

"What is it you're worried about?"

"I don't know...sometimes he seems too intense," I said, surprising myself. "Like he's trying to control me or something."

Grandpa narrowed his eyes and looked right at me. "Are you worried he might be like Don? Don't be. He's not. I can tell."

"What?" I jerked back.

"Bob!"

"Becky, it's obvious what she's worried about. Can you blame her?"

"Retta, I'm sorry," Grandma said. "But he is right. Jack seems like a normal teenage boy. With Don, we always knew he was troubled, but we thought he'd outgrow it. He seemed to for a while. But then the summer Max was killed, Don changed."

"What do you mean by 'troubled'?" I asked, glad to have stumbled onto this conversation.

Grandma said, "There was an incident with his high school girlfriend. But he got better when he went off to college. After the accident he was different, angry all the time. He got into a fight in a bar and was facing prison. We managed to get a good lawyer, and he served nine months."

My mouth hung open. "Wait, he hurt somebody? You knew something was wrong with him?"

"Honey, he's our son," Grandma said while Grandpa looked off to the side. "We thought he was in trouble, and we could fix him. He had therapy for his anger, and we thought he was cured."

Grandma turned her head away. "He was such a sweet boy. Just sensitive and sweet. He adored Max. He called her his little princess."

Princess. I blanched.

Grandpa cleared his throat. "I still think he must have suffered some kind of brain damage in the accident."

Grandma nodded at him. "I think so, too. He has never been the same."

"So what did Mom do when she found out about all this?"

Grandma looked at her with sad eyes. "I don't know if she ever knew it all. They weren't dating until after he went back, and I don't know if he told her. He was embarrassed by the bar fight and sure he'd never do anything like it again."

"Where did she think he'd been?"

"Honey, you have to realize we thought he was better. Your mom was such a good influence on him, and we thought it would always be like that."

My blood started a slow simmer. I remembered what Samantha had told me, about his disappearance and the mysterious car wreck. They'd known something was wrong with him; they'd known! They knew he was violent and angry, and they let Mom marry him uninformed.

I pushed my plate away and stared at the table in an attempt to stay calm. "I'm going to my room," I announced before sliding the chair back more roughly than I meant.

****

Later that evening, I still fumed. I thought about the family I'd been stuck with. Okay, these grandparents were obviously an issue, but Mom's family was fine. Annoying but not horrible. Samantha and Nana were trying to be nice and supportive. Frankie was a decent enough kid. I found it hard not to like a kid who loved books as much as I did.

Suddenly, I knew why Tracy bugged me. The girl was living the life I'd been denied when I'd been growing up. She went to school, got to play outside, had friends and family. She was what could have been, and she didn't even appreciate all the freedoms I would have given anything for.

That was what it was: I was envious of a little girl.

I felt like the worst human ever. The crappy way I'd treated the girl…before I knew it, I was crying.

That was it. I was done being a jerk. I had to come back to the living again. But first I was going to make these assholes take me home.

Then I was struck with a powerful idea. Maybe I could find out about Mom, after all. This was perfect. My sanity depended on it. I pulled out my laptop and frantically Googled colleges around central Wisconsin. For this plan to work, I'd have to find what I needed quickly, and Jack would also have to cooperate. He just might.

Chapter Thirty

Jack arrived in his mom's Prius at about eight Sunday morning. I told my grandparents I was going with him to visit his grandparents' farm. We drove off with Grandma waving.

"So," Jack said, "it will be several hours before my mom wonders where I went with her car. What's your plan, genius?"

"Just drive to Appleford, Wisconsin," I said.

"Are you serious? How far is that?" He pressed the trip mileage reset.

"Over eleven hours." I turned to grin at him. "So get comfortable. Just take I-35 north for about seven hours."

"What, to Des Moines? And then let me guess, we'll head east and go right past Buckley?"

"Yes," I said sheepishly.

"Holy crap, we're going to be in so much trouble by the time this is over." Jack had a wide-eyed look that could be taken for terror or joy, or maybe both.

"Sometimes breaking rules is fun."

"Yeah, I guess." He shook his head and grinned. "So what is it we're doing exactly?"

"I'm going to get more answers about my mom."

"That doesn't clear things up for me," he said, comfortably holding the wheel with just his left hand. "Why don't you just talk more with Samantha?"

"She doesn't know the answers. I want to know where we went after Oklahoma up to when we moved to Buckley. I mean, it's possible we lived there even before moving into the house."

He glanced over at me. "Um, just so you know, I don't think you did. I asked around, and your mom started working at the school right about the time you moved in."

"When were you going to tell me this?"

"I was going to. We never talk anymore. You don't answer my calls."

"You could have told me yesterday!" I looked at him while he stared ahead, both hands tight on the wheel now.

"I know. I'm sorry. I got all flustered after being such an idiot about the…uh…thing."

It didn't matter for now. "So who'd you ask?" My heart sped up in anticipation.

"I ran into Dale Bird a week ago and stopped him. He had no idea who I was but got all friendly at your name. Your mom had just gotten to town. You were staying at the Buckley Inn when she started working at the school. Dale's wife befriended her or knew her or something—she volunteers at the school—and she mentioned they had a house to rent, so that's how you ended up there." He paused. "He told me a little more, too."

"Yeah?" My heart beat faster.

"He said his sister used to run a daycare, and you stayed there until your mom found an older lady to watch you at home."

All this detail was stunning, and I lost the ability to speak for the moment.

"Once you were old enough, the same lady started homeschooling you. But you probably remember that part."

I coughed. "I do. I don't remember the inn or the daycare." My mind was absorbing all of this, and I couldn't say anything else. I should remember the daycare. I'd been old enough.

Jack was quiet for a moment before saying, "So are we going to see one of the ladies who drove you?"

I nodded.

"Isn't that dangerous for them?"

"Not in this case, I think. I have a cover story. Nobody will know."

"Okay," Jack said, though doubt remained in his voice. "What's your cover story?"

"Just that I found her online and admired her work and wanted to meet her. I read a couple of her papers last night."

Jack was quiet a moment. "That doesn't seem like a very good excuse."

"I know." I sighed, deflated. "Tell me if you think of something better."

He nodded. I cycled between stewing over Don's parents' betrayal of Mom and feeling wonderment over the new information from Jack. How could they not have warned Mom? Why hadn't I sought Dale Bird out myself when I'd been in town to pack up the house?

Either way, this had to work. It *had* to.

Jack said, "Retta?"

"Hmm?"

"Have you thought more about the GED idea?"

I had. Jack had suggested I take the test this year instead of finishing high school next year. I could go to

Iowa State with him in the fall. Thinking about it made my stomach churn again. Was this a bad sign about Jack? I glanced over at him. "A little. I'm not sure."

"It would just be so perfect. Otherwise we'll never get to see each other."

"Yeah." He seemed so sincere. And Grandpa's point about Jack being different from Don made me feel better about it. But I was still so conflicted.

He looked over at me and smiled.

I couldn't help but return it. "How far have we gone?" I asked.

"About…ninety-three miles," he said.

I checked my watch. "It's only ten to ten. How much time before you need to call your mom?"

"I'll wait until she calls me. She probably thinks I'm still sleeping. She's going to kill me for stranding her."

"How's she going to get back?"

"Maybe she can rent a car. My dad's going to kill me, too." He gave a slightly high-pitched laugh.

"Did you just giggle?" I asked, cracking up.

"Shush," he said, face reddening. "It was a very manly giggle."

I leaned against the window, still smiling. Why couldn't I make up my mind about him? Everything appeared great, but how could I really know? I caught myself chewing on a thumbnail again.

****

We were just outside of Des Moines. Jack's mom had already called, and he was indeed in loads of trouble. She was having to rent a car to get back. But she wasn't going to report him as a runaway or the car as stolen, so that was something.

Jack pulled into a gas station. "I'm going to go inside to get some food. Do you want anything specific?"

"Whatever's fine," I said. "I'm going to call Samantha."

"Good luck with that." He laughed nervously.

"Thanks," I said as he shut the door and started setting up the gas pump.

I took a deep breath and dialed. "Samantha, hi."

"Retta. What's going on? Is everything okay?"

"Okay," I said, taking another breath. "So you're going to be mad."

"Okay," Samantha said slowly.

"I'm with Jack, and we're going to Wisconsin." I glanced back and saw him pumping gas.

"What!"

"There's something I need to do there."

"Where are you?" Samantha demanded.

"Just outside Des Moines." I made my voice almost chipper. "But don't worry—we're going to come back. I just have to talk to someone there. And then I'll come back."

"Retta! You can't do this!" she shouted, sounding panicked.

"Samantha, did you know they knew Don was violent? He had a history of it, even before Mom."

"What are you talking about?" She was still loud.

"He attacked someone in a bar the year he was gone and spent almost a year in prison. They knew all this and never told her! And they also said something happened with a girlfriend he had in high school."

"What?" Samantha cried. Then calmer, she said, "Wait, don't change the subject. What are you going to

277

do in Wisconsin?"

"I need to talk to someone," I said.

"Who?"

"I can't tell you."

"Retta!" Samantha exclaimed.

"It has to do with when I got away from Iowa that night. It's a woman."

Samantha was silent for a moment. Then she sighed. "I need to know where you are. Call me every hour. Send me pictures of road signs along the way."

"Okay." I could see Jack inside looking at a shelf. "Samantha?"

"Yes?"

"How do I know Jack isn't going to end up being like Don?"

"What?" Samantha asked in a low voice. "Are you scared of him now? Is he forcing you to do this?"

"No! He's fine. I just wonder, because you all thought Don was fine."

"Honey, we were young. And there were powerful warning signs. And of course the story of the accident and his missing year. Does Jack ever make you uncomfortable?"

"Not when I'm around him. But I wonder sometimes. He told me once that he used to watch me when I was running, even before we met. Isn't that sort of creepy?"

"Maybe. Not necessarily."

"He seems too enthusiastic sometimes." I could see Jack was at the end of a long line to check out. "Like he's too into me. Like he doesn't have control."

"Retta! Does he try to make you do things you don't want to do?"

"No, no, nothing like that," I said, blushing. "I just mean, like he was desperate to come visit me in Kansas."

"Are you trying to give me a heart attack? Lord." She paused and took a breath. "You are supposed to be a couple, right? He probably just wanted to see you."

"I guess," I said, frustrated because I was having trouble explaining myself.

"I think what you are worried about is not a problem Jack has. I knew Don, and Jack is nothing like him from what I've seen and what you've told me. Don was always very protective of my sister, once they started dating, which seemed sweet to me at the time. But I was so young—it's also a classic mask for jealousy, which is what drove his anger toward her. He accused her of looking at other men a few times, and both times they laughed it off, but even then I didn't think it was a joke. I just never said anything. Does Jack worry about you with other guys?"

I was struck by the complete foreignness of this question—he'd never done anything remotely like that. I remembered Rachel's boyfriend getting so mad at the bonfire. Jack was nothing like that.

"No."

"Well, that's a good sign. Maybe he just saw you when you were younger and has always liked you. He can't help that, and there's nothing wrong with it. Don't hold it against him."

"Okay." Jack was paying now.

"But," Samantha added, "if you do feel uncomfortable when you are around him, you should pay attention to that."

"That's the thing. When I am with him, I like him a

lot. But when I am not with him, I start to question everything about him."

"I see. I think you are just responding to what happened to your mom, which is understandable. I think you should talk to your therapist about this. It's not fair to Jack to punish him, and if you don't want a relationship, you should let him know that." She paused.

Before she could say anything else, I said, "Samantha."

"Yes?"

"I don't blame you for not telling Mom what you thought about Don. It's not the same as them."

"Thank you." She sniffed. "I appreciate that. But Retta, just don't do anything dramatic on this trip. Anything you might regret. Be safe."

I sighed. "I'll send you the pictures. Bye."

Jack got in the car with two bags of stuff, which he dumped at my feet. "Snacks!" he said, smiling. "Also, a phone charger."

"Cool."

"How'd it go with Samantha?"

"Fine." I smiled back at him, thinking Samantha was probably right. I opened a bag of nacho cheese Doritos and thought, *no, she's definitely right.*

Chapter Thirty-One

We were approaching Appleford. It had been dark for a couple hours already, and I strained to see the signs.

"So," Jack said, "What are we going to do all night? I don't think we can find this lady tonight, can we?"

"Can't we just get a motel room?"

"I'm not sure. I've heard you have to be eighteen at most places."

"Oh. Well, maybe there's a Denny's. It's too cold to sleep in the car."

I used my phone to direct him to the Denny's. We saw a sign for a Super 8 down the road, so we drove there first. I stayed in the car and watched Jack go in and have a short conversation with the guy at the desk.

He shook his head when he returned and said, "No luck. They can't let anyone in unless at least one person is eighteen. He said they're all like that, but told me a couple places that might not ask for ID if I paid cash." He handed me a piece of paper with a couple of motel names on it.

I mapped both places, and since they were a ways off, we decided to eat first. Jack handed the server his dad's credit card to pay once we were done.

"He's so going to kill you for all this," I said.

"I know. I'll have to do all sorts of extra chores

around the farm to pay it off." He laughed.

"Oh, sorry," I said. "It's all my fault." We smiled at each other until the server brought the card and receipt back.

"Are you a good tipper, Jack?" I asked after the server walked off.

"I think so." The skin around his eyes was still crinkled.

"You better be—food service is hard work." I lightly kicked his foot under the table.

"Okay, okay. Is four enough?"

"Make it four-fifty and I'll still like you."

"Okay, you're worth two quarters." He grinned wider before writing the tip in and signing the receipt.

The first motel we went to turned Jack away even though I stayed in the car. But the second one let us— well, Jack—check in. I ducked down in the seat when we drove past the office on the way to the room.

"The guy didn't even look," Jack said. "I don't think he cared."

"This probably isn't the safest motel in the world."

"Don't think I'll be telling my mom about it."

I laughed.

Jack pushed open the door, and I followed him in, switching on the light. "Oh," Jack said.

"What?" I peeked around him. "Just one bed." I blushed as I said it.

"I didn't even think to ask." He looked at me guiltily.

"Well, since you're supposed to be by yourself, that's probably a good thing." I bit my lip.

Jack fell into the chair by the little table on the other side of the bed. "No big deal. I can sleep here."

He yawned. "I'm beat."

I didn't know what to say.

Jack was leaning forward with his elbows on his knees and his chin resting on his palms, his eyes closed.

"Well," I started. "Maybe I should be the one to sleep in the chair, since you drove all day."

He lifted his head. "No, I'm not going to make you do that."

I sat on the bed and held my arm out over it. "It's big. There's room for both of us."

"I'm not sure," Jack said. "It might be weird." I thought there was color in his cheeks, though it was too dark to know for sure.

Jack took his boots off and leaned back in the chair.

"Are you sure?" I asked.

"Yeah, the chair will be fine." He nodded.

"If you say so," I said, pulling my own shoes off. Then I peeled back the bedspread and climbed in on the side opposite Jack.

I looked over at him just as he got up and headed over to the window. "I'm going to turn the heat up. It's cold." He hit the light switch on the way back to the chair, cursing once as he tripped on the boots.

I lay in the dark, thinking about Jack only a few feet from me, almost close enough to touch. And I really wanted to touch him now. I heard him shift in the chair.

Surely Marilyn would be able to find out about Mom. She said she was asked by somebody she already knew to get involved in the network. She could check into it. She must know people who knew people...

I could hear Jack breathing. He wasn't asleep yet.

He shifted again, the chair squeaking. I couldn't believe he'd driven me all this way. He was probably going to be in way more trouble than I would be. Samantha was still extra cautious around me.

The chair squeaked again.

I wondered if he'd be the same after this trip. All the way until we were at Iowa State. What would it be like there?

A rustling sound came from the chair as he shifted again.

I laughed. "Jack."

"Yeah? I keep making all this noise."

"This is stupid. Why don't we both just sleep on top of the bedspread. We're fully clothed."

He was quiet for a moment. "Okay. Just promise you won't take advantage of me."

I laughed and got out from under the covers. We pulled the comforter back into place and both lay down. There was two feet between us, which seemed chaste enough to me. I wished—just a little—that it was a smaller bed.

"Thanks," Jack said. "For the record, I recommend never trying to sleep in a chair."

"Sound advice," I said.

Having him even closer to me made him more distracting. He lay very still, so I did, too. Eventually, I fell asleep despite the many possibilities flitting through my mind.

****

In the morning, I woke covered in a sheen of sweat. Jack must have cranked the heat to the max. I got up to turn it back down.

I wanted to see the new day, the one on which I'd

hopefully learn something more about Mom. Since I wasn't supposed to be in the room, I was slightly afraid to open the heavy and dingy burgundy curtains like I wanted to, just in case somebody saw.

Marilyn didn't know anything herself. But surely she knew someone who did. Surely. I put my face between the curtains and looked out. The sun was shining, and a pile of dirty snow was collected next to the dumpster our room overlooked.

I turned back around to look at Jack, lean and long, stretched out on the bed. One leg was bent but his other foot nearly hung off the end of the bed. I could see his sock had loosened, and the end was folded over his toes. One arm sprawled over his head, but the other, the one that had been next to me, was by his side, palm up, like he'd been waiting for me to take it.

I clutched my stomach to keep it from fluttering away. Then I lay back on the bed, just touching Jack's shoulder. He stirred, and I glanced over at him.

He rolled his head toward me and sleepily said, "Morning, sunshine," before leaning forward to surprise me with a kiss on the forehead and rolling onto his back again.

The butterflies in my stomach started acting up again, and I smiled, but he'd turned his head back, though I could see him blush. I took his hand. "Do you know what time it is?"

Jack picked up his phone with his free hand and said, "Six twenty."

"Let's go somewhere and get toothbrushes."

"I already bought some, yesterday. In the bag with the snacks."

"Oh, aren't you Mr. Prepared." I glanced over at

him, but he wasn't looking at me.

"Well, you know, I am mature enough to rent a motel room now." He paused. "When do we go meet your mystery lady?"

"I guess we could go over to the campus at eight thirty or so."

"Campus?" he asked.

"It's a small women's school. Taggart College."

"Oh, is she a professor?"

"Yeah."

He said, "That explains the papers you mentioned." We were both quiet for a few moments.

"Jack?" I said. We were both looking at the ceiling.

"Yeah."

"If Samantha agrees, I'm going to do the GED and go to Iowa State this year."

"Really?" He turned toward me. "That's awesome."

I looked back at him and blinked. Then, in what seemed like slow motion, I leaned forward and touched my lips to his. I closed my eyes as I felt his lips moving against mine, and my insides turned to molten gold, shiny in the sun I knew was everywhere, everywhere.

He pulled away, and I opened my eyes and saw him looking at me with such raw intensity that I couldn't move at all. He leaned back in and kissed me again and again, running his hand through my hair, which sent a shiver down my spine. My hand found his chest, where I felt his heart singing the sweetest song for me.

Jack pulled back. "We should probably get going if we want to get breakfast," he said. But he was looking at me like I was made of honey.

My lips felt like they'd known their true purpose for the first time, and I had to will them to say, "Okay, good idea."

We let go of each other's hands, and Jack rolled off the bed. I lay there wondering if I'd be able to stand, I was trembling so much.

****

Jack and I climbed the steps of a large red brick building with white wood accents. He pushed open the heavy white door, and we found ourselves in a wide hallway. Fortunately, I spotted a sign. "Sociology this way," I said, dragging him by the hand.

We climbed to the third floor and found the little room after wandering down one wrong hall. The door was ajar. I looked at Jack with wide eyes and had to force my mouth shut.

He laughed and whispered, "You didn't think it'd be this easy, huh?"

I shook my head. Now that I was here, I knew this was a terrible idea. What if she couldn't find anything out? Or refused to try?

But I had to find out what I could.

I took a breath and tapped on the door. There was no answer, so I peeked in. Bookshelves lined the walls of the narrow office, and a large wooden desk sat close to the window opposite the door. The light was off. Jack still stood right behind me, his hand in mine.

"Can I help you?" I heard from the hall. I turned and saw Marilyn standing there, holding a mug.

Her head jerked, and she stepped back. Coffee splashed on the floor from her mug just as I caught a whiff of it. Marilyn glanced at Jack.

"R—hi, I'm Professor Wilkins. Are you looking

for me?" she asked tensely.

"Hi," I said. "Can I talk to you? I, uh, read a couple of your papers and was interested in your research."

Marilyn glanced at Jack again. "Just you?" she asked.

"Jack, will you wait for me out here?"

He nodded and wandered off toward a bank of chairs.

Marilyn still looked shocked, but she forced a smile and motioned for me to go into her office.

"Retta, what are you doing here? Is everything okay?" She walked to her desk and put her mug down. She leaned against the side of the desk.

"I just...had some questions. Everything's okay." I felt very stupid for coming. Would anyone she could talk to remember more than the motel lady?

"Aren't you living with family in Oklahoma now?"

I nodded. My hand covered my mouth, and I wavered a bit on my feet.

"You're a long way from there. You really should not have come." Marilyn took a sip of her coffee. "It's risky."

"I had a cover story."

"I think I heard that. Perhaps your future is not in subterfuge." She laughed. "Since you're here, how are you, really?"

I blushed. "I'm okay. My new family is nice. I'm just—I'm just trying to understand who my mom was. I know who she was for as long as I remember, and I know who she was before she had to leave Oklahoma. But everything in the middle is gone. I just can't stand it!"

Marilyn nodded, a sympathetic look on her face,

and took another sip of coffee. "But you know I don't know anything that can help you."

I was miserable. "But I thought you could maybe try to find out? Can you ask anyone who might have been around then? I was two, and she was probably wearing these tall blue Doc Martens when she left."

"Retta, I don't know." She was quiet for a moment, hand on her face. She took a breath. "I can try. But I can't make any promises, and it will take some time. Maybe months. It's not like I can send an email out—I'll have to inquire directly when I see certain people."

My heart lifted. "Thank you so much."

"But Retta, please be prepared to find nothing. Some things are just unknowable."

I nodded.

Marilyn walked around to her desk chair and motioned for me to sit in another chair. "Since I've got you here, I might as well do what I do. So, Retta, how are you doing in school? If I recall, you're a bit of a language scholar, right?"

"Oh," I said, my hand going to my mouth again. "Um, well...I finished last semester in Iowa, and that was fine. All As. But I started school this month in January and just got suspended for hitting back after this girl pushed me into the lockers."

"That's no good."

"If I can get my aunt to agree, I'm going to take the GED and go to Iowa State in August."

"This year? Aren't you just fifteen?"

"I'm sixteen now. I already know what I want to do."

"Still, that's pretty young for college. What is it you exactly plan to do?"

"I'm good at languages, so I plan to major in linguistics and minor in some specific language. Probably Spanish. Maybe an Asian language, too."

"Really? Are you quite academically inclined, then? Thinking of going on beyond your BA?"

I nodded. "Maybe?"

"Well, if I might present you with another option. Consider coming here. It's competitive, but if you spent another year in high school and worked with me on a project, I'd be willing to write you a reference."

I was speechless again. I'd never imagined going to a fancy liberal arts college. "But—isn't it expensive?"

"Most of our students get substantial financial aid and scholarships."

"Why would I have to wait another year?"

"You need a stronger record than a GED, plus I'll need some time to get to know you if I am to recommend you."

"That's nice of you. I don't know what to say. I'll have to think about it. But I really, really appreciate the offer." I stood up, anxious to get back to Jack.

"Give me your phone number," Marilyn said, "and I'll call you if I can find anything out. In the meantime, think about what I said and let me know if you're interested. Get in touch by June if you are, though. We'll need some time."

"Okay," I said, smiling but feeling awkward. I wrote down my number for Marilyn and handed it to her before leaving.

Jack lounged in an orange plastic chair, leaning back against the wall. His eyes were closed. *Just look at him—and he's all mine.*

Chapter Thirty-Two

Samantha hugged me when she picked me up from the airport. She was quite the hugger. The trip home had been less fun than the trip out, especially the awkward night I had spent at Jack's house. His dad had been the one to take me to the airport because Jack was in school, and his mom was at work. All things considered, he'd been pretty nice, seeing me all the way to security and wishing me a nice flight.

"You are in so much trouble," Samantha said.

"I know," I said.

As soon as I got home and had a shower, I tapped on Tracy's door.

"Hi, Tracy."

The girl didn't say anything, just looked at me in confusion, mouth hanging open.

"I was wondering...didn't you say you had a horse game for the Wii?"

"Yeah! Do you want to play?" Tracy asked with wide eyes.

"Sure."

Later that evening, after the kids were in bed, Samantha called me downstairs. "We have something to show you," she said.

Samantha and Nana sat with me and started up a DVD. It was a montage of videos and photos they'd put together while I was gone with "Smells Like Teen

Spirit" playing over it. It started off with a big question in black and white: "Who is Retta Brooks?" The words "Beautiful daughter" flashed on the screen followed by lots of pictures of me as a baby, some with Mom holding me but none with Don, fortunately, and then continued to several of the ones Mom had hanging on the wall in our house in Iowa.

I didn't know what to say.

The word "Runner" appeared on the screen before stills from the video of me running in my jeans and then additional shots of people in large running races. Then "Reader" and pictures of books followed by "Polyglot" and images of language dictionaries. "Friend" overlaid a picture of Jack and me standing with the other kids in front of the movie theater in Buckley.

I was still speechless, but some kind of unidentifiable emotion was working its way up.

"Traveler" came into view on a screen with a couple of the road shots I'd sent Samantha. This made me laugh through emerging tears. After that, a screen showing pictures of Frankie, Tracy, Samantha, and Nana came up before being replaced with a blue screen with the words, "And finally, cousin, niece, and granddaughter."

I sat there in stunned silence, staring at the screen.

When it ended, Samantha said, "Does that help at all?"

I was still staring at the screen, which was frozen on the last slide. It was...I couldn't begin to describe how I felt, and without warning, I burst into tears. Samantha hugged me, and Nana joined the hug from the other side. Now I recognized the emotion. It was despair. I just sobbed. "I didn't find out."

"You didn't find out what?" Samantha asked.

"What really happened when we left." The tears were unstoppable, dripping off my nose, soaking my shirt.

Nana said, "Retta, we didn't want to upset you, but we need you to know you are already somebody special, particularly to us. We care about you and want you to be happy. We want to help you figure out what you need to do to make that happen."

"You can be whoever you need to be," Samantha said. "Retta, Frances, somebody else. But you should know that we'll love you regardless."

That just made me cry harder.

We sat there in our group hug until I calmed down. My brain started working again.

I pulled back from the hug. "So does this mean that you are open to me making decisions?"

"What do you mean?" Samantha asked.

"Well, I hate going to school. We'd talked about other options before."

"You mean homeschooling?" Nana asked.

"Maybe, or I am thinking of just doing the GED."

"Retta, I don't think that's a good idea," Samantha said, but Nana put her arm over Samantha's. "But okay, we'll consider it."

"Okay."

"I'll tell you what," Samantha said, "why don't you seriously think about it and come up with a specific plan, and get back to us on Sunday?"

****

I had to go back to school the next day, but I spent all my spare time that week studying for the GED. On Saturday I took a practice exam I found at the library, which I aced. I could do that. But what about Marilyn's offer? Going to Taggart would be awesome, really. I'd never considered a small liberal arts college before. I'd checked it out, and one of the few women's sports they had was cross country, so I could still do that, even if it wouldn't get me a scholarship. For what I wanted to study, it did make loads of sense. And the idea was exciting. Mom would have been so proud; I knew she would have been.

But then there was Jack. I already missed him so much.

Sunday morning I got up and went for my long run, came back, and showered. I felt invigorated like I always did after a run. I'd also made my mind up about what to do.

I played Wii again with Tracy. It was kind of fun, much to my surprise. I could imagine Mom and me playing Wii games if we'd had one. At lunch Samantha said Nana was coming over at four, and I could let them know then what I'd decided to do.

Four o'clock came, and Samantha ushered the kids upstairs. I sat across from her and Nana in the sitting room and felt on the spot, but only for a second. I pulled Wes off the couch cushion and into my lap and absentmindedly petted him.

"I love how you've taken to our little Wesley," Samantha said. "Giles ignores you like he does everyone else."

"Giles and Wesley," I exclaimed. "The Watchers from Buffy!"

Samantha laughed. "Yeah, I'm a fan."

"Mom was, too. Huge."

"Yeah, I saw all the DVDs at your old house." She

smiled. "We probably were watching them at the exact same time."

Nana put her hands together. "Please tell us what you've decided, sweetie."

"Okay. So yesterday I took a practice GED exam and made nearly a perfect score on it," I said. "That is what I want to do. Take the GED and never go back to high school."

Nana looked surprised. "But don't you want to go to college?" Nana asked, leaning forward with her hands in the air.

"That's the point. I want to go to college this fall," I said.

"Oh," Nana said, sitting back.

Samantha said, "Let's just let her have her say, Mom, and we can respond afterward."

Nana nodded.

I continued. "I want to go to Iowa State. I already checked, and I can go ahead and apply now—as long as I have the GED before classes start, it's fine."

Nana's eyes narrowed in confusion.

I said, "I know you know, but I'm running the marathon here in April."

Samantha and Nana smiled like they were proud of me, which annoyed me. It's not like they'd had much to do with it.

Then I felt guilty for thinking that.

"And I am not going to go by 'Retta' anymore. You said I could do that, right?" I said, looking at Samantha.

Samantha's eyes widened. "Oh. I don't remember. But, sure, if you want. I don't see why not."

Nana asked, "What are you going to go by?"

I shook my head. "I haven't decided yet."

"What are you thinking of?" Nana asked.

"I'm not going to say yet."

Nana and Samantha nodded.

"There's one more thing," I said. "I'm not able to forgive Grandma and Grandpa right now for not telling my mom about Don's problems."

Samantha nodded, and Nana's face turned dark. "Good," Nana said. "I never wanted you seeing them."

"Mom, please," Samantha said. "Do you plan to tell them this, Retta?"

"Yes," I said, nodding.

"That might be a little cruel, sweetie," Samantha said.

"What's cruel about it, Samantha?" Nana asked.

I didn't say anything and instead looked out the window.

Nana got up and went into the kitchen.

"We still need to talk about these things," Samantha said, putting her hands on her knees.

"What?" I asked.

"First, I feel obligated to point out you may forgive your grandparents someday. So handle that gently."

"Okay."

"Also, I didn't promise I'd let you do the GED. I said I'd consider it. But I think changing your name is not a bad idea." She looked toward the kitchen, where Nana was making some noise with a pot or pan or two.

"What about the GED?" What if she didn't let me do it? Now my heart was set on it.

"I need to see you pass a couple more practice tests. I looked into it, and you have to drop out of school before you can take it, and I don't want you to do that and then not pass it."

"There's no way I could not pass it! You have no idea how easy it is."

She looked back at me and crossed her arms. "Okay, but still. Let's order some practice books and tests online, and then you can do them. So you'll need to keep going to school for a few weeks longer. And don't slack. Besides, don't you want the extra practice for your language classes?"

I sighed. "But you're saying I can take it and then go to Iowa State in the fall?"

Her eyes narrowed as she thought about it. She stared right at me before saying, "Yes. But there's one condition."

"What?" I was nervous again.

"You have to come home for all the breaks."

"Oh, that's it?" That was fine. Where else would I go? "I can do that."

"But, Retta—you'll have to take out loans, you know. There probably won't be scholarships available this late. You can look for scholarships for the spring and next year. I'll help you out as much as I can, but I'm not in a position to pay all your tuition. You can try out for cross country, though."

"Yeah." I smiled. I could do that.

Chapter Thirty-Three

The next day, I found Samantha in the kitchen. "I have an idea. The marathon is a fundraiser, right?"

"Okay," Samantha said, "if you say so." She was chopping carrots for dinner.

"It is. And I'm supposed to set up a page on this fundraising site. Hopefully you guys will donate." I grinned.

"I'm sure we can manage that," Samantha said, smiling back.

"But the thing is, there are loads of different kinds of fundraising projects on the site, including some memorials for people."

Samantha stopped chopping and looked at me.

"So I was thinking," I continued, "I want to set one up for Mom."

Samantha blinked. "That is a great idea. I love it. How would it work?"

"I'd select a charity to benefit—I think one that helps fight domestic violence in some way. I have to set a goal dollar amount and create the page. Then I have to write up a description or explanation of what it's for and include some photos or video. And then it's just a matter of getting the word out."

Samantha poured the carrots into a bowl and began cutting new potatoes. "I absolutely love it."

"Cool. I'm going to do it."

Samantha watched me with what looked like pride, but she also seemed to be tearing up. I left before she could be sure because I didn't want my good mood ruined.

I went back upstairs to try to get in touch with Jack because I wanted his help on the video. But then I remembered his parents had taken his phone and computer away.

The video expert wasn't going to be able to help me, I realized—not any time soon. I'd have to do it all myself.

So I did. Over the next couple of weeks, I set up the page and created a slideshow of pictures of Mom that Samantha and Nana had given me. The next thing I knew, it had taken off—I was interviewed by a couple of Oklahoma news stations, and then some of the national news networks picked it up, and now it came up in online searches.

****

My hand trembled as I answered my phone, unable to hide the excitement in my voice at seeing Jack's name pop up for the first time in three weeks.

"Hi, Retta—how are you?" Jack was talking fast, like he was also excited.

"I'm good. I've really missed you." I blushed, but it was so true.

"Me, too. I heard about your fundraiser—what's it up to now?"

"Over sixteen thousand bucks! People are donating from all over the country. It's crazy."

"Yeah, but awesome." I could hear his smile.

"Jack, I've wanted to ask you something."

"Yeah?" He dragged it out.

"Do you ever feel like you don't know who you are? You know, since you have two names?"

"Oh." He paused. "I guess not really. It's more that I feel like I am two different people. Around here, I had to learn to be the Iowa farm boy to survive. But when I was with my cousins, I could be the Indian me, even though I didn't know what that was at first." He laughed. "It was nice, but I don't mind being the other me."

"I still don't know what to do. I told Samantha and Nana that I wasn't going to go by 'Retta' anymore."

"Really? Then by what?"

"I don't know yet. I'm thinking of using 'Frances.' I was also thinking of 'Bobbi,' after Bobbi Gibb."

"Who?" he asked.

"The Boston Marathon crasher," I explained.

"Oh, right. I think either is good. They're both nice names. You should do whatever feels best."

"But that's what I mean. I don't know."

"Well, if it helps, you really were Frances for a while. Your mom probably always thought of you that way."

Tears welled in my eyes. "You're right." I paused. "But I don't feel like Frances."

"But you don't know, right? Maybe try it out?"

****

A couple weeks later, Samantha knocked on my door after school. "They made a plea deal with Don this afternoon." She put her hand on my arm, and my stomach flipped. "He pled guilty to second-degree murder. The sentencing hearing will be in March."

"Oh, my God," I whispered. "What does that mean?"

"I don't know, exactly, but I hope he will be in jail for the rest of his life." She squeezed my arm. "It's good news about Don. It means you don't have to testify."

I nodded again. I still had to fill in the blanks. Maybe Marilyn would still come up with something.

Once Samantha had left, I Googled to see the story for myself. That's when I found out more details of the crime had come out. It wasn't my fault we'd been found, after all. Someone who knew Don and Mom in Norman had been visiting relatives in Buckley when he'd spotted Mom at Walmart. Word eventually got back to Don. He claimed he hadn't gone there to kill her—just to talk.

It wasn't my fault at all. I felt so light and free that I was almost floating.

Of course, right afterward I crashed and cried for hours.

A few weeks later, Don's sentencing hearing took place. He got the max for murder two—fifty years, even though the prosecutor told us he'd likely serve only about twenty-two years. It was as over as it could be.

Chapter Thirty-Four

I loaded the dishwasher after dinner a couple days later while Samantha rinsed. Frankie and Tracy stood there, their dish-carrying duties fulfilled.

"Oh, go on, you two," Samantha said.

They ran into the den, where I assumed they were setting up the Wii.

"Retta."

"Yeah."

"Thanks for helping with the dishes. I'm glad you're helping us around the house. We all have our chores, and I think laundry would be yours. What do you think?"

"All of it?" I couldn't really say no, but still, it sounded like a lot.

Samantha nodded. "I'll help out, but I want it to be your responsibility."

"Okay, I guess." I shrugged.

"Great. I'll show you how this weekend."

We finished the dishes soon afterward, and I followed her into the den.

Tracy's face lit up as she stood there with a controller in her hand. "Are you going to play with us?"

I didn't feel like such an outsider anymore. "Sure, I guess I will."

Samantha arched her eyebrows and said, "Are you all ready to get whooped?"

"You wish!" Frankie said.

Samantha laughed and hugged him and then Tracy. She took the controller Frankie handed her, and then she surprised me with a hug, too.

"Hugs all around," she said.

It felt good.

****

When Samantha got home the next day—from the meeting with the school principal about me dropping out—her grim face let me know something was wrong.

"What is it?" I asked before she could put her purse down on the counter.

"The principal refused to sign the document," Samantha said. "He said he did not believe it was in your best interest to leave school to take the GED. I'm sorry, honey." She patted my shoulder as we stood in the kitchen.

"How can he do that? What does he care?"

"It's the law. He has to believe it's in your best interest, and he apparently doesn't."

"But—"

"Retta, the man wasn't unhelpful," Samantha said. "He pointed out that you almost have enough credits to graduate already. I wrote down what you need. After this semester, you'd only need English and history, which you can do via independent study this summer."

"What about homeschooling again?" I asked.

"Yes, he mentioned that, too. You could. I think Nana's still willing."

"I wouldn't need her for anything much. I can go back to what I was doing before this year—basically studying on my own and only getting help from Mom when I needed it."

A week later I was doing just that. I had to do three semesters worth of English, one semester of US History, two semesters of World Civilization, one semester of Chemistry, and one of Trig, and then I'd be done with high school and be able to move on to real life.

But I also contacted Marilyn and started working on her research project, which was pretty awesome. I was reading Spanish and French sociology articles looking for specific topics. It was fun using my language skills in a real way for once, and if I ever wanted to do real research in college, I'd have some official experience.

A week before the marathon, my fundraising had topped twenty eight thousand dollars. The results had been bolstered by Don's sentencing, which got the story back in the news again.

****

Everything I had read about marathons was spot-on. I was over ten miles in, making good time and still feeling great. My pace was perfect. I could be running faster, but I couldn't afford to do that if I wanted to finish.

I kept going and going. I passed the marker for Mile 13, still feeling good. I took an offered water cup and downed it and then pulled some Skittles out of my waist pack and ate them one at a time over the next mile.

At Mile 16, with just ten miles to go, I got a side cramp I first tried to run through. I ended up slowing down to a walk for a couple minutes, but it didn't get any better. So I started running again, grimacing and even groaning to cope with the pain.

At Mile 17, I realized the cramp was gone. I grinned, which loosened more sweat that went straight into my right eye. I wiped it and my forehead and concentrated on the motion of my feet.

They were feet of incomprehensible power. *Bam bam bam bam*, they sang.

The next thing I knew, I was passing the Mile 20 marker. I felt renewed. I imagined each drop of my sweat that exploded onto the pavement was one of the bad things that I'd been through in the last seven months. All the fighting with Mom—*splat*. Don—*splat*. Those locker bitches—*splat*. My legs were on autopilot and could do no wrong. Mile 21. Mile 22. Mile 23.

I had no sense of time and was getting queasy. My legs no longer felt like powerful rubber bands catapulting me step after step. They were lead sticks. I was slowing down. I was about to hit the wall. I had to prepare. I ate my last three pieces of energy bar.

I recited my phrase, out loud: "I am the greatest, I am the greatest, I am the greatest."

I hit the wall. It was ten times worse than the depression I'd gone through after first moving to Oklahoma. My legs were still doing their job, but only just. Now I was crying. "I am the greatest," I sobbed, over and over.

I was moving in slow motion. But I was moving. A little past the Mile 24 marker, it cleared. I felt better and better with each step until I was able to run a decent pace again and feel okay. Not great, but good enough. Just two miles left.

I wiped the tears and sweat off my face and noticed that the backs of both my sweaty hands were now streaked with red from the dust that floated around on dry, windy days. The wind was nice, though. It was already pretty hot. Summer here would be awful.

Mile 25.

Still going.

There it was. Mile 26. So close, but so incredibly, impossibly far away.

As I neared the end, I saw news cameras aimed at me. Maybe there was somebody famous running near me. Or maybe the news stations filmed every runner that came in, in case somebody was interesting.

There were some cameras not filming me—there was a group of them clustered around somebody in the crowd past the finish line.

A little girl emerged from the cluster of cameras and pointed at me. It was Tracy. All those cameras swung around toward me.

I crossed the line.

I tried to slow down. I saw Tracy and Samantha and Frankie, but I couldn't stop, and all the cameras panned as I went by.

I finally was able to stop running and just walk. I kept walking until I thought it was time to sit down, and that's what I did. I sat with my legs straight out and leaned back on my palms. My whole body shook.

I was immediately surrounded by reporters and cameras. They were saying things to me, but I couldn't really make anything out, and I stared ahead. I couldn't see past them. Then Samantha pushed some of them out of the way so she could squeeze through, with Frankie and Tracy right behind her.

Samantha crouched down to give me a hug. "Retta, you were amazing! Just amazing."

"Oh. Cool."

"Retta, Retta!" Tracy said, hugging me.

Frankie hugged me as well. "You're all wet!" he said.

"It's sweat, you dummy!" Tracy said. She sat down next to me and hooked her arm through mine.

Samantha talked to reporters, managing to keep them away.

I held my arm up to Samantha when she returned. "Help me up, please."

"Okay," Samantha said, pulling on both my arms, her eyes glowing. "I am so proud—or impressed. You were incredible, Retta."

"Actually, you can call me Frances now. Frances Retta Brooks."

Epilogue

My phone rang.

"Hello, Retta?"

"Yeah?" I sat up on my bed, knowing exactly who this must be. "Marilyn."

"Yes." She sounded surprised. "Can you talk?"

I glanced over at my roommate, who sat at her tiny dorm desk, head-bopping to whatever lame pop music leaked out of her pink headphones. "Yes," I said quietly, just in case.

"So as not to torment you, I'll cut to the chase. I did manage to get a little information about your mother. Unfortunately, it's not much."

My heart sped up, and I leaned forward. "Okay."

"When you two first left Oklahoma, you went to Omaha, Nebraska. There was someone there able to help you get settled. Your mom got a job as a waitress, but my contact couldn't remember where. You only stayed a few months because your mother got spooked."

I held my breath.

"Unfortunately, that's it. They don't know where you went after that."

I exhaled. "Lincoln, I think," I managed to say.

"Honey, you'll never know for sure. Some things we just can't know."

"I know," I said, nodding. "I know."

After a moment of quiet, Marilyn said, "So how is Iowa State? I'm still disappointed you didn't hold out for Taggart. You did good work for me."

"It's good. I like my classes."

"Good for you, then. Are you happy?"

"I think so."

"That's good." She paused. "Okay, honey, I'm going to go. Let me know if you ever need a reference for undergraduate research."

"I will. Thank you again…for everything."

"You are welcome. And I'm sorry it wasn't a better result."

I nodded and said, "It's okay. I understand."

And I did understand. I understood I'd never know enough about Mom's—and my—past. After I hung up, I lay back on the bed and cried. Knowing that much more felt better and worse at the same time. That was all I'd ever know. I'd never know where we were for those two years, or what Mom really had to go through.

But it was okay, it really was—because I knew where and who I was now. I knew Mom would have been proud of me. And I knew what I was capable of.

Author's Note

A couple of years ago, I pitched this book to an agent who gave me a confused look and said that there are plenty of organizations out there to help women get away from abusive situations, so what was the point of the one in the book being secret? This is a common type of misinformation and one I hope we can eventually correct.

Although this book is about Retta's mom's abusive relationship, Retta questions whether Jack might be potentially abusive. She's not wrong to worry. Most people think of domestic violence as an adult problem, but the highest rate of dating violence (almost three times higher than other groups) is among 16-to-24-year-olds. It can also impact teens even younger than 16.

People often wonder why a woman or girl doesn't "just leave" an abusive relationship. Often they feel there's no way to get away. That's why many women don't leave—because it's even riskier than staying. The single most dangerous time for any abused woman is when she leaves. There's an additional complicating factor when children are involved.

Despite these facts, what Retta's mom did was a crime (kidnapping, basically). If she'd been caught, Retta's father might have been given custody. Real organizations that help abused women advise against trying to "go underground," both because there really isn't an underground and because it would be unethical—and because it's the best way for a woman to lose custody of her kids.

Still, in many ways, things are better than they used

to be. The backstory of the book takes place in the 1990s, when the police often did very little about abuse as it was considered a "private" issue. Retta's mom didn't know how to fix her problem. In 1994, the Violence Against Women Act (VAWA) was passed, and by the 2000s, there was evidence of a change in thinking among law enforcement and the courts, and some programs supported through federal funds.

The most important issue to understand about domestic violence is that the real problem is with the abuser, not the victim. There are a few programs nationwide that address the toxic masculinity of convicted male abusers in an effort to change their behaviors. But there aren't enough of these, and despite passage of VAWA, police departments don't always handle incidents effectively, fairly, or safely. Additionally, at the time of this writing, VAWA is at risk of being defunded by the government.

The single best way to avoid ending up in an abusive situation is to know the warning signs of an unhealthy relationship and get out sooner rather than later. Not every abuser is the same, and I'm focusing here on abuse by men toward women—the most frequent type, but definitely not the only type of relationship in which violence occurs. There are some classic signs that show up early on in relationships that later involve abuse. One problem is that our culture has a myth that true love is intense and overwhelming. Real love involves respect. Abusers are often narcissists, incapable of looking at things from the other person's perspective. Below are some warning signs and characteristics of abusive relationships that many mistake for signs of passion and "true love."

1. Intensity. Abusive relationships often begin quickly and rapidly escalate in intensity. This can feel exciting at the time, but it's still a red flag to consider. He might want to be with you and only you all the time. He may tell you he loves you or use excessive flattery surprisingly early.

2. Jealousy. This can be on the part of the potential abuser (he is jealous, especially of your other friendships) or can be manufactured by him, to make you feel jealous and worry about the status of the relationship.

3. Violence. While this one seems obvious, people often write off what they see as "minor" incidents, such as damaging things you own or grabbing you, as signs of passion.

4. Control. Any effort to control what you do is a big red flag. It might be that he wants to always know where you are, that he makes you feel like you need to ask permission to do things, or that he wants to keep you from wearing certain types of clothes.

There's a good Huffington Post article by Bonnie Koehn ("Early Signs of an Unhealthy Relationship") that summarizes even more of these warning signs. (Google the article title to find it.) These apply equally to adults and teenagers.

Despite all the warnings above, know that it is still possible to get away, however difficult it may seem. Even though it can be very hard, ask for help from those who care about you. If you or someone you know is potentially in danger, the National Domestic Violence Hotline 1-800-799-SAFE (7233) can also help.

A word about the author...

Kelly Vincent wrangles data weekdays and spends the rest of her time playing with words. She grew up in Oklahoma but has moved around quite a bit, with Glasgow, Scotland being her favorite stop. She now lives near Seattle with three cats who definitely help her write her stories and make progress on the MFA she's currently adding to her collection of advanced degrees.

Find her at kellyvincent.net and @kvbooks on Instagram and Twitter.

CPSIA information can be obtained
at www.ICGtesting.com
Printed in the USA
LVHW011047270120
644893LV00002B/27